LETHAL PROTECTOR

NEW YORK TIMES AND *USA TODAY* BESTSELLING AUTHOR

KAYLEA CROSS

LETHAL PROTECTOR

Copyright © 2021
by Kaylea Cross

* * * * *

Cover Art and Print Formatting:
Sweet 'N Spicy Designs
Developmental edits: Deborah Nemeth
Line Edits: Joan Nichols
Digital Formatting: LK Campbell

* * * * *

This book is a work of fiction. The names, characters, places, and incidents are products of the writer's imagination or have been used fictitiously and are not to be construed as real. Any resemblance to persons, living or dead, actual events, locales or organizations is entirely coincidental.

All rights reserved. With the exception of quotes used in reviews, this book may not be reproduced or used in whole or in part by any means existing without written permission from the author.

ISBN: 979-8592385896

For my brave Canadian warriors and those who love them. Thank you for your service.

Author's Note

Friends-to-lovers is one of my very favorite romance tropes, and I can't wait for you to see how Tala and Braxton's story unfolds. I loved bringing these two together after everything they've been through!

Happy reading,
Kaylea

PROLOGUE

"Is this seat taken?"

At the sound of that deep voice next to her at the base mess hall table, Tala looked up from her lunch tray and gasped in delighted surprise. "Brax!"

She jumped out of her chair with a huge smile spreading across her face, and barely resisted the urge to throw her arms around him. That kind of fraternization while in uniform was a definite no-no. "What are you doing here in Kandahar?" The latest rumors she'd heard had placed his unit up north somewhere.

His sexy grin made her heart somersault. He looked incredible, tall and broad-shouldered, his shirt hugging the sculpted muscles in his chest and shoulders. His honey-toned skin had deepened with his tan, and his full, dark beard made him even more ruggedly masculine. "Just got in early this morning. Heard from Tate that you were here, so I thought I'd track you down and say hi."

Her brother was friends with him and Braxton's best buddy, Mason. "I'm glad you did. You're looking good." Even more gorgeous than she remembered, and she thought about him a lot more than she should.

"Thanks," he murmured, looking uncomfortable at her compliment. He gestured to the chair beside her. "May I?"

"Yes, of course." She sat back down, put an elbow on the table and propped her chin in her hand to admire him, touched that he'd taken the trouble to come find her. "How long are you here for?"

"Couple days, maybe, just depends."

On whether they get actionable intel on their next target. "Is Mason with you?" They were both JTF2 operators, members of Canada's tier-one, elite counterterrorism unit. Hence the beard, due to relaxed grooming regulations in the SOF units.

"He's around. Not working with him directly much right now, though."

Braxton was a master sniper. He worked with small teams mostly, attached to a JTF2 assault squadron or another SOF element. "Ah. Well, tell him I said hi when you see him."

"I will." He leaned back in his chair a bit, giving her a slow smile that heated her insides. And she was almost positive he had no clue he had that effect on her. "Everything good with you?"

"Yeah. I've only got another five weeks before I rotate home. I can't wait to see Rylee." Her teenage daughter back in Kelowna, right in the heart of British Columbia's lake country. "We video chat a lot, but it's not the same." Seeing Braxton made her feel homesick, reminding her of all she'd left behind.

"No. She staying with your parents?"

"Yeah, they're taking good care of her. They even moved into our place so she could stay in her own surroundings while I'm over here." Her parents were awesome, had always been there for her, including supporting her as a single teenage mom trying to learn how to take care of a baby.

He nodded, opened his mouth to say something else, stopped, and pulled his phone out of his pocket. He gave the screen a cursory glance, then tucked it away with a sigh. "Really sorry, but I gotta go." He stood.

"I do too." She wished they'd had more time together. But duty called. "Hey, if you end up being here for a few more days and have some time to kill, drop me a text and we'll meet up for a coffee or whatever. If you want," she rushed to add.

"I'd like that." His deep brown eyes were warm as he gazed down at her, the corners crinkling slightly with the hint of a smile. He was fond of her, but she wasn't sure if there was anything more for him than that. She wished there was. "Take care of yourself."

"Yeah, you too." She allowed herself to watch him walk away for a few seconds before forcing her attention back to her half-eaten meal. Except her appetite was now gone. Seeing Braxton reminded her too much of home—and also what she could never have.

Braxton was married to his unit, and tended not to let anyone in. There was no place in his life for anything else, including her. And for some unknown reason that still wasn't enough to make her stop dreaming of him or imagining them together.

Returning her tray to the stack by the door, she left the mess hall and hurried back across base toward her barracks, anxious to get this next patrol over with so she could enjoy some downtime tomorrow. Rylee had exams this week and would no doubt be up late cramming. Maybe they could have a quick video call tomorrow.

Seated in the back of the APV fifteen minutes later, she found her concentration fragmented as they headed outside the wire and out of the relative protection of the base. Their mission today was to provide security for some brass on the way out to some rural villages to foster relations with the local farmers in the region.

Communication buzzed back and forth between the officers in charge up ahead of them in the convoy, and the sergeant riding shotgun in her vehicle. She stared out the small armored window at the dun-colored landscape, her mind wandering back to Braxton.

Twenty-plus miles into their trip, the vehicles slowed as they approached a large village. EOD teams had been busy here during the night, clearing the road of any mines or IEDs in preparation for their arrival today. Still, Tala tensed, her pulse speeding up as she tightened her grip on her C7 rifle.

She jerked when bullets raked the side of their vehicle, sucking in a sharp breath as her heart rate shot up.

"Contact right, two hundred meters," her sergeant barked into the radio.

Tala glanced around, looking for signs of the enemy. More rounds pinged off the armored plating and kicked up puffs of gray-brown dust as they hit the ground.

The sergeant twisted around in his seat to say something, face tense, but a fireball exploded at the front of the convoy. The force of it shook their vehicle.

The radio traffic surged as the two vehicles in front of them opened, the soldiers pouring out to assume a defensive position. Tala forced back her fear and exited her vehicle with the others, rifle to her shoulder as she searched for a target. She flinched and ducked when another explosion rocked the air, another vehicle ahead of them going up in flames.

Her sergeant was yelling at them over the noise, ordering them away from the vehicle. Tala reacted immediately, glancing around for the nearest cover. She was in a bad spot, out in the open, midway between the road and the irrigation ditch to the left.

Tala ran for it.

She only made it a few steps before a blast of heat seared her back. The air rushed from her lungs as the force of the nearby explosion shot her forward, lifting her off the ground.

She landed hard on her side and scrambled upright, her ears ringing, and did a quick assessment. The APV she'd just been standing next to was a burning mass of metal. Two people were lying on the ground.

People all around her were running for cover. She had to help the wounded.

You're not hit. Get up.

Shaken, she rolled to her feet and rushed for the closest casualty.

Brilliant white light seared her retinas a second later. More heat, this time beneath and in front of her. Then she was airborne.

The world turned upside down. She hit the ground hard on her back and lay there staring up at the smoke-filled sky. It took a moment for her brain to kick back online, the world spinning around her, the stench of cordite stinging her nostrils and her mouth filled with dust and blood. Shit. Had she been hit?

Get up. Get up.

But she couldn't. Could only push up on her elbows, her mind reeling, her body refusing to obey. She was hurt.

Rylee.

Her daughter's face flashed in her mind, galvanizing her. Have to get behind cover.

Through the thick cloud of dust, a figure appeared above her. A man. Kneeling down beside her. "Tala."

She blinked up at him, stunned but recognizing that voice. Braxton. Where had he come from?

She tried to respond but only a wheeze came out. Something was wrong.

He was reaching down, past the limited field of her blurry vision toward her legs. She felt tight pressure around her right calf. "Medic!" he shouted over his shoulder. "I need a medic over here!"

Tala went rigid, her heart shooting into her throat as her gaze snapped to his broad back, blocking her view. Was she injured? She didn't feel anything except the stinging from where the blast wave had hit her in the face and hands.

She struggled to lift her head, tried to see what had happened to her, but Braxton was in the way. Two more people ran up to help.

And then Braxton spun around to straddle her torso, leaning down to cup her face in his hands. They were slick with blood. The metallic scent of it turned her stomach. He stared down at her, face grim, his dark eyes holding her immobile. "You're gonna be okay. Just keep looking at me."

He was trying to prevent her from seeing her lower body.

Fear tore through her. Gunfire rattled all around them, the stench of blood and burning metal stinging her nostrils. She struggled to turn her head to see past him, see what the other two people were doing to her.

And then the pain hit. Vicious and hot. Searing through her right calf.

She sucked in a ragged breath, eyes squeezing shut as a cry of agony came out. She instinctively thrashed, trying to escape it. *My leg…*

Strong hands held her in place. Braxton was pinning her shoulders down, his weight anchoring her hips. His urgent voice echoed in her ears but she couldn't understand him, couldn't focus through the pain and terror.

Oh God, oh God, oh God… She was shaking now. Freezing cold in spite of the heat, her stomach roiling.

"Don't move, Tal. Just stay still. You're gonna be okay."

Tala forced her eyes open, shock taking hold. Was he lying? She was hyperventilating, the fear and pain colliding. She met his gaze for a second, then slid hers to the left.

Through the dust and smoke she saw a boot lying in the dirt a few meters away. Several inches of bloody bone and tissue were sticking out of it.

She stared at it in horror, reality hitting her like a sledgehammer.

Oh my God, that's my foot.

Gagging, she rolled her head to the side and retched onto the bloodstained ground.

CHAPTER ONE

Four years later

Butterflies swarmed in Tala's stomach when the Missoula airport came into view down the highway, the buildings awash with the reds and golds of sunset. Behind them, reflected in the passenger side mirror, the soaring mountains cut a jagged purple silhouette against the glowing horizon.

When they picked up Braxton in just a few minutes, she would finally be face to face with him for the first time in sixteen months. It seemed like an eternity.

She'd flown down here from Kelowna last week to spend the Christmas holidays with her daughter and brother in Rifle Creek. And the prospect of seeing the man who starred in all her romantic and erotic fantasies had her all tangled up inside.

"When's the last time you saw Braxton, anyway?" she asked Mason as he drove them in his Jeep. Her eighteen-year-old daughter Rylee was in the back with Mason's service dog, Ricochet. The Aussie shepherd-border collie cross had his head stuck over the front seat, his chin resting on Mason's shoulder so he could look out the windshield at the passing scenery.

"Almost a year now. He was on a short leave between deployments and came to visit me in Calgary. What about you? I know you guys talk all the time."

"Not all the time." Maybe a few times a month. Not nearly as often as she'd like. "Mostly we email or text, with the occasional video call thrown in there."

She tried to make it sound casual, though for her it wasn't casual at all. Her feelings for Braxton were as serious as they came.

"And the last time I saw him was at my parents' place last August when you guys came to see Tate," she added. She and Tate shared a father. They had grown up together as kids and had remained close in spite of having spent so many years living apart—her in Kelowna and him down here in Montana.

"I remember that," Rylee said. "Uncle Tate got so drunk, you guys had to carry him to bed."

"Oh, yeah, *that* time," Mason mused with a fond smile. "And you weren't supposed to see that. I thought you were fast asleep in the other guest room."

Rylee snorted. "Not like I could help it with how loud you were all being."

Tala smiled. Being able to spend time with her daughter again was a Christmas gift in itself. They'd always been close, but things hadn't been the same since Rylee had started college down here in August. Tala missed having her at home.

"That was a fun day," she said with a faint smile, remembering that day last summer vividly.

They'd all gone out onto Okanagan Lake together on her dad's boat. The guys had waterskied. She'd spent the afternoon secretly staring at Braxton's bare, sculpted chest and arms from behind the safety of her dark sunglasses. Everyone had been in swimwear except for her, because she'd been uncharacteristically self-conscious about him seeing her prosthetic on full display.

After Mason parked the Jeep, they walked into the terminal together and went to the baggage claim area. People from Braxton's flight were already gathering their luggage.

Tala scanned the crowd, searching for him, excitement bursting inside her when she spotted him. "There he is. Braxton!" She waved her arm over her head.

He looked up and locked gazes with her across the busy space, and her belly fluttered at the smile he gave her. The nerves rushed back, mixing with anticipation. She needed to make sure to hide her feelings for him while he was here, though that was getting harder all the time.

He looked away for a moment to grab his Canadian Forces-issued duffel from the conveyor belt. Hefting it over one broad, muscular shoulder, he started toward them.

Tala's pulse beat faster as she drank in the sight of him. He was taller than Tate and Mason, wider through the chest and shoulders. And by far the most reserved of the three. He looked even better than she remembered. Bigger. Sexy enough to make her remaining toes curl in her left boot.

She couldn't wipe the grin off her face as he came toward them, and stepped forward to hug him when he got close. "Hey, it's so good to see you."

He dropped the duffel. Then, to her surprise, he wrapped his arms all the way around her, lifting her off the ground as he hugged her in return. "You too," he said, his deep voice and the faint, woodsy scent of his cologne making her senses go haywire. He had a disconcerting way of making her feel like a teenage girl with a raging, painful crush.

But just for a moment, Tala allowed herself to close her eyes and cling, absorbing the feel of his embrace. Soaking up the honesty of the rare display of affection from him. As if he'd missed her so much that he couldn't help himself.

A rush of complex, tangled memories and emotions hit her.

He'd been there for her during the worst day of her life. Had literally helped save her life, and then cheered her on during the long and grueling recovery process that followed. Including when she'd done a stint in San Antonio at the Center for the Intrepid, because Canada was unable to provide that level of care for its amputee veterans. Braxton had sent a big bouquet of gerbera daisies and checked in with her whenever he could.

He was remote and hard to read, but his usual cool demeanor always seemed to melt away for her. Unfortunately, that didn't mean what she wished it did. He only saw her as a friend, nothing more.

Braxton released her and turned to grin at Mason. "Hey, man."

"Get in here, brother," Mason said, grabbing him in a tight, back-slapping thing men considered to be a hug. "Flights good?"

"Got me here in one piece, so can't complain." Braxton finally turned to Rylee, who was standing off to the side a little. "Hey, kid."

"Hi." She held out a hand. "Nice to see you again."

His eyes warmed, the touch of a smile playing at the edges of his incredibly sexy mouth. "You too." He shook it, his expression turning to surprise when Rylee stepped in to hug him. He returned it, but gently, as if he was secretly afraid of breaking her. "You been behaving yourself at college?"

"Mostly. It was a pretty traumatic start to my first year, though."

"I heard that. Glad you and Nina are both okay."

Tala wrapped an arm around her daughter's shoulders. Tate's fiancée and Rylee had both been targeted by a dirty cop preying on women at the University of Montana. They were both lucky to be alive. Rylee's former roommate hadn't been so lucky.

"You ready to get outta here?" Mason asked.

"Good to go." Braxton reached down for his duffel.

Out in the parking lot, Tala got into the back of Mason's Jeep with Rylee, allowing Braxton to ride shotgun and give his long legs more room up front. Ricochet hopped on the seat between her and Rylee, his tail and rump wiggling like mad as he stuck his head between the front seats to greet Braxton.

"Ric, my man. How's it going, buddy?" Braxton ruffled his fluffy ears affectionately.

Ric was practically vibrating in excitement, his front paws dancing on the armrest in his ecstasy. "Still totally neglected and unloved, I see," Braxton commented dryly.

"So neglected," Mason answered, and started the engine. "My furry wingman."

Braxton turned his head to look at her and Rylee. "You guys been hanging out together for the entire holiday so far?"

"Rylee and I are both staying at Tate's," Tala answered. "But we see Mason and Avery pretty much every day."

"That's because we like you," Mason said as he turned onto the main road leaving the airport.

"And it's got nothing whatsoever to do with Uncle Tate and Avery being work partners," Rylee said in a dry voice. "Or that you guys are trying to organize your business, so you need to get together all the time."

"Nope," Mason said. "Only because we like you guys."

"Did you have a good Christmas?" Tala asked Braxton as they drove toward the highway.

His slight grin disappeared, like the sun vanishing behind the clouds, and she was suddenly sorry she'd asked. He never said much about his family, and she'd never pressed him about it. "It was okay. How was yours?"

"Good. We stayed up late Christmas Eve watching movies and eating all the treats Nina made us while she had a long video call with her whole family back in San Fran to celebrate with them. We slept in Christmas morning, then opened presents, and we all pitched in to get the turkey done on time for dinner. You're gonna love her, by the way. And Avery, too."

"I'm sure I will. What about your training? How's that going?"

It meant a lot that he'd asked about her biathlon training. With Rylee gone, she purposely kept busy these days to stave off loneliness, working full time as a personal assistant, and training five days a week. Conditioning, strength training, skiing, shooting at the range. "Pretty well. Still have a lot of things to work on, but I'm trying hard."

"Didn't you have a competition a few weeks ago?"

"Yeah. I placed eighteenth out of twenty-two. So, better than last time, but still not where I need to be if I want to make the national masters team." In the biathlon world, at thirty-four she was considered old. If she wanted a spot on the national squad, the masters category was her only shot.

"If you keep working as hard as you have been, you'll get there."

She wasn't hard up in the self-esteem department when it came to her abilities, but that kind of unwavering support and belief from Braxton carried a hundred times more weight than it would have from anyone else. She was grateful that he didn't see her dream as cute or amusing, and that he didn't pity her.

Outside of her family, she generally didn't give a shit what anyone else thought of her. But if Braxton felt sorry for her, it would crush her.

"If you're up to it while you're here, maybe you could help train me a bit," she added. She wanted to get a few good workouts in during her holiday, to keep up her conditioning. She'd worked too hard to backslide now.

He met her gaze again. "What kind of training?"

"Shooting." She'd started training for real in biathlon over a year ago after she'd tried an intro course and loved it. Her coach was amazing, but who better to get hands-on help from than a JTF2 sniper? And getting to spend quality time alone with Braxton was her idea of heaven. Even it was on a platonic level.

"Of course, but doesn't Tate help you?" he asked, frowning slightly. "Or you?" he said to Mason. They'd served together in JTF2 for years, before Mason had been injured in a helicopter crash and forced to medically retire from the unit and then the military soon after. He'd done security contracting work with Tate for a while, then left that too.

"They're both so busy these days," she said before Mason could answer. "Tate's doing double duty between his detective work and getting Rifle Creek Tactical up and running, and Mase is taking on everything Tate can't right now. Plus, they're both disgustingly, ga-ga in love right now, so I'm not going to drag them away from their better halves to help me fine tune my technique during the holidays."

"Avery's *definitely* my better half," Mason agreed.

"No shit," Brax deadpanned, then looked back at Tala. "Yeah, sure I'll go with you."

She hoped he hadn't agreed because he felt obligated. He was tough to read, even for her sometimes. "Great. But you let me know how you feel later on. I don't know what you guys have planned for the week. You're here for nine days, right?"

"Technically eight. Then I need to report back to

base in Ottawa. Heading back overseas a couple days after that."

She nodded, fighting a wave of cold as his words dredged up unwelcome memories of heat and dust and blood. She could still smell it, still taste it as she'd lain there bleeding into the dirt. Therapy and constant effort on her part had helped with the worst of her PTSD, but loud noises could still trigger it, and she still had nightmares sometimes. "How long will you be gone this time?"

"Little under three months left on this contract."

Are you going to get out after that? She bit the question back. It was a personal question, and he was the most private person she knew. But after this contract was done, he needed to decide whether he wanted out, or whether he wanted to re-up. And if he chose to continue, it was yet another reason why he wasn't for her.

She'd sacrificed enough to the military already. She didn't want to be in a relationship that forced her to give up even more, not even for him.

"You hear anything about your work visa yet?" Braxton asked Mason.

"Yep, mine came through last week. Big relief, because that was a major hurdle, and Avery and I getting married next year helps my case for getting a Green Card, too."

"Good." He glanced back at her. "Tate still nagging you about working for them?"

"He's mentioned it a few times." She was actually toying with the idea of working for their adventure ranch/training facility company—Rifle Creek Tactical—at least part of the year if her biathlon dreams didn't pan out. Doing the same kind of thing she was now in her private sector day job, organizing everything and then keeping everyone on task.

"I told him I'd think about it, but of course, immigration is a huge issue since I don't have dual citizenship like

Tate does," she continued. "I could probably do a lot of the work remotely if I wanted. I should know within the next four-to-six months or so if my biathlon career is going anywhere. I'll have a better idea of where I'm at after that."

"Guess you haven't seen Tate's place yet, have you?" Mason said to him.

"Just on video calls."

"It's a great house. And I hope you're hungry," Tala added, "because Nina's been cooking for the past two days in anticipation of your arrival."

His half-smile softened his whole face. "Looking forward to it. And to give them my congratulations in person."

"That's right, we've now got two weddings to celebrate next year," Tala said, patting Mason's shoulder. He and Avery had gotten engaged at Thanksgiving, and Tate had popped the question to Nina on Christmas Eve.

"You're coming to my wedding, right?" Mason asked him.

Brax screwed up his face as though he was thinking hard. "When is it again?"

Mason punched him in the shoulder. "You know exactly when it is, asshole."

"Refresh my memory," he said, glancing at Tala with a mischievous glint in his eye.

"July third, so it's right in between Canada Day and the Fourth of July." He shot another look at Braxton. "You seriously forgot the date already?"

Braxton grinned. "No, of course not. I already put in a request for the time off. But you know I can't promise anything."

Mason nodded and took the turn for the highway that would lead them up into the mountains. "I know. But it means a lot that you're trying."

The mention of the weddings dimmed Tala's mood

a little. While she was thrilled for everyone involved, especially her brother, having two members of her inner circle get engaged so close together made her feel more alone than ever. Especially when the object of her secret fantasies was sitting right in front of her.

No, she told herself firmly. She had to stop dreaming about him and be realistic. Her true feelings for him didn't matter, because she had zero chance with him. They lived in different worlds now, and besides, if and when she did risk getting into a relationship again, she wanted someone physically present and emotionally available.

Unfortunately, Braxton would never be either of those things.

CHAPTER TWO

It had been way too long since Braxton had hung out with Mason. He hadn't met Avery yet, but Braxton was thankful for her, because he hadn't seen his best friend so much like his old self since before the helo crash that had nearly killed him and ended his military career several years ago.

But as great as seeing his buddy was, getting to hang out with Tala this week was even better. She was on his mind constantly and he'd missed her like hell.

"So this is Rifle Creek, huh?" he said as Mason drove them down Main Street.

"Yep, the heart of the town right here," Mason answered. "As you can see, it's a happening place."

Brax grinned. "Looks like." There were exactly three people out on this cold, late December evening, two of them walking a dog.

The town itself looked nice, though, like a Hallmark movie setting all done up for the holidays. Rows of neat brick and timber buildings lined the town center, shops and restaurants and small businesses all decorated with wreaths and strands of lights that sparkled on the few inches of snow on the ground and rooftops.

"You like quiet anyway," Tala said from the backseat.

He could smell the faint scent of her perfume. Something light and sweet that teased his senses. It had been a long time since he'd seen her in person. Too long. He'd missed her, and all his senses were focused on how close she was now. Close enough to touch, yet still out of reach, no matter how he wished things could be different.

He inclined his head. "I do." He was introverted and liked his own company, a big plus considering his job meant spending a lot of time alone or with just a handful of others in dangerous, forward areas. But he'd make an exception for his buddies, and Tala. She was one of the few people he felt at ease with and could really be himself around.

Tala and Rylee were quiet as Mason chatted away, pointing out various places they passed, including a haunted restaurant called Poultrygeist that served the best chicken in town. Braxton wanted to check it out while he was here.

As soon as they got beyond the town center, things got even quieter. The houses began to thin out, the lot sizes becoming increasingly larger away from town, some with wooded areas in between.

"So now we're technically out in the country," Mason announced a few minutes later as he made a left turn into another residential neighborhood full of what mostly looked like well-kept historic homes. "Tate's place is just near the end of this road."

The sun had set almost an hour ago now, leaving the twilit sky stained purple and studded with bright stars. The beam of the Jeep's headlights illuminated the snowy street ahead, making the crystals sparkle. On either side of the road, the houses were all lit up with holiday lights, some of the windows aglow with lamplight.

Something stepped out into the middle of the road

ahead of them and Mason automatically hit the brakes. "Is that Reggie?" he said.

Braxton was aware of both Tala and Rylee leaning forward between him and Mason to stare out the windshield with him, and of the scent of Tala's perfume intensifying. "It's a goat," Braxton said, for a moment wondering if the jetlag was making him see things. But no, that was definitely a goat, and he was pretty sure it was—

"Wearing a...Santa hat." What the hell?

The animal stood in the middle of the road, either too stupid to move or defiantly standing its ground against the Jeep, Braxton wasn't sure. "Oh, Reggie. Stop him, Mase, and I'll take him home," Tala said.

Before Braxton could make sense of what was happening, Mason leaned on the horn.

The goat jerked once, its unblinking gaze fixed on the Jeep, then keeled over there in the middle of the street.

"Oh, shit," Brax muttered, pretty sure that Mason had just killed someone's pet.

"No, he's fine," Tala said, and jumped out.

He didn't look fine.

Brax hopped out after her, zipping up his jacket against the biting cold and hurried after Tala, wanting to help. The goat was still lying there like road kill, its stiffened legs sticking straight out as if it was frozen solid.

"Reggie, you bad boy," Tala said as she neared it, her chocolate-brown waves flowing down her back. He'd imagined stroking his fingers through them so many times before kissing her, of fisting them in his hands while he buried himself inside her and she cried out his name. "How did you get out of the yard again?"

The goat seemed to be starting to recover. Moving around a little and weakly trying to get to its feet. But when Tala got close it jerked again and toppled over.

Jeez, maybe it had epilepsy. "Need a hand?" he asked Tala.

"Sure, if you don't mind carrying him." She moved out of the way.

Braxton eyed the goat as he got close. The thing was staring right at him through one weird-shaped pupil, the little red Santa hat covering its other eye, an elastic strap holding it in place beneath his bearded chin. "What's wrong with him?"

"Nothing," she said on a laugh. "Reggie's a fainting goat."

He glanced at her in surprise, got lost for a second staring into her big brown eyes, and swore he read silent yearning there for a split second. Her face was so close, and the intimate way she watched him made it damn near impossible to keep his hands off her. The way she'd hugged him at the airport had filled the empty void he'd been carrying around inside him for too long. Holding her for those few precious moments had made his whole chest ache, but he hadn't been able to stop himself.

She was dangerous. Testing his self-control to an extent no one else ever had, even though he had to keep his hands off her and never let her know how much he wanted her. For reasons he was well aware of.

Realizing he was staring, he snapped back to the present and responded to what she'd just said. "For real?"

"Yep. Tate's neighbor raises them. Come on, I'll open Curt's gate and you can put him back in the yard."

Braxton bent to gather up Reggie. The little goat bleated but didn't struggle, staring up at him, his body rigid.

Braxton straightened and started carrying him down the street behind Tala, lit up by Mason's headlights. He couldn't help but admire the sexy shape of her lithe, toned body, or notice the way her jeans hugged her ass just below the edge of her thermal jacket. The slight hitch in her gait from her prosthetic was barely noticeable now. She'd come so far in her recovery, and was now a competitive biathlete. She was one of the strongest people he knew.

Christ, he was totally gone over her. And he needed to make sure no one ever found out.

Mason followed behind them slowly, lighting their way. "That's Tate's place there," Tala said, pointing to the right.

He glanced over. Tate had told him the two-story log home had originally been a cabin back when the town had been home to a booming timber industry. It had since been renovated and expanded to include a deep wrap-around porch.

The windows along the front glowed with warm light in the growing darkness, a Christmas tree full of multi-colored lights filling one. A column of smoke curled from the stone chimney in the sloped roof, promising a real wood fire.

Braxton couldn't wait to unwind in front of it later with a whiskey and catch up with everyone. It had been a long few days of travel getting here from overseas and he was looking forward to unwinding. Hopefully with Tala, though being alone with her was a double-edged sword that brought both pleasure and pain.

"Curt's right next door," Tala said, continuing past Tate's driveway to the next house, a two-story wood craftsman-style with a front porch lit by a single strand of white lights.

Mason pulled into Tate's driveway. Braxton followed Tala up to the gate, inhaling her sweet scent as it carried back to him on the light wind. He made himself stand back while she opened it, the whole time imagining backing her up against it and kissing her until she was weak and clinging to him.

"Just set him down inside."

Braxton did, holding onto the animal until it got its feet under it. Reggie gave a little bleat and wobbled precariously. He looked okay until Tala closed the gate and the metal latch caught with a clang.

Watching over the top of the fence, Braxton shook his head as Reggie once again jerked and fell over. "Damn, that's gotta suck," he said, trying not to laugh.

Tala chuckled. "Reggie's quite the character. So's his owner."

No sooner had she said it than the front door opened and a man stepped out, his bearded face and long, gray ponytail lit by the porch light. "Who's there?" he growled.

"It's Tala, Curt. Tate's sister. Reggie got out somehow. We just put him back in the yard."

The man's scowl disappeared. "Oh, thanks so much. How the hell did he get out this time?"

"I don't know, but the Santa hat is a riot."

Curt grinned. "You should see the antlers I got him. But I had to take the bells off them. He kept fainting every time he moved," he said with a chuckle, then lifted his chin at Braxton. "This your man?"

Tala's pretty eyes shot to Braxton. "No, he's—"

"I'm Braxton. I'm a friend of Tate's," he said. Though, hell yeah, if circumstances had been different, he would have given anything to be Tala's man.

"I'm Curt." He eyed Braxton's jacket. "You a vet?"

"Still active duty."

He gave Braxton an approving nod. "Marine?"

"No. Canadian Forces."

"Oh, another Canuck. Well, welcome to Rifle Creek, northern neighbor. Tala, tell your brother to come by tomorrow for that holiday drink I promised him."

"Will do. You still seeing Mrs. Engleman, by the way?"

One side of his mouth turned up. "Maybe."

"Good for you. Have a good night." She turned to Braxton as Curt went in and shut the door. "See? A character. And just wait until you meet Mason and Avery's neighbors."

"Can't wait," he murmured, bemused. Rifle Creek might be quiet, but was the furthest thing from boring so far.

"Come on, Nina's probably got dinner waiting."

They walked side by side back up the road to Tate's place, the cozy-looking log house situated near the front of a large lot surrounded by a mix of trees. He itched to be able to wrap his arm around Tala or at least hold her hand. He liked just being close to her. Liked that it was only the two of them, and that she felt comfortable enough in his presence not to fill the silence with chatter.

Tala was comfortable in her own skin. She knew who she was, knew what she stood for, and what she wanted. Those were the things he found sexiest about her, though it was a long list. There was no one like her. And if he wasn't so fucked-up inside and unsure what his future held, he might have had a chance with her.

I want someone who will put me first, she'd told him once, and it had stuck hard. He wasn't in the position to offer her that, and didn't know if he ever could due to his career.

Then there was the additional factor that none of his previous relationships had ever worked out. As in, ever. Every single time he'd gotten involved in one, the woman had ended it, frustrated that he couldn't or wouldn't give them what they needed.

They'd told him he was emotionally closed-off, that he didn't know how to open up or let them in, and then, of course, he was gone for up to a year at a time because of his job. He'd never been good at showing emotion, and his training had made it worse. The hell of it was, while being able to disconnect from his emotions was what made him good at his job, it also made him a walking disaster in a romantic relationship.

The simple truth was, he wasn't equipped to make one work. And the last thing he wanted was to risk losing

Tala because of it. So he was forced to worship her from afar. Including her body. And he definitely shouldn't have imagined her naked, or getting her underneath him or the look on her face when he made her come.

Oblivious of his thoughts, Tala led him around the side of the log house and through the door off the porch. As soon as he stepped inside, Braxton drew in a breath and groaned. "Smells great, whatever that is."

"It'll taste great, too. Nina's our little domestic and cosmic goddess of sunshine."

He hung his jacket on a hook on the wall beside hers and followed her through the mudroom toward the voices beyond the entryway. The whole place felt homey and cozy, welcoming. As soon as they stepped into the kitchen, a recently remodeled and upgraded space that suited the rustic style of the house, he spotted Tate standing at the counter.

"Hey, you finally made it," Tate said, grinning as he came forward to hug him. "How's Reggie?"

"Hopefully vertical again by now," he answered, clapping a hand on Tate's back.

Tate stepped away and reached for the pretty Latina woman standing at the granite-topped island. "This is Nina. Nina, Braxton."

"Hi. So glad to meet you in person finally," the curvy brunette gushed, and before Braxton could even open his mouth to reply, he found himself engulfed in a floral-scented hug.

He returned it a bit awkwardly, meeting Tate's amused gaze. "Hi. Congratulations on your engagement."

Nina beamed up at him. "Thank you. It was so romantic, the way he asked me." She leaned into Tate, looking up at him adoringly.

Braxton raised an eyebrow at Tate, who was smirking. Romantic, eh? That was something he wouldn't associate with Tate, but she would know better than him.

"And this is my Avery," Mason said, pulling a tall, striking strawberry-blonde toward him.

Avery made a scoffing sound. "I can introduce myself," she told Mason wryly, then turned to Braxton with a polite smile. "Hi. Nice to meet you." She held out a hand, her gaze direct, no-nonsense.

"You as well," he answered, biting back a grin as he shook with her. Mason needed a firm hand. Looked like he'd found exactly that in Avery.

Nina clapped her hands and hugged them to her chest, her face all but glowing with happiness. "Everything's ready. Who's hungry?" She'd set the entire meal out on the island, buffet-style. "Everyone help themselves. Guests first," she said, handing Braxton a plate with a smile.

He murmured a thanks and moved to the first platter, a mixed salad with fruit and cheese and nuts. Six other dishes were laid out beside it. Meat, pasta, several kinds of vegetables, potatoes, bread. "Wow," he said.

Tala hummed in agreement as she stepped up beside him with her plate. Just that fast, awareness tingled across his skin and in his gut. Her cheeks were still pink from the cold. He drank in the sweep of her dark lashes, the light smattering of freckles across her nose, her lustrous, deep brown hair falling past her shoulders.

He wanted to kiss each one, then dip down to explore that sexy mouth. Wanted to lift her up, turn and pin her to the closest wall so he could settle his hips against her core and drink in all the sounds she made as he gave her pressure and friction exactly where she needed it.

If she were his, he would show her exactly how beautiful and sexy she was by worshiping every inch of her body until she was crying out his name and clenching around his fingers and tongue as he made her come. Then he would ease his cock into her slick heat and ride her slow and steady until she exploded again, claiming her completely.

"This is what Nina does," she said, jerking him out of his wayward thoughts. "She always goes all out with food." Rylee was next in line beside her, followed by Mason and Avery.

At movement near ground level, Braxton glanced down to find Ric sitting at his feet, staring up at him with intelligent eyes, one brown, one blue.

"He's looking for the weakest link in the treat train," Mason said, a bottle of root beer in one hand as he grabbed some cutlery for himself and Avery from down the island. He'd stopped drinking during his recovery from the injuries he'd sustained in the crash, realizing he was in a downward spiral with booze. Braxton admired him for recognizing it and taking action. "Don't be the weak link, Brax."

Braxton blinked down at Ric, torn. He looked so hopeful, and he was so cute and fluffy. *Just one bite*, those eyes seemed to plead. *One little taste, I won't tell. It'll be our secret.*

"Just ignore him," Tala advised with a soft laugh that sent heat curling through him. "And you'd better fill your plate up, or Nina will fill it for you."

He tore his gaze away from Ric, cleared his head of all sexual thoughts of Tala, and dutifully began scooping portions of everything onto his plate. Nina had set the table in the dining room, so Braxton carried his plate there, waited to be told where to sit, and pulled out Tala's chair for her since she was seated next to him.

She smiled her thanks and scooted in toward the table, giving him a little sidelong glance that had him curling his hands into fists to keep from reaching for her.

It took everything in him not to lean over and kiss that tempting mouth right here in front of everyone. She had him all tangled up inside even though he knew damn well nothing good could come of crossing that line.

The sudden flare of impatience at not being able to act on his impulse caught him off guard. It was totally unlike him. His control was legendary within his unit. He was known for being calm, level-headed, cool under pressure.

Tala made him feel exactly the opposite, and those little hints of interest from her made it worse. Just by being close to her, she stoked the secret fire burning inside him until it raged right below the surface.

God. He wanted her more than he wanted his next breath. But he couldn't have her. Not if he didn't want to lose her, and possibly Tate too, along with their business Braxton had signed on for with him and Mason.

The conversation flowed easily around the table while they ate, even as the incessant hunger hummed through him. Mostly it was Nina and Mason carrying the conversation while the others piped in occasionally, and Braxton mostly observed, way too caught up in his head because of the woman next to him.

He consciously relaxed his muscles. Being here felt so strange, a kind of culture shock, but in a good way. This was a different world from the FOB in northern Syria he'd been living in for the last few weeks, sleeping only in short snatches and eating field rations. Facing enemy rocket fire every night, and far worse every time they went outside the wire.

Here it was safe. Peaceful, and everyone under this roof was connected by bonds of family and upcoming marriages—except for him. Sitting around this table now made him acutely aware of his status as an outsider, that he'd been included in this cozy circle as a kind of honorary member. But he wasn't one of them. Not really.

The cold, hard truth was, he was alone. Even his family wanted nothing to do with him.

He pushed the thought aside and kept eating, too focused on Tala beside him, and the continual tide of hunger she created inside him. The flashes of interest he'd seen from her tonight and on their recent video calls made this even harder.

He was way too attached to her as it was, stemming back to the day she'd been wounded. Expert as he was at masking his feelings, he had to work twice as hard to hide his feelings for her. He'd managed it this long. He could make it another week without cracking.

"So, Braxton," Nina said, turning the conversation to him with a smile from down the table. "What did you do for Christmas?"

He swallowed the food in his mouth, his hand tightening around his fork a bit as six pairs of eyes settled on him expectantly. He hated being the center of attention, and this topic was one he'd rather avoid. "I was on base at Dwyer Hill. They put on a turkey dinner there with all the trimmings."

"Oh." Nina glanced at Tate uncertainly, then back at Braxton. "So you... No family holiday then?"

"No." He was aware of Tala shooting him a compassionate look, and hoped the hell she didn't feel sorry for him.

Braxton forced a small smile at Nina. She didn't know she'd hit a sore spot. Or that he'd swallowed his pride and tried the whole family Christmas thing again last year, flying home to Vancouver to show up to his mother's place Christmas afternoon. It had gone exactly as well as he'd expected.

When he'd arrived she'd already been drunk to the point of unconsciousness, lying on the couch while some romantic movie played in the background, a sea of bottles and food containers around her. His brother had been long gone, off with the latest woman he'd moved in with to support his drinking habit, even though he'd known Braxton was coming—having just returning from a fucking war.

He shrugged. "We're not close, so..."

"Oh. Sorry." She set down her fork and grabbed the closest dish—pasta. "Here, have some more. There's plenty," she told him with a gentle smile, an unspoken apology in her eyes.

Braxton took it, returning the smile. Nina had a soft, kind heart. No wonder Tate had fallen for her so hard and fast despite his gruff edge.

"And some of this," Tala said, reaching for the scalloped potatoes in the center of the table. "I know they're your favorite."

Speaking of kind hearts... Tala's was both strong and soft. She was a force of nature, could be intimidating, endearing, and downright adorable by turns. The thought of never being able to make her his set off a searing ache inside him.

"So when do you think you might be up for taking me shooting?" Tala asked him.

The question threw him for a second. "Whenever you want, as long as it works with whatever meetings the guys have set up." He glanced at Tate and Mason, part of him hoping they would say it wouldn't work out.

Mason shook his head. Tate waved his hand in dismissal. "We'll make it work. She's been desperate to ask you."

Desperate? He shifted his gaze to her.

"No, I haven't," Tala said, but her cheeks flushed and she wouldn't look at him.

Why was she embarrassed? He'd love to take her shooting, which was why he'd downplayed his reaction when she'd first asked him earlier. Spending time alone with her would be a form of torture, but he'd withstand any amount of pain to be with her.

"I'm in," he told her, gratified when she met his gaze again. She had the most gorgeous eyes, a soft, velvety brown with golden flecks.

"Okay," she said, a smile stretching those full lips that he'd imagined kissing and doing other X-rated things to more times than he could count.

He banished those thoughts, but they refused to stop tormenting him. "What time?"

"I'll call you tomorrow and we'll set something up."

"Sounds good." He just hoped his legendary self-control wouldn't fail him when they were alone together.

CHAPTER THREE

It was late by the time Avery and Mason brought him back to their place after dinner, a big, brick Victorian closer to the "downtown" area. Having grown up in the busy and increasingly crowded Lower Mainland south of Vancouver, Braxton found that term amusing when used to describe Rifle Creek's little business and shopping district.

"I know how you love your privacy, so we're putting you in the downstairs suite instead of upstairs with us," Mason told him, leading the way down a set of stairs from the kitchen.

The suite had Mason's stamp all over it, with his blade and weapons collection mounted on the living room wall. "This is where you lived when you first moved in, huh?" He missed Tala already, and he'd only left her ten minutes ago.

"Yep. Just set your stuff in your room and then let's head back up so we can talk business for a while."

Braxton had been hoping to avoid this conversation until tomorrow after he'd had a solid night's sleep, but Mason was clearly impatient to start now. "Sure."

He'd just set his bag on the foot of the queen-size bed

when the doorbell rang upstairs. "Let me guess, it's the neighborhood watch," Mason muttered from the doorway, then reversed direction and motioned for Braxton to follow.

They took the stairs back to the kitchen. "Yup," Mason confirmed when he turned the corner and saw whoever it was through the long sidelights on either side of the front door.

Braxton stood back a little as Mason pulled it open to reveal two elderly women standing there with identical gray hairdos. "Well, if it isn't my favorite sister neighbors," he said.

The woman in front beamed at him. "Mason, hi. We saw you pull in and wanted to come straight over with a little something we made for you and your guest." Her gaze cut directly to Braxton, the avid interest there impossible to miss as she thrust a basket at him. The other woman peered shyly over her sister's shoulder, her blue eyes magnified behind the thick lenses of her glasses.

"I'm Pat," the first one said. "And you are…?"

"Braxton," he said, stepping forward to take the basket from her. What was going on right now? "Uh, thank you. This is really nice of you."

Pat's smile gleamed in the glow of the porch light. "It's no trouble. We just wanted to introduce ourselves and welcome you to the neighborhood. Well." She waved a hand. "It's late. You enjoy that, and feel free to drop by for coffee anytime while you're here. We're just across the road, you can't miss us."

Umm… "Thank you."

"You're welcome." She glanced from him to Mason. "Well, goodnight."

"Goodnight," he and Mason chorused.

Mason shut the door, snickering under his breath. "Knew they wouldn't be able to resist the temptation long."

"What just happened?" Whatever was in the basket smelled awesome, though.

"Our adorable neighbors. Avery mentioned to them that I had a buddy coming down to stay with us for the week. Guess they wanted to check you out in person."

"It's almost midnight."

"Pat was probably waiting by the front windows all night, watching for my Jeep. Anyway, her sister is an awesome baker. What'd they give you?"

Braxton pulled aside the red-and-white checked cloth. "Muffins."

Mason glanced at them and inhaled appreciatively. "Mmm, blueberry cinnamon streusel. Bev's specialty. Come on, I'll put on a pot of decaf and we can have one by the fire."

"Sounds romantic."

Mason laughed. "Whatever, man, I'm off the market now, even for you." He paused in the living room to light the fire. "Make yourself comfy. I'll be right back."

Braxton settled himself on the velvet-tufted couch and stretched his legs out in front of it. He was glad he'd decided to come down here for his leave. He'd missed Mason, missed serving and training with him. Leaving JTF2 and then the military had almost crushed his friend. Mason had been in a really dark place for a long time afterward, and Braxton had been worried as hell about him until Avery had come along.

When they were both settled with hot cups of decaf and a fresh muffin, Braxton set aside two for Avery for the morning and Mason got straight down to it. "Things are really rolling with RCT now."

Rifle Creek Tactical, the business Braxton was a third partner in with Mason and Tate. They wanted him to be more than just a silent partner and financier, however. "You think you'll be up and operational by spring?"

"Definitely. Main lodge will be finished by March,

and April first is the initial booking date we're looking at. But before we start finalizing everything I wanted to get your take on what you wanna do."

Meaning, was Braxton going to stay in the military for another contract, or leave at the end of this current one. "I'm leaning toward reupping," he said, feeling uncomfortable. Talking about this with Mason was hard. Braxton knew how much his friend missed being part of the unit. Mason had their emblem inked on his forearm, and Braxton had the unit's motto on his.

Facta Non Verba.

Deeds, not words. That was exactly right.

People could say all kinds of bullshit. What mattered was their character, and how they chose to act. Actions always spoke louder than words.

As the silence expanded, Mason watched him with those piercing blue eyes. "How hard are you leaning?"

"Hard." He was making over six figures a year now. Giving up that kind of guaranteed salary at the pinnacle of his career for all the uncertainty that came with joining a start up, was too big a risk. Even if it came with the perk of working with his best friends.

Mason nodded. "I get it. And I'm not gonna lie, leaving will be the hardest thing you ever do, so when it happens, make sure you do it for the right reasons."

Braxton lowered his gaze, uncomfortable with the turn in topic but there was no avoiding it. Both Mason and Tate were waiting on him to make up his mind about what his future plans were. And while he hated keeping them in limbo, he flat out wasn't ready to leave the military. "I know."

It made him think of Tala. He was already thirty-five, a year older than her. She wanted a solid partner who was there for her, not someone who was gone for months at a time facing dangerous situations he could never tell her about. She wanted security, and he didn't blame her one bit.

There were a few other guys in the unit in their mid-to-late thirties, but Braxton was well aware that he was reaching the end of his time in the field. The years of physical punishment were already taking their toll on his knees, lower back and shoulders. He might only have a handful of years left before he'd be looking at some kind of transition into a training or admin position for the unit.

The idea made him mentally cringe. He shrugged, trying to make light of his decision. "I always just figured I'd know when it's time to hang it up, you know?"

Mason nodded. "Think you'll stay in long enough to work your way up the command chain? Become part of the brass one day?"

He made a face. "No, I'd hate it." He'd put his heart and soul into the unit, into being a JTF2 assaulter. Had dedicated half of his life to it. To be taken out of the action, to have his main sense of purpose stripped away from him, was gonna suck. Hard. But at some point it was going to happen.

"I think you would too." Mason shook his head. "It's so damn weird, isn't it? The job's hard. A lot of it's the shits, but when push comes to shove and you're forced with the prospect of having it all taken away, you miss it so fucking bad."

"Yeah," Braxton said quietly.

Some days he got weary of it, and yet he wouldn't trade it for the world. And he was doubly hesitant to leave because he knew damn well that once he did there was no going back. He'd feel lost, like an outsider. Watching Mason struggle with those same issues had been sobering, and Braxton wasn't looking forward to when it came to be his turn.

"Getting out's a big decision," Mason added. "You gotta be certain about what you want and do if for the right reasons, so I get it. Just know we'll always have a place for you here if you decide you want to do more than bankroll the business."

"Thanks."

Mason inclined his head and popped another bite of muffin into his mouth. "And you can still be a part of it even if you don't wind up moving down here. The immigration thing is tricky. Anytime you want to come down and teach a course, we'll make it happen. Whatever you want, we can market it to whatever kind of group you want to teach."

"Sounds good." It would likely have to do with sniping skills or outdoor survival, his specialties. He was looking forward to using both when he took Tala out tomorrow. Although keeping his feelings locked down around her and denying his baser impulses was the ultimate exercise in self-control.

"Did Tala seem interested in a position when you guys approached her?" he asked after a pause. "She's detail-oriented, and with her personality and organizational skills she'd be the perfect manager." She would definitely keep everyone on task and on schedule, make sure everything ran smoothly.

"I think she's on the fence about it. Maybe if Rylee decides to stay down here after graduation in another few years, Tala might change her mind."

Braxton nodded. "Makes sense." Her home was in Kelowna, but she loved her daughter more than anything.

The day she'd been wounded was branded into his memory. If his unit hadn't left base late, if he hadn't already been out of his vehicle and laying down suppressive fire while he rushed toward the ravaged convoy, he never would have reached her in time to help. He was thankful he had. There was nothing he wouldn't do for her.

Including keep his feelings and hands to himself, even if it killed him.

He couldn't give in. He would only wind up disappointing her, then losing her. She deserved better than that.

She deserved better than him.

****

"Move over, you're hogging the bed," Tala complained in the darkness, shoving her daughter with her hip. She was tired, but restless, unable to stop thinking about Braxton.

Rylee snorted at her and inched a bit more toward her side of the mattress. "Any farther and I'm gonna fall off."

"I can get a camping mattress from your uncle if you want to sleep on the floor."

"Or you could sleep on the floor."

"Not happening, sweetheart. I was in labor with you for twenty-three hours. You owe me for life. Literally." She shifted, getting comfortable as she draped her right knee over the pillow she'd tucked there. It helped ease the pressure on her stump.

"So, Braxton looked good, eh?" Rylee said after a minute.

Tala opened her eyes to stare at the wall, frowning. "Yeah. Why?"

"No reason. Just wondering if I need to act as chaperone between you two while he's here."

She rolled onto her back and turned her head to stare at the back of Rylee's head. "What's that supposed to mean?"

Rylee rolled over to face her and gave her some serious side-eye in the dimness. "Please."

"Please what?" She'd been careful to hide her feelings for Braxton from everyone. Or she thought she had. But Rylee had somehow picked up on it.

She hadn't dated anyone seriously since Rylee came along, and never introduced her daughter to any of them. She'd been too busy staying afloat, taking care of Rylee while working a full-time job, and being a reservist. Then she'd been injured and romance had been the furthest thing from her mind ever since—with one notable exception, and now he was here in Rifle Creek.

"All right, be that way." Rylee turned back over to face the opposite wall.

Tala poked her in the shoulder, eaten up with curiosity. And hope. Always that stupid bubble of hope that refused to go away where he was concerned. "No, seriously, what did you mean?" Had Rylee noticed something from Braxton that she hadn't?

"I'm just saying. I see what I see. And you two were sparking all over the place from the moment we picked him up at the airport. Or when he picked you up, I should say."

Her heart swelled, but she instantly scolded herself. Him wanting her that way wasn't the same as wanting *her*. "Whatever."

"Seriously. You like him, right?"

Like? She was practically obsessed with him. "Rylee. Go to sleep."

"That's not a no." She poked Tala in the back. "Come on, you totally do! You like him. Just say it."

There was no point in trying to ignore this, because Rylee knew her better than anyone, and would never let it go until she relented. "Yes, fine, I like him. Now go to sleep."

Rylee didn't answer, but Tala could practically feel the smug glee emanating from her daughter. "I like him too," Rylee said a minute later. "A lot. And so do Nana and Papa, by the way. And of course, Uncle Tater."

"Good to know," she muttered, pretending to be irritated even as her heart beat faster. It meant a lot that her family liked Braxton. He was solid, protective, and though he was reserved, he cared deeply about the people he was close to. He was the embodiment of dependable, motivated and brave.

And sexy. Sweet lord in heaven, he was so insanely sexy he revved her dormant libido just by standing in front of her.

Her mind drifted back in time to the first time they'd met that frigid winter day in Kelowna. She'd rushed straight over to her parents' place after receiving Tate's text that he'd just arrived in town.

Taking off her winter coat in the mudroom, she hurried for the stairs. "Hey, where's my welcome hug, jerk?" She rushed upstairs, expecting to find Tate at the top, then stopped dead at the sight of the stranger standing there instead.

A big, dark, gorgeous stranger.

"Oh, hi." She glanced around. Seeing no sign of her brother, her gaze strayed back to the man before her. Definitely military, she could tell by his bearing. "Sorry. I was talking to Tate before."

His lips curved slightly in the midst of his thick, dark stubble, his deep brown eyes locked on her in a way that made her heart beat faster. "You must be his sister."

"Tala," she said, offering her hand. The instant his closed around hers, a shock of awareness zipped through her.

"I'm Braxton."

Recognition flared. "Oh, you're Mason's friend." They served together, and met Tate during a deployment in Afghanistan. "Nice to meet you. Is he here too?" Tate had probably wanted to surprise her.

He dipped his head in acknowledgment. "Out on the back deck with your parents."

She slid her hands into her back pockets and leaned back on her heels, curious about him and already sensing that he was a man of few words. "What brings you guys to Kelowna?" Had to be a military thing.

"Training."

He didn't elaborate, but she guessed it must be for mountain and winter warfare training. She could get the details out of Mason later.

"There she is."

She swung around to see her brother walking toward her. "Tater." She rushed at him, threw her arms around him and laughed when he gave her the bear hug she'd been craving.

"I see you've met the straggler Mason brought with him."

"I did." She squeezed him with all her strength, not wanting to let go. "Ohh, it's so good to see you."

"Tater?" Braxton said behind her.

She let go of Tate as he answered. "Yeah, and only she and Rylee get to call me that, so don't try."

"Perk of being his big sister," she said to Braxton, a ribbon of heat curling through her when that dark gaze locked with hers.

He'd been totally magnetic, even back then. That hadn't changed.

And he was still quiet and mysterious. Controlled. Oh, so much iron control.

It made her wonder what it would take to make him lose control. The naughty part of her would love to rattle his chains and see what happened. Or find out just how he exercised it in bed.

She mentally shook herself. There was no point in carrying the thought any further than pure fantasy. She wasn't going to make the first move even if he suddenly showed an interest, and wasn't willing to throw everything between them away over what could only ever amount to a fling. Because Braxton was about the most unattainable man she'd ever met.

CHAPTER FOUR

Jason rushed up the stairs of the old apartment building, urgency pumping through him. He was exhausted and half-frozen after his latest trek back from the mountains. But almost everything was ready now. Only a few more things to take care of, and then they would finally be free.

Exiting onto his floor, he hurried down the old carpeted hallway that smelled of stale cigarette smoke and cooking grease. He could hear TVs blaring in a few of the apartments he passed, and shouting from his next-door neighbor, who was probably drunk again.

What a shithole. He couldn't wait to leave this dump behind. Leave Missoula and this whole fucking state behind, and start over in the land of sunshine and palm trees.

He unlocked the apartment door, quickly stepped inside and locked it behind him, then set his loaded pistol on the kitchen counter. He might not have much going for him, but thanks to an old veteran neighbor when he was in his teens, he was a deadly shot and a skilled outdoorsman, able to go off grid and survive even in the harshest conditions.

LETHAL PROTECTOR

He was also smart. Gifted, actually, at least according to the aptitude tests they'd given him back in school. But being smart didn't put food on the table or keep you safe when you were a kid. So he'd dropped out and made money with a local gang to support him and his sister.

"Mel?" he called. She wasn't in the kitchen or on the couch.

He walked farther into the apartment. The tiny Christmas tree he'd bought with her at a tree lot last week stood in the corner of the cramped living room, its sparse, thin branches sagging beneath the weight of the single strand of lights, and the handful of ornaments his sister had made. That and the two stockings hanging from the fake fireplace mantel—the only keepsakes from the childhood they'd both mostly rather forget—were all they had for holiday decorations.

Next year, he would give Mel the kind of Christmas she deserved.

She appeared in her bedroom doorway a moment later, her long, dark hair tousled around her face. "What?" she mumbled, looking half-asleep. Little wonder, since she'd worked the graveyard shift and had only gotten home a few hours ago.

"Come out. I need to talk to you." It had been just the two of them for the past ten years. Ever since the day Jason turned fifteen and they'd left their abusive, addict father behind in South Dakota. She was four years younger, and he'd made it his mission in life to protect and provide for her, by whatever means necessary.

At his somber tone, the sleepy haze cleared from her eyes. She tugged her robe tighter around her and came out to perch on the arm of the couch, her expression anxious. "What's wrong?"

He'd thought about how to tell her on the way home. But there was no good way. No way to break it to her gently. "You have to leave today." They'd discussed the plan at length before this. Now the timeline had been moved up.

Her eyes widened. "What? When?"

"Tonight. Because it won't be safe for you here after that."

She shook her head, her face tight with fear. "Jason, what did you do?"

"I can't tell you." The less she knew, the better. "But don't worry about me. I've got everything planned out."

"Don't worry about you? How can you—"

"It'll be all right." He had arranged everything carefully. "I just need to take care of a few more things." He softened everything with a smile, trying to soothe her fear. "Only a few more days until New Years. Then we'll be starting a brand new life out in California."

She sat frozen on the arm of the couch, staring at him with apprehension. "Are you going away again?"

"Not yet. Not until I get you out of here." He crossed to her and drew her into a hug, his heart squeezing. She was all he had in this world. The only person who loved and cared about him.

He was sick of the life they'd been forced to live here. Sick of the constant danger he'd created for himself. It wasn't who he wanted to be. He had dreams, same as everyone else. It was time he left this whole mess behind him and went after them, to help secure some kind of stable future for his sister.

"I don't want anything to happen to you," she whispered, her hair smelling of bitter coffee from the café where she worked one of her jobs.

"I'll be okay. But go pack now so you're ready to leave. I'll be back in a little while." He kissed the top of her head and left, his heart heavy but filled with resolve.

Outside, the cold night air sucked the breath from his lungs. The city was dark, the lack of light adding to the chill as he pulled up the hood of his jacket and caught the bus to his next destination.

The public pool was about to close when he got there. With only minutes to spare he entered, the weight of the pistol hidden in the back of his waistband comforting as he made his way to the lockers. He took out the backpack, paused just long enough to pull open the main compartment and check that the cash was still in it.

Zipping it back up, he shrugged the backpack on and left, taking a different route back on foot. He kept his head down and his hands in his pockets, staying aware of his surroundings even as his pulse thudded in the side of his throat. By now they would know what he'd done. The gang had eyes everywhere, and people would be looking for him. He had to get Melissa clear, and then leave town forever.

As he passed a long brick building, a cold voice spoke behind him.

"That belongs to me."

His heart shot into his throat as he froze, fear curling inside him.

"Turn around, you traitorous motherfucker."

It was too late to try to run. Alex was the head of the most powerful and feared gang in the region. He would have backup either with him or nearby.

Slowly, Jason turned around to face the man he'd betrayed, bracing for the impact of bullets at any moment. But to his surprise, Alex seemed to be alone.

"You stole my money," the other man growled out, his face cast in shadow.

"It's my money. You went back on your word," he snarled back.

Alex took a menacing step toward him, coming into the pool of light cast by a nearby streetlamp. "Your money is *my* money. Every fucking penny of it. If it weren't for me, you'd have *nothing*," he spat.

Jason tensed and readied himself to reach for his

weapon, wrenching his gaze from Alex's face to his hands just in time to see the other man begin to reach downward.

No!

His own hand flashed back to draw his weapon and aim it at his target. They both fired at the same time.

Jason ducked to the side just as a hot, searing pain burned across the outside of his left shoulder. He squeezed the trigger twice more, the shots exploding in the quiet. His aim was dead on.

Alex jerked and fell to his knees, staring at his chest in shock. Jason stared too, stunned as Alex's pistol fell to the ground with a clatter.

Those cold, dark eyes lifted and pinned Jason where he stood. "You're a dead man," he sneered, a hideous smile revealing teeth covered in blood. It dripped from his mouth, spread down the front of his shirt. "They'll hunt you down. You and your sister." He slumped over, falling on his side while a pool of blood stained the snowy ground around him.

Shaken, Jason whirled and raced off into the darkness. Holy fuck, he'd just killed Alex Kochenko, the man even the cops were afraid to go after. Word would spread fast. Jason was on borrowed time. Everyone would be coming after him now, to avenge their leader.

He gasped for breath as he ran, heart pounding, legs burning as he raced back to the apartment building. Blood seeped down the sleeve of his shirt, warm and sticky, the wound burning. He had to get home before the others came for him. Had to get Melissa out of there.

Damn, he wished he'd had the chance to send her away before he took the last of the money he'd been squirreling away from various drug deals a bit at a time, but there'd been no time. An irresistible opportunity had presented itself with no warning, one he couldn't pass up, so he'd taken it. Sneaking money from another deal when everyone else had been distracted.

And after killing Kochenko, he'd just made his own sister a target too.

He struggled his way up the steps, his mind screaming at him to hurry, hurry. His hands shook, his fingers stiff and frozen as he turned the key in the lock. He shoved the door open and stumbled inside, shutting and locking it behind him. Holy shit, he'd never imagined this happening. "Mel!"

She shot out of the bedroom, a gasp tearing from her when she saw him. "Oh my God, you're bleeding!"

He didn't care about the gash in his shoulder, only protecting her. He held up a hand when she started toward him. "No. Get your stuff. We're leaving now."

She hesitated. "But—"

"*Now*, Mel. Hurry."

She turned and fled back into her room. Jason swept through the apartment one last time, cramming everything he needed into the backpack. There was no time for another trip back. He could never return here. Might not make it out of the city alive as it was.

When he had everything he could carry, he shoved it all into the backpack and forced the bulging zippers closed. The weight would slow him down and drain his strength more than he could afford, but he would just have to deal with it.

"Mel, let's go!" he shouted, his heart knocking against his ribs. They were coming. His skin was crawling.

She hurried out of the bedroom a moment later, face pale, visibly shaken as she dragged her beat-up rolling suitcase he'd bought her at a second-hand store last year, wearing her own backpack and carrying another small duffel in her free hand. "Okay, I'm ready."

He opened her backpack and began shoving stacks of money into it. Enough to keep her fed and housed for a few months if necessary. "These are in twenties. Keep it all hidden. Don't show it to *anyone*, reserve as much of it as you can, and when you get somewhere safe, hide the rest. Keep your phone on you at all times. When it's safe, I'll contact you."

She whipped her head around to stare at him, horrified. "I'm not leaving you behind."

"You have to." He couldn't go with her when the most dangerous gangsters in the state would be gunning for him. He would never endanger her that way.

She shook her head, tears pooling in her eyes. "I can't do this by myself!"

Fuck this. There was no time. He took her face in his hands, instantly silencing her. "Yes, you can. Because there's no other way." He'd been preparing her for this moment for the last year. Talking about the plan, various things she needed to do to keep herself safe until he could join her. "Now let's go."

As soon as he released her, Melissa rushed over to the fireplace to grab their tattered Christmas stockings. She sniffed and wiped her eyes as she turned back to him, shoving the damn stockings into her coat pockets. The sight of her tears and knowing she was afraid, shredded him.

"It's gonna be okay," he promised. "Everything will be different for us in California. Just remember the plan. I'll meet you wherever you are." He shut off the lights, took one last look at the Christmas tree in the corner, then grabbed his sister's arm and escorted her out of their home.

He was on the run from the law now too, but the biggest threat he faced was from the men that until recently, he'd called his brothers.

It didn't matter who came after him. He was ready. No one was going to stand in his way. He'd killed before and he'd do it again, whatever it took to get away and start a new life with Melissa far away from here.

CHAPTER FIVE

Four years earlier

Tala woke groggy and disoriented to find herself in a strange room filled with medical equipment. She blinked, struggling to focus on her surroundings as a soft, rhythmic beeping filled the room. Everything was blurry. She felt so weak she could barely keep her eyes open.

"Corporal Baldwin, hi." A man wearing pale blue scrubs appeared in her line of vision, standing beside her bed. "How do you feel?"

"I'm..." Her heart lurched as she remembered the explosion. Of Braxton trying to prevent her from seeing her leg. And her boot holding what remained of her right foot.

Her gaze shot to the blankets covering her legs. Oh, shit, was the bulge beneath the right side shorter than the left? "My leg," she managed, her stomach twisting.

A gentle hand grasped hers. She clenched her fingers around it, fear and dread ripping through her. "The doctors preserved as much of it as they could. You just came out of surgery."

Oh God, oh God...

She started to shake. Tremors at first, rapidly changing to more violent jerking until her teeth were chattering. She was aware of the man talking to her in a low, calm voice, but she couldn't make out what he was saying.

More people came into the room. Medical staff. Tears flooded her eyes. She squeezed them shut and clamped her jaw tight, hating that everyone was witnessing her breakdown. This couldn't be happening. It couldn't be real.

She ordered herself to breathe. To calm down. She was alive. That was the main thing. She'd lost a foot, and while that sucked, it could have been a lot worse.

A warm, tingling sensation began crawling through her body.

"I know this is a shock," another male voice said close to her as she began to float.

The shaking faded, that sense of warmth blissful, taking away the fear and panic. The voice told her about the rest of her injuries. Shrapnel wounds across the front of her body, concentrated on her legs. Some burns, and a concussion.

"But you're stable now," the voice continued. "You're going to be fine. In another day or two you'll be on your way home to Canada."

Home. She forced her heavy eyelids open, desperation gripping her. "My daughter," she croaked out. "My family."

"Your parents and brother have been contacted, and know you're okay."

I'm not okay, I just had my foot blown off.

Another face appeared above her. A woman with kind brown eyes. "We've given you something to help you sleep. Just rest now."

It was a relief to let her eyes close, let herself drift on the warm current and allow it to pull her under where there was no more fear. No pain. No horror.

All too soon she was awake again. Someone was there changing the dressing on her leg. She swallowed, her heart tripping, hands clammy. She didn't want to look. Couldn't bear to see it and confirm this was all real.

She made herself look anyway.

At the blunt stump covered by a thick padding of bandages at the end of her right calf. Her stomach pitched. She wrenched her gaze away, her chest constricting as her mind struggled to accept the irrefutable evidence she'd just been confronted with.

She was an amputee. Another statistic from the war.

After a while, the visitors started coming in. First, her direct boss and commanding officer. Other members of her unit from the 3rd Division, including her two closest friends here. They didn't stay long, and did everything they could to comfort and reassure her, try to lift her spirits, but she could already feel herself sinking into a black pit of despair.

She didn't want to see anyone. Didn't feel like talking, even to her own family on the phone. All she wanted was to be left alone, and to sleep so she could escape this horrific new reality she couldn't face yet.

She dozed again, and woke when another nurse came in to check her dressings.

"Someone else has been waiting to see you," a nurse said as she changed Tala's dressings. "Sergeant Hillard is leaving soon with his unit. He's just outside."

Hillard? Tala glanced over the woman's shoulder and her heart squeezed as he appeared around the edge of the curtain. "Braxton," she said, her voice cracking. She was so glad to see him.

He edged into the room with a half-smile on his handsome face. "Hey, Tal."

The nurse tucked the blankets around Tala's hips and straightened. "I'll just give you two some privacy."

Tala pushed up onto her elbows as he walked to her bed. An immediate lump formed in her throat. She felt it quiver there, the hard knot in the center of her chest starting to melt, bringing a hot rush of tears to her eyes.

It was the most natural thing in the world to reach for him. He set something aside and bent over to gather her to his chest. The instant those strong, familiar arms closed around her, she buried her face in his shoulder and let go of her grip on control.

Deep, painful sobs racked her, muffled by his shoulder. Braxton didn't try to make her stop crying or say ridiculous, unhelpful things like *it's okay*, or *you're going to be fine*. He simply held her, both arms locked around her, one big hand cradling the back of her head. Letting her vent her grief.

When the worst had passed and she was able to get her breath back, she wiped at her face and flopped back against her pillow. "Sorry." She was exhausted. Utterly drained.

"Nothing to be sorry for." His dark brown eyes scanned her face as he pulled a chair over to the bed and sat on it. He reached for her hand, curling his large, warm fingers around hers. "I talked to Tate right after you were admitted. I thought it best your parents and Rylee heard it from him, instead of your CO. I hope that was okay."

She nodded, blowing out a shaky breath. She no doubt looked like hell right now, but she was so glad to have him here. "Thank you."

"Of course." He was silent a moment, watching her, rubbing his thumb across the back of her hand. "Is there anything I can do?"

She shook her head. "No, and you've done more than enough for me already. The surgeon told me that if you hadn't got the tourniquet in place so fast, I would have been in big trouble. What did you use, anyway?"

"My belt."

She vaguely remembered him reaching down to waist level before he tended to her leg. "I don't even know what hit me. What was it, do you know?"

"You stepped on an anti-personnel mine."

She absorbed that in silence, rage beginning to burn in the pit of her stomach. Some cowardly asshole must have planted it in the ambush area after the EOD teams had left near dawn. Now she was lying here without a foot, and facing a long, arduous road to recovery.

She blew out a breath and focused on him. "So, I hear you're headed out again?"

"Within the next few hours. I have to get to a briefing soon, but I wanted to come by and see you first, in case they transferred you before I'm back."

"I'm glad you did." He was the only visitor she'd been glad to see. A piece of home. Someone who truly cared about her on a personal level.

"I'm sorry this happened," he said quietly.

She met his gaze. "Thank you." He was the first person to say that to her. "I'll be okay, though." Not today, or anytime soon. But someday.

"I know." He said it with quiet conviction, as if he didn't have the slightest doubt. "You'll get there."

She was lucky to have a loving, supportive family waiting for her back home. The road ahead of her seemed long, lonely and endless right now, but at least she had her family to help her. And when she thought of Braxton heading outside the wire again, facing untold dangers, her chest tightened.

"You be safe out there, yeah?" She couldn't bear it if anything happened to him.

"I try to be," he said with the faintest hint of a smile. "I'll get in touch when I can, check in with you and see how you're doing."

She forced a smile, wishing he didn't have to go. "I'd like that."

He nodded, withdrew his hand and stood. "Oh. I, uh…got you something." He reached behind him and picked up something. "Maybe it's stupid, I don't know, but I saw it and…" He shrugged and held out a teddy bear.

She had no idea where the hell he'd gotten it, but it was the same dark brown as his eyes, with big amber eyes and a shiny black nose. A real smile spread across her face as she took it from him. "It's adorable. Thank you."

"Welcome." He shifted his stance, looking a little embarrassed, then he met her eyes again. "Take care of yourself, Tal. Stay strong. One day at a time."

It was good advice. She wanted another hug before he left, but she'd already clung and wet his shirt with her tears. "I will. Bye."

"Bye." He gave her one last smile that made her insides ache, then he was gone.

An awful emptiness took hold after Braxton left. She didn't know if she'd ever see him again, and that hurt more than the unbearable pressure in her chest.

She hugged the bear to her and closed her eyes. The nurse found her like that the next time she came in to change Tala's dressings a few hours later.

Tala fiddled with the bear while the nurse worked, using it to distract her through the pain of having her mangled limb manipulated, lost in thought. She needed to call her parents and Rylee, then Tate. She'd had enough time to absorb the initial shock, and Braxton's visit and more sleep had helped make her feel stronger.

She studied the bear's arms and legs, its perfect four little paws. And sudden inspiration struck.

It was gallows humor, sure, but it seemed fitting and Braxton would approve.

She touched the nurse's arm to get her attention. "Any chance you could bring me a sharp pair of scissors and a sewing kit?"

CHAPTER SIX

"You didn't bring Stumpy with us?" Braxton asked her as he drove them in Tate's truck to the closest shooting range several miles out into the country.

Tala grinned. "It's *Sergeant* Stumpy. And no, he's at home resting on my bed at Tate's place. But next time I will. We need to get some pictures of the three of us on an adventure together."

"I can't believe you named him that."

"What? That name is awesome."

He shook his head, the hint of a grin playing around the edge of his lips. "How did he wind up losing his foot, anyway? You never told me."

She relayed the story. "So, yep, he lost his foot the same day I did," she finished.

"*That's* how Sergeant Stumpy came to be?" Braxton asked, looking scandalized. "You literally took a pair of scissors and hacked his foot off the same day I gave him to you?"

"Well, you wanted to know." When he shot her a horrified look, Tala laughed. "I was lying there looking at him, and I thought it would be fitting if we could go through rehab together."

He eyed her a moment. "I had no idea you were so savage."

"Don't worry, it was all very humane. He didn't feel a thing, I made sure, and one of the surgeons offered to do the suturing for me after. He's got a perfect little stump under the prosthetic they made for him at the rehab facility."

"Well, I'm glad he kept you company through everything."

"Me too." Sgt. Stumpy had first accompanied her on the long flight home from Kandahar, then through the grueling process of her rehab, and a lot of places since.

Now she took him with her whenever she traveled or went on little adventures, then took a picture of him and sent it to Braxton. She had all kinds of shots of her little stuffed companion on airplanes and in hotels, out in the boat with her in the summer, or in his custom-made biathlon gear when she trained.

He pulled into a parking spot near the range building. The lot was empty, apparently all the local shooters home enjoying the holidays. "I liked the photo you sent me of him when you carved pumpkins at Halloween."

She smiled at the memory. "First time Rylee wasn't there to carve with me, so I wanted the company." She'd dressed Stumpy up in a little Jason mask and taken pictures of him holding a toy chainsaw and covered with orange bits of pumpkin. "I used a Dremel tool to carve the designs, so it looked like a pumpkin slaughterhouse in my kitchen. There were even pumpkin bits on the ceiling fan and windows at the end."

"It was a picture that said a thousand words." Braxton shook his head, his lips curving in amusement as he turned off the ignition. "Can't believe you still have him."

"I could never get rid of Sergeant Stumpy, we've been through too much together. And, he reminds me of you."

Those deep brown eyes cut to her and held, and she blushed as an answering wave of heat swirled through her. She hadn't meant to say that last bit out loud, but it was true. That bear symbolized Braxton for her, and had helped her through a lot of hard times.

"Why, because we're both dark and furry?" He ran a hand over his scruffy jaw.

She laughed, thankful he was letting her off the hook so easy. "No. Because you're both good listeners, and you've both supported me through everything."

He continued to hold her gaze for a long moment, and that all-too familiar yearning began to expand inside her once more. "Well then, I'm glad."

"Me too. So," she said, changing the subject to a safer topic. He'd been busy all morning with Tate and Mason, visiting the building site on the property they'd bought for Rifle Creek Tactical. Now it was almost three, giving them only another hour or two of daylight to work with.

"What do you want to get out of this session today?" he asked her. "I know you've got something specific in mind."

As a matter of fact, she did. "By the time we leave, I want to be hitting all five targets consistently from a standing position."

He shot her a knowing look. "By consistently, you mean always."

Her lips quirked. "That'd be nice. How do you want to do this?" She reached into the backseat to grab her custom .22 biathlon rifle. Tate had ordered her ammo and targets as a Christmas gift so she could train while she was down here.

"Want to start inside, or just go straight to the outdoor range?" he asked.

It was cold and the wind was icy, but no worse than

what she'd face in a lot of competitions. "Whatever you think's best. You're the expert." There was no one better to help improve her shooting. As a master sniper, Braxton was one of the best shots in the world, and knowing she was about to get personal instruction from him had her giddy with excitement.

Of course, her excitement level was also in part because he was the sexiest man alive and she was about to have his undivided attention for the next few hours.

"Let's start inside, so I can watch you there and see what we're working with," he said.

"Okay. I won't be able to simulate everything perfectly, because I've got a special prosthetic for my skis. Sometimes after I finish a tough sprint, I'm a little wobbly when I come into a range on a course, especially near the end of a race when I'm exhausted."

He nodded. "I'll take a look at your positioning."

The idea of having his eyes on her so closely was simultaneously thrilling and nerve wracking. But he wasn't here to admire her figure or stare at her booty, he was a professional who'd come at her request to offer her critical feedback on her shooting. Hopefully the nerves buzzing in her stomach would disappear once they started working.

The range master was expecting them, since Tate had called ahead to inform him they were coming. He introduced himself, set them up inside the empty indoor range, then went back to his desk.

"Bet you've never seen one of these up close before, huh?" Tala said to Braxton as she took her rifle out of its case, then added proudly, "A custom .22 with non-optic sight and a straight-pull-bolt action."

"No, never." He accepted it and checked it over with practiced motions, and just seeing him holding her rifle sent a shiver of longing through her as she imagined those hands handling her instead.

She would bet he was just as confident and controlled with a woman as he was with a rifle. It was so unfair that she'd never find out firsthand.

"How much does it weigh, around ten pounds?"

"Mine's just under eight. Extra mags are stored in the stock, and each clip holds five rounds."

He handed it back to her, his eyes full of interest. "Zero it out, and let's see what you've got."

Right. Down to business. "In para biathlon we shoot from the prone position at ten meters, and the targets are one-point-eight inches wide for prone. Just so you know. But there aren't many para events for me to attend in B.C., so I've mostly done regular ones and shoot from fifty meters. Also, my wrist can't touch the ground when I shoot prone."

"Got it." He folded his arms across his chest, momentarily distracting her with the way his deep blue sweater clung to the muscles in his chest and shoulders.

She thought about the hug at the airport, when she'd been held against all that male power, and went a little weak at the knees. She wanted to rub her face all over his chest like a cat. "Okay, I guess I'll start standing, since it's my weakest stance."

Damn, she was way more nervous than she'd anticipated. Maybe this wasn't such a good idea. Maybe she should have asked Tate and Mason to come with them, to have a buffer. Improving her shooting enough to give her a shot at making the national masters team was her new dream—and then maybe the Paralympics. This was important to her.

Pushing all of that and Braxton's distracting presence from her mind, she focused on the task at hand. Conditions inside the range were optimal, so she didn't have to compensate for temperature, wind and poor light conditions.

But when they finally got around to moving outside,

that was another story, and it was where Braxton would really shine. He had an incredible amount of experience and knowledge to draw from in compensating for a myriad of conditions. She couldn't wait to pick his brain about all of that.

She adjusted the paper row of five small, circular targets she'd brought and moved it out to fifty meters. Once ready, she assumed her stance, aimed, and fired two shots. Both missed the first two circles slightly up and to the left.

Her face heated, embarrassment washing through her because Braxton was watching everything. As an elite military sniper he routinely took shots from a distance of up to a kilometer or more with a large caliber weapon, and here she'd barely hit the paper target fifty meters away.

She bit back the urge to babble about being much better than this usually, and quickly adjusted the rifle's sight, the metal hand-screws clicking with each turn. Two clicks down, two clicks right. With that done, she put the butt of the weapon into position against her shoulder, tried to shove Braxton from her mind and awareness, and fired again.

"Almost dead center," he said from behind her, the impressed note in his voice warming her to her bones.

She relaxed a little. "Obviously, I'm much better at ten meters. And normally I do this after finishing a hard ski when my heart rate's through the roof, I'm gasping for breath and my hands are freezing. I find standing position a lot harder than prone. Mostly because of my balance when I get fatigued."

He nodded. "Try again and I'll watch your stance closer."

Tala faced the target, ignored the new little butterflies swirling in her stomach, and cleared her mind. She focused on her breathing, sharpened her aim, and fired at the last three targets. She hit two of them, but not center, and the last one missed a half-inch to the right.

LETHAL PROTECTOR

She lowered the rifle, her pulse picking up when Braxton approached her from the side. Without a word, he reached out to grasp her upper arms and turned her upper body slightly, the innocent contact sending a rush of heat through her.

Then he grasped her hips, gently pushing her forward a little, and her belly flipped at his touch, her mind imagining his hands moving over other parts of her. "Widen your stance. More weight on your left leg, bend your knees a bit more, then tuck your chin down a little farther."

She did as he said, feeling the warmth of his hands through her clothes even after he removed them. Hell. She exhaled and centered herself. "Like this?"

"Little wider, and more weight on your left leg."

She complied, automatically bending her right knee a bit more to compensate. "Okay?"

"Try it."

The paper targets were all marked up, but it didn't matter for now. She loaded a fresh clip, took aim at the first target, and fired. This time she hit all but one circle.

Lowering her weapon, she looked over at him and smiled, surprised but excited by how quickly he'd been able to help her. "Okay, you're the best shooting coach *ever*."

One side of his mouth kicked up, his dark eyes warming. "Yeah?"

"Without a doubt." Just those small adjustments had improved her aim and balance so much. Her coach was great, but Braxton was elite on a rifle, and he'd been able to see subtle problems no one else could have in such a short time. A product of a lifetime spent honing his skills, and conducting joint missions with the world's most elite SOF units like Delta and DEVGRU.

Energized and feeling more confident, she loaded another clip and fired at the targets again. This time she hit all five.

Grinning, she faced him again. "Well, then. Let's hope I can replicate this outside during a race." Conditions were much trickier then, but what he'd taught her so far was definitely helping.

He grinned back, and her heart damn near did a somersault under her ribs. He was a gorgeous man, but when he smiled... Damn, he took her breath away. "Happy I could help. Wanna try prone now?"

"Yes." Pumped, she loaded a new clip and lay down on her stomach. Assuming her firing position with her legs spread out in a V, she hooked the rifle's arm sling to a firing cuff on her upper arm and took aim. This time she hit three out of five targets.

"You're faster prone," he remarked.

"Being prone helps steady everything, but it's still hard for me to slow my heart rate down during a race. I'm still learning how to slow that and my breathing when I ease into a range after a ski segment." It was a damn hard sport, but that's why she was so hooked on it. She loved the challenge of it, pushing herself and competing against the elements as well as the other athletes.

He nodded again, as if that made perfect sense. "Do what you normally would during a race, and hit it again."

She focused back on the target and snugged the butt of the rifle against her shoulder, pretending she was in a race. Body relaxed, breathing slow and easy, she counted her heartbeats and squeezed the trigger between two.

Three shots hit close to center. The other two, barely within the edge of the circles.

She glanced over at him. "See? There's definitely more room for improvement." He made her feel scattered.

Her pulse kicked as he approached her again, anticipation curling inside her as he crouched next to her left side and grasped her hips in his hands. Sparks tingled across her skin, a dozen erotic images exploding into her mind. Of them both naked, his hands closing on her hips with firm authority as he positioned her how he wanted her, his lips caressing the side of her neck as his deep voice caressed her like velvet.

You're gonna come for me, Tala.

Oh, shit. She shook the thought away, annoyed that she couldn't control her wayward thoughts around him.

Braxton's grip tightened on her hips. "Relax," he murmured, jostling her gently.

His touch and nearness made relaxing impossible, because her entire body was going haywire. She forced out a breath and consciously relaxed her muscles, aware of the sensual warmth sliding through her, like warm honey.

"That's better. Now come up just a little more on your elbows and settle into the position. Yeah, like that." His hands closed around her shoulders, firm and sure, steadying her as he squared them more. "How's that feel?"

Distracting. And really damn arousing, because it made her want his hands on more of her.

"Good," she managed, hoping the hell he couldn't tell what was happening to her. She was acutely conscious of his eyes on her as he stepped away, and that forbidden curl of heat deep inside her that she couldn't quite ignore completely as she focused on improving her aim.

She lost count of the number of rounds she fired as the lesson progressed, but finally she was down to her last clip. She managed to hit all five targets with it, and finished with a real sense of improvement and accomplishment.

When she started to get up, Braxton was there, gripping her left hand to help her to her feet. "That was really great, thank you," she told him, trying not to stare at him at such close range. He smelled delicious, and she recalled with acute detail every touch of his hands.

"I barely did anything. You were already solid, we just needed to make some subtle tweaks."

She loved that he said we. "Maybe next time we can try it out on the trails, if you're up for some cross country skiing while you're here."

The corner of his mouth lifted, and she wanted his lips on hers so bad she almost moaned. "I'd like that." He glanced at his watch, breaking the spell. "We'd better get back. Mason and Avery are making me dinner."

"Oh, sure." Squelching her disappointment, she quickly packed up her stuff and followed him back out to Tate's truck. They talked about shooting on the way back, but she was preoccupied, her mind still back in that shooting range.

It was getting harder and harder for her to conceal the depth of her feelings for him. And sometimes when she caught him watching her, she'd wondered if maybe there'd been a glimmer of interest there, but it had to have been just wishful thinking. In all the time she'd known him, he had never hinted at being attracted to her, and he'd certainly never made a move.

Somehow, she had to accept that they would never happen. He was married to his unit. The last thing she wanted was to make things awkward between them going forward, or to be hurt later on.

Braxton meant too much to her. She would rather live with this constant ache in her chest than not have him in her life at all.

****

Tate grabbed his keys from his desk in his office at the station and stopped by Avery's door on the way out. She glanced up from her computer when he knocked. "Hey. You heading out?" she asked.

"Yeah." He walked in and stopped in front of her

desk. "You see the new alert that just came in?"

"I glanced at it, but didn't read it yet. Why, bad news?"

"It's not good," he allowed. "You should take a look." He waited for her to pull it up on her computer.

She frowned slightly as she read it. "Jason Fenwick. Twenty-six, gang member with a long rap sheet, currently based out of Missoula." She glanced up at Tate. "Let me guess, the Red Phoenixes?"

"Yep." The gang had reorganized itself early last year, and had become a force to be reckoned with.

For months now they'd been embroiled in a turf war against local biker gangs in the state and surrounding region, but had recently concentrated their power base in Missoula. They'd taken over a lot of territory, at great cost. The body count continued to grow each day, and the sudden explosion of gang violence in the city had been all over the news for the past several months. Authorities there were trying their best to stop it, and getting nowhere fast.

Avery went back to reading aloud. "Wanted for murder now in addition to multiple weapons and drug charges." She looked at Tate. "He's a suspect in the killing of the Red Phoenix leader last night? And now he's missing. Go figure."

"*Reported* missing, and rumors say he was killed in a shootout late last night. Missoula PD dragged a burned body from the river early this morning. Still waiting for confirmation from the coroner whether it's him."

She leaned back in her chair and arched a strawberry-blond brow at him. "And you're concerned about this because…?"

"Because I just got a tip from a concerned local who saw the story on the news today. He reported seeing someone matching Fenwick's description close to Rifle Creek late last night—well after the alleged shootout with the

Red Phoenix leader, and before the guy they pulled from the river was killed. I looked into it, and apparently Fenwick stopped in town briefly to get food, then was sighted later walking along a trail leading up into the mountains."

She nodded, her jaw tightening. "So we might have an armed killer in our town."

He didn't like it any more than she did. They'd dealt with more than enough dangerous shit here over the past few months, and he didn't want any more of it in his town. "Yeah."

"I'm guessing you've alerted the department, so the on-duty officers can check it out?"

"Two officers are following up on the lead now. In the meantime, we have no confirmation that Fenwick is dead, so he definitely could be in the area. Until we can either confirm he's dead or bring him in, everyone needs to keep a sharp eye out."

CHAPTER SEVEN

"You sure you don't wanna play?" Tala asked him with a sweet smile the next morning.

Braxton had thought about her nonstop since their shooting lesson yesterday. Including last night when he'd finally crawled into bed and stroked himself off while imagining her naked and on her knees, taking the length of his erect cock between her lips.

He cleared his throat. "I'm sure. But thanks." He stayed put in his easy chair in the corner of Tate's living room. He'd come over with Avery and Mason an hour ago for a brunch thing that had somehow transitioned into games.

Games weren't his thing, and charades was about the worst one he could think of. He'd rather stick something sharp in his eye than have to get up in front of everyone and make an ass out of himself, even his closest friends and their significant others.

"Aww, are you sure? I know you hate being the center of attention, but it's all in good fun," Tala said, looking disappointed.

And as gorgeous as ever in black leggings and a body-hugging red sweater, her long brown hair falling in waves around her shoulders, shining in the lights of the Christmas tree in the corner opposite Braxton. She looked happy and relaxed, like Christmas itself, and while he would do pretty much anything for her, he drew the line at charades.

"Positive." The whole thing made him feel awkward and out of place. Besides, in the interest of fairness, both teams should have the same number of people, and he would make seven.

"Okay then, you're keeping score." Mason shoved a notepad and pen at him, already marked with the names of the two teams at the top. "And no cheating. No giving the ladies more points just because they're better looking than us."

"Hey," Rylee complained. "I'm better looking than you guys too, but I'm still on your team."

Mason grinned and hugged her to his side. "You're gorgeous. But even with you, we're still not winning in the looks department against those three." He nodded at Avery, Tala and Nina.

"You're not going to win, period," Tala said, her competitive side starting to show. She liked to win. "You guys are going *down*."

"Talk is cheap," Tate fired back, looping an arm around Rylee's shoulders so she was sandwiched between him and Mason. "Let's see who's talking trash at the end of the game."

The ladies went first, and things got spirited right from the outset. Braxton was amazed and amused by how into it everyone got. There was shouting and laughing and whoops and high-fives, along with groans and complaining.

Avery threw a decorative pillow at Mason for a comment he made, then so did Nina and Tala. Braxton threw one at him too for good measure, beaning his buddy in the side of the head when he wasn't looking.

Mason whipped around to stare at him, a look of betrayal on his face. "Hey."

"You've had that and a lot worse coming to you for years, and you know it. Be glad it was only a pillow."

Everyone burst out laughing, and Mason grinned. "Yeah, okay, I'll concede that point. What's the score, anyway?"

"Ladies lead eight to five."

Mason frowned and grabbed the paper from him. "That can't be right. You're giving them extra points." He studied the tally.

Braxton yanked it back from him. "It's right. Go save your team, if you can."

The game resumed, with both teams intent on winning. Observing everything from the corner, Braxton felt a pang in his chest.

His family had never played games like this. Most of his childhood memories were of him being alone. His brother was ten years older and hadn't wanted much to do with him. His mom had been lost in her own booze-soaked haze of depression.

He'd learned early on to amuse himself and be content with his own company, taking long bike rides or playing in the woods. Sometimes he'd join up with some neighborhood kids to play road hockey, but he'd been too young for them to bother with most of the time.

Watching everyone now, he realized he envied what they had. They were all so comfortable with each other. They had a sense of belonging he'd only ever felt in the military. Maybe that's why he'd bonded so fast and hard with Mason during the selection phase. Neither one of them had known the love and security of family.

The game finally reached the last round, with the ladies up by one. "You guys need to win this to tie," Braxton informed the other team.

"Yeah, yeah," Mason muttered, distractedly waving

a hand at him as he walked into the center of the room and put the piece of paper containing the prompt into his pocket. "Don't let me down, guys," he said to Tate and Rylee.

"Don't let *us* down," Rylee retorted, making Tate chuckle.

Braxton started the timer on his watch. "Go."

Mason dropped to the floor on his stomach and started slithering around the rug.

"Snake!" Rylee shouted. "Worm! Salamander!"

Mason put his hands to his neck and started fanning them as he slithered on the floor, now kicking his feet. Ric got up from his bed by the fire and rushed over to lick at his master's face, back end wiggling like crazy.

"Cut it out, Ric," Mason said with a laugh, and gently pushed him away to resume his act.

The room went silent. Then Nina gasped, her face brightening. Avery smacked her arm and gave her a warning look. Nina sat back, biting her lip as she watched Mason and his team.

"Tadpole?" Tate guessed.

Mason shook his head and got to his knees, making a weird expression with his face. Eyes bulging, mouth opening and closing as he kept his wrists stuck to the side of his neck and waved his hands. Braxton smothered a chuckle at the ridiculousness of it all.

"What the hell is that?" Tate demanded.

Everyone started laughing. Tala laughed so hard she snorted. Braxton glanced over at her, unable to hide his smile as she broke into an infectious belly laugh.

"Trying to win over here," Mason said to her, a sarcastic edge to his voice.

"You just look s-so rid—ridiculous," Tala choked out through her laughter, then grabbed a throw pillow and held it against her face to muffle it.

Meanwhile, Mason continued whatever it was he

was trying to convey, now shuffling around the coffee table on his knees, watching his team earnestly. Nina was still biting her lip, glancing from Mason to his team, clearly thinking she knew what he was portraying.

"Mutant!" Rylee finally shouted in desperation, frowning in intense concentration as she focused on Mason.

"I don't know *what* the hell it is, but he looks like he's in pain," Tate said, shaking his head. "Are you in pain, Mase?"

Mason shot Tate a dark look and finally climbed to his feet to walk around, first bent over a bit with the fishy fins at his neck, then lumbering around with his arms swinging like—

"Bigfoot," Tate said.

Mason rolled his eyes and straightened as he kept walking around the room, now lifting his eyebrows at his team in a disbelieving *come on, it's obvious* way. Both Rylee and Tate stared at him with identical blank expressions that made Braxton grin. Nina shifted restlessly on the couch, looking ready to explode.

"Time," Braxton announced when the final second ran out.

Mason groaned and sagged dramatically, shooting a frustrated glower at his team. "It was—"

Nina jumped up from the couch before he could finish. "Evolution," she shouted, all excited.

Mason gestured to her with his hands, eyes wide as he confronted his team. "Yes! Thank you. You see?"

Rylee made a strangled sound. "Wh-what? *That's* what that was?" She burst out laughing, and Tala joined in with her.

"Jesus, Mase, that was terrible," Tate said over the laughter filling the room. "I mean, how in hell did you expect us to figure that out from what you were doing?"

"Uh, I was so clearly *evolving*, right before your eyes

in the space of a single *minute*. Everyone knows life started out in the primordial ooze and then into the ocean before moving onto land."

Nina nodded, face sober now. "He's right. I knew exactly what it was as soon as he transformed into the first fishy thing."

"Thank you," Mason said, lifting his chin.

"Aww, bad news, guys," Avery told him and his team with a look of fake sympathy. "Losers gotta do the dishes."

"Rules are rules," Tala agreed, looking extremely pleased with the outcome.

"Fine," Mason muttered. "But I'm never teaming up with Tate for charades again. He sucks at it."

"I can live with that," Tate said with a grin as he followed Mason and Rylee into the kitchen to start the cleanup.

Setting aside the tally sheet and pen, Braxton rose to go with them.

"Where do you think you're going?"

He froze and looked over at Tala, who was curled up on the end of the couch with the pillow in her lap, watching him with an appreciative gleam in her eyes that made his insides tighten. "To help clean up."

"I was hoping you might be up for doing something else instead."

Oh, she had no idea what he was up for where she was concerned. And even though he should be keeping a bit of distance from her now to avoid tempting fate more than he already had, he couldn't. Didn't want to. "What've you got in mind?"

"I was hoping you might want to go cross country skiing for a couple hours this afternoon. Rylee's already warned me not to ask her, and the others want to just chill at home for the rest of the day. Meaning, they want some *alone* time."

If she were his, he'd want the same damn thing. For as long as he could get. "Then skiing it is."

Her smile lit up her whole face, and all he could do was stare. "Good. Let me go find Tate's gear. You're taller, but it should still fit you okay." Then she was off.

Braxton headed into the kitchen, his gut telling him he was making a mistake by going out with her alone, but the rest of him was desperate for it. The others glanced up at him as he took a dishtowel from the oven door handle. "I'll help dry, but then Tala and I are heading out to do some skiing."

"Good, but keep an eye on her," Tate said as he washed a pan in the sink. "She tends to overdo it and push farther than she should with her leg."

"Runs in the family, huh?" He liked that Tate was protective of her. It was clear to anyone with eyes how much he and Tala adored each other. And Braxton knew that Tate had hero-worshipped his big sister for his whole life. He'd wound up joining the Marines because of her example.

Tate grinned. "Guess it does."

Braxton answered when spoken to as he helped tidy the kitchen, but his mind was already jumping ahead to the moment he'd be alone with Tala again. His exes had all accused him of being too remote and unfeeling, but maybe they'd been wrong, because he felt things for Tala that he'd never experienced before.

The deep craving for her wasn't easing up. If anything, being here had intensified it.

Looking back, he could pinpoint the exact day it had started. That hot August afternoon last summer when he'd visited her in Kelowna with Tate and Mason. They'd all gone out on the boat together to waterski. Tala had declined, sitting at the stern.

When it was his turn, he'd jumped in the water and put the skis on, then grabbed the rope. Looking up once he was in position, he'd found her watching him, floppy-brimmed hat shading her face. Even through the dark lenses of her sunglasses he'd felt her gaze on him like an electric charge throughout his body. He'd made that initial run with a raging erection pressing against the front of his swimming trunks.

On the final jump he'd attempted to impress her, he'd wiped out pretty bad. He surfaced just as Tate circled the boat back around for him, wiping the water out of his face. A hand reached down for him. He grabbed it without thinking, expecting it to be Mason's, but the slender structure made him look up in surprise to find Tala there.

Her grip was solid, but it was the look on her face that made something shift inside him. She'd taken off her sunglasses. Those pretty eyes were full of concern, and a tenderness that drove the air from his lungs. Her expression made it seem like he truly mattered to her.

Staring up into her eyes, he felt his heart go into freefall.

"You okay?" she'd asked him, anxiously scanning his face.

"Yeah, I'm good." Perfect, now that he was the focus of her undivided attention and concern. If her brother and Mason hadn't been watching, he would have reached up to curve a hand around her nape and pull her down to claim those tempting lips right then and there, and to hell with the consequences.

That moment was still so clear in his mind. As clear as the moment he'd realized how close he'd come to losing her forever the day she'd been hit. Seeing it happen, then visiting her in the hospital later, had triggered all his protective and possessive instincts. They fit. He'd never felt smothered or craved space when he was with her. That said it all.

He'd almost blurted out the truth to her the night following that day on the boat, but his relationship track record and her being Tate's sister had stopped him cold.

It took a moment for him to come back to the present fully. When he did, he realized that the kitchen had gone quiet. He glanced at Rylee, who was watching him expectantly near the sink. "Sorry?" Had she said something?

Her lips twitched. "Nothing. Your mind is clearly elsewhere." Her eyes twinkled. "What's her name?"

He wasn't touching that one for a million bucks.

"You keeping something from us, Brax?" Mason asked, his expression full of interest. "You seeing someone?"

He opened his mouth to say something sarcastic, but Tala stepped into the kitchen. Her gaze moved from Mason to Braxton, and he would have sworn that was sadness he saw in her eyes. "No. I'm not seeing anyone," he answered, watching her intently, his muscles tightening.

Relief flashed across her face, so fast he almost missed it. But a huge part of becoming a sniper meant learning to notice tiny details others missed, and he knew what he'd just seen.

He went dead still, his fist locking around the dishtowel. Holy fuck, if she was actually into him…

Without warning, a tidal wave of hunger and possessiveness crashed over him. He struggled to rein it in, his pulse picking up, the urge to plunge his hands into her thick hair and kiss her until she couldn't stand up on her own.

Then she smiled, a private smile just for him, and it was suddenly hard to breathe. "I've got the stuff. You ready?"

Somehow he unlocked his jaw enough to respond as blood rushed to his groin. "Ready." He tossed the damp towel at Mason, not even watching to see if his buddy caught it. He was already following Tala to the door, his gaze locked on her ass as his pulse thudded in his ears.

He shouldn't touch her. Couldn't risk crossing the friends line with her.

But if she wanted him, God help him, he didn't think he'd have the strength to hold back.

****

The sun was still high overhead, but it was cold, and as soon as the sun dipped below the treetops, the temperature would start dropping and it would get dark fast. He needed to be inside his meager shelter long before then.

Jason paused at the crest of the hill, gasping as he bent over to catch his breath, hands on his knees. The air was thinner up here at this altitude, and the sharp cold made his lungs ache.

The gash across the outside of his left shoulder had opened up again. He could feel the blood seeping through his sleeve, and his upper back burned from carrying the heavy backpack all the way up here from the small town of Rifle Creek. He couldn't stop yet, though.

He blew on his fingers in an effort to warm them in his gloves, but they'd gone numb a while ago. Getting out of Missoula alive had been the easy part. Now it was him against the elements, and he had to be smart. Mother Nature was a cruel bitch, especially in these mountains in the dead of winter. Mistakes up here could be deadly.

Good thing he was more than prepared to meet the challenge.

Straightening, he ignored the exhaustion weighing his limbs down and forced his tired legs to carry him down the far side of the ridge. The snow was deep here, his boots sinking through the dry powder with each step, quickly draining what was left of his endurance.

His stomach growled, reminding him that he hadn't eaten since early that morning when he'd grabbed a quick meal at a café in Rifle Creek before beginning his trek up here. He pushed aside the cold, the hunger and sense of desperation eating at him, focused on the only thing that mattered.

Survival, and the new life waiting for him on the other side of these mountains.

He thought of Melissa alone on a bus right now, heading to the West Coast and facing an uncertain future all by herself. She was depending on him to fulfill his promise and meet her in California in another few days.

She needed him. He was all she had. He wouldn't let her down.

He'd walked this same route a dozen times now during previous supply drops over the past several weeks, and knew the area by heart. This part of the mountain was deserted, accessed by only the occasional hunter or hiker. Any bears would be deep in hibernation now, so the only animals he had to worry about were cougars.

He was a lot more worried about the human predators out there.

Members of his former gang would be hunting him. Looking for any clue that might lead them to him. He'd been careful, but someone might have seen him, and there would be a sizeable, internal reward offered by the gang for killing him and avenging Alex. All it took was one lead, one sighting of him in Rifle Creek earlier that someone reported to the cops, and the gang's most lethal enforcers would be on his tail.

The tiny wooden shack appeared through the evergreens up ahead when he rounded the corner of the snow-covered trail. It was built of old timber from the forest, hand-hewn and silver with age, its roof sagging under the weight of another winter snowfall. Some hunter or prospector must have built it more than a hundred years ago. Jason only cared that it was empty, isolated, and that the old, cast-iron potbellied stove still worked.

There were no other tracks in the snow leading toward or away from the shack. The wooden door creaked when he pushed it open, scraping along the uneven floorboards. Breathing hard, he groaned in relief as he shrugged off the backpack and let it drop with a thud at his feet to look around. Everything was exactly as he'd left it the last time he'd been up here a few days ago.

It was freezing inside so he put some wood into the stove and lit it, standing close as he surveyed his secret cache in the glow of the flames. Survival gear. Clothing. Food, water and emergency supplies. Enough to get him through another few weeks as he began his trek through the mountains and evade anyone looking for him.

And enough weapons and ammo to take out anyone stupid enough to try.

No one would ever find him out here. Not his former gang, and not the cops. All he had to do was make it to the other side of the next peak, and he'd be safely on his way to meet his sister.

Jason lowered himself to the old, bare floorboards and held his hands toward the flames, deep in thought. He was ready to see this through, prepared to do whatever it took to make it happen. His gaze strayed to one of the stolen rifles propped up in the corner. The one with the high-power scope that would give him an edge over anyone hunting him.

A sound from outside made him freeze. The sharp call of a white-tailed ptarmigan, followed by the startled flurry of wings. He would have missed it if he hadn't been so attuned to his surroundings.

Someone was out there.

He shot to his feet and grabbed the ballistic vest. As soon as he had it on, he reached for the rifle in the corner, loading a full magazine into it before heading for the door. Pressing his back to the wall beside it, he waited. Listening.

Moments later, he heard it again. More birds being startled into the air near the shack.

His heart slammed into his ribs, anger and fear twisting inside him. Someone had come for him. But if they thought he was an easy target, they were wrong.

Dead wrong.

Flinging open the door, he rushed through it with the butt of the rifle to his shoulder, his eyes scanning the area near the shack. His peripheral vision caught a flash of movement to his right.

The sharp crack of a gunshot exploded in the silence, a bullet slamming into the side of the wood siding behind him a split second later.

He pivoted to face the shooter and fired a burst of two shots, then dropped to one knee.

Silence.

His pulse hammered in his ears as he waited, every muscle in his body tense. But there were no more shots. No other movement, or even sounds, just the sighing of the wind and the faint creak of branches overhead.

Moving cautiously, he got up and crept toward the shooter, ready to fire. He spotted the body lying behind a tree trunk. A man, on his back.

Jason moved closer, keeping his finger on the trigger. But when he got closer, the man's sightless eyes were staring up at the swaying treetops, the snow around him rapidly turning red.

He swallowed, nausea churning in his stomach as he stared down at the dead man's face. One of the most feared of Alex Kochenko's lethal enforcers. The man had somehow tracked him all the way up here. Would have killed him, if Jason hadn't been so alert.

He glanced around, cold crawling up his spine. Enforcers usually worked alone, but there could be more coming. And when this one didn't return, someone would follow to find out what had happened. Jason had to get rid of the body.

Slinging his rifle across his back, he dragged the dead man by the feet through the forest. Deep into the woods where no hiker or hunter was likely to go.

He covered the body with snow and a pile of branches, then left it for the carnivores and the winter snows would bury it. Before long, there would be nothing but a pile of bones, and by then Jason would be in California with his sister.

He started back to the shack, rifle at the ready, gaze moving restlessly around the quiet forest. Ready to dole out the exact same fate to anyone else who posed a threat to him.

CHAPTER EIGHT

Okay, coming up here had been a fantastic idea. And Tala had definitely made the right choice in inviting Braxton to join her.

"Isn't it gorgeous out?" She looked up at the patch of brilliant blue sky framed by the tall evergreens surrounding them on either side of the trail they were skiing on. Pure freedom.

"Sure is," Braxton agreed as he came up alongside her.

He'd been quiet since leaving Tate's place, but that was nothing new. Even so, she sensed some sort of tension coming from him and couldn't tell what it meant. "Feels good to stretch my legs again."

They'd driven Tate's truck to the Rifle Creek Tactical property, put on their boots and skied out to the trails from the parking lot at the building site. Now the hammering and noise from the power tools was barely audible in the background, replaced by the quiet swish of their skis over the snow in the silent forest.

"You look pretty comfortable on those," she told him, admiring his technique. Smooth. Powerful.

"Had some practice over the years," he said with another of those sexy half-grins, his lips tugging upward. "Did a lot of it when our unit came out to do mountain warfare training at SilverStar when we first met."

The mountain resort about an hour's drive from Kelowna. "Figures."

"Yeah. Until then I'd only done downhill and some snowshoeing."

"So what do you think? Which do you like better?"

He thought about it a second. "Downhill's more fun. Cross country's a better workout."

"*Yeah,* it is," she agreed. It was great to build cardio and endurance, especially at this kind of altitude. "And I've got the advantage over you, because my biathlon skis are shorter and stiffer than regular cross country skis."

"I'll try to keep up with you," he teased.

She raised an eyebrow at him. "That a challenge?"

He met her gaze, and she felt an electric thrill race through her. "What if it was?"

"Then I'd be forced to leave you in the dust."

"And I'd make sure I caught you."

She almost stumbled on her skis at the sexy way he said it, and the unmistakable heat in his eyes. It was there and gone in an instant, just a brief flash, but it stunned her.

She jerked her gaze back to look ahead of them while her heart thumped against her ribs. Had she just imagined it? Was she reading something into it that wasn't really there? Because holy hell, she'd give anything for that interest to be real.

"Looks like someone beat us up here earlier," he said.

She followed his gaze to the right and spotted a set of footprints in the snow. They hugged the trail she and Braxton were skiing on for a few hundred meters, then cut through the trees. "Hunter maybe?"

"Could be. Or just someone looking to get away from

civilization for a while."

The tracks disappeared into the trees where the shadows swallowed everything, while the trail ahead of her remained clear. "The others don't know what they're missing, huh?" she said to change the subject, still off-balance about his previous comment and wondering if she was losing it.

"I like that it's just the two of us."

That made her look over at him again to try and read his expression, but as usual it was neutral, giving nothing away. It was frustrating as hell. Then again, he'd never come out and told her he liked spending time alone with her before.

Stop with the wishful thinking. You're going to get hurt. "Me too. Did you ski growing up?"

"Just on school field trips. My mom's not an athlete."

No, she was an alcoholic. "What about your brother? Did you do any sports with him?"

"No. He'd already graduated and moved out long before I started getting into any sports in school."

She was silent a moment, absorbing that. He never said much about his family, but from the little she'd pieced together, it hadn't been a happy home, and it didn't sound like he'd grown up with much support around him. It made her sad to think of him being lonely as a kid. "Do you ever see your dad?"

He shook his head, his gaze focused on the trail ahead. "Not since he left when I was five, and that's good with me."

"Oh." She shot him a curious glance, hoping he would continue, but not about to push him. Braxton was the most private person she knew.

"He's the one who turned my mom onto the bottle," he said after a moment. "And she's always blamed me for him leaving."

Ouch. And so fucking messed up, to put that all on

an innocent kid. That would be like her blaming Rylee for her sperm donor taking off.

No wonder he was so quiet and had a tendency to come across as remote. They were protective mechanisms he'd learned young. "We don't get to pick our families. I'm lucky I was born into a good one, although we've gone through our share of dysfunction too."

He shot her a curious look. "Yeah, what's the story with your parents, anyway?"

One side of her mouth kicked up at his puzzlement. "It's quite a story. They split up when my mom found out my dad got Tate's mom pregnant. I was a toddler. My dad married Tate's mom, but they eventually divorced when Tate was ten, and my parents got back together about a year after that."

She shrugged at the surprise on his face, knowing how messed up that must sound. "It all worked out in the long run. Tate and I spent most weekends together with my dad before his mom moved him down here after they divorced, and thankfully my mom never held a grudge against him. She adores him, as you've seen."

"He's lucky."

"Yeah, but who doesn't love Tate?" She was eighteen months older, had loved him from the first moment she'd seen him, and his gruff façade was all show. He was a total marshmallow with the people he loved, and she was thrilled that he'd found Nina.

"Your mom's an amazing lady."

"She sure is. And she's a lot more forgiving than I am. I love my dad, but if he'd been my husband, I wouldn't have taken him back. If anyone cheated on me, we'd be done. End of story."

"Good to know," he said thoughtfully, and again she couldn't tell what to make of it, or what was going on in his head. "What about Rylee's father? You've never said anything about him. Is he still in the picture at all?"

"No. He took off when he found out I was pregnant and I refused to have an abortion. His family moved him back east somewhere and none of them have made contact since. Rylee knows his name and could look him up if she wanted to. She's talked about doing it, but she said it's more of a curiosity thing for her. She's not interested in having any kind of relationship with him, since he couldn't be bothered to reach out to her over the past eighteen years."

He nodded. "How old were you when you had her?"

"Sixteen."

Man, that had been hard. Looking after a baby while trying to finish high school. When she'd gotten pregnant almost all of her friends had dropped her like she was some kind of pariah. She'd never been ashamed, though. And she'd never regretted keeping Rylee. "I couldn't have done it without my parents. They've been there for me through everything. And of course, I love my kid more than life itself."

"She's a pretty great kid. Takes after her mom."

She smiled and glanced over at him, warming at the compliment. This whole conversation so far was longer and deeper than any they'd shared before. "Thanks. I like to think so."

"You're right, though. You are lucky. To have your family."

"They're your family too, Brax."

His gaze shot to hers, and something dark and desperate moved in his eyes. As though he secretly yearned for the same connection and bond she had with her family. Her heart squeezed.

"They are," she stressed, wanting him to believe it.

"That's good." But the smile he gave her didn't quite reach his eyes. Had she said something wrong?

They lapsed into silence after that. At first she was a

bit uncomfortable, wondering if she might have inadvertently put her foot in her mouth, but Braxton was quiet most of the time, so she decided not to worry. The uphill section of the trail she'd picked lay ahead. It was long, the steady incline pushing her endurance to its limits.

"We can slow down," Braxton said, and she was gratified that he was breathing hard too.

She shook her head, not wanting to waste precious oxygen by replying, and kept going. By the time they reached the top of the climb and neared their destination, she was tired, but at least her stump wasn't that sore.

"Lookout spot should be just up here," she panted.

He made an affirmative sound and kept pace with her, but the uphill section had been a challenge for him too.

The trail ahead curved sharply to the left. Suddenly the trees began to thin out, letting fingers of sunlight pierce between the tall trunks to slant over the snow in front of them. Tala turned left and found herself at the top of a high cliff with a 270-degree panoramic view all around her.

"Wow," she said as Braxton came up beside her.

It looked like a painting. Pure silence surrounded them like a blanket. Rifle Creek cut through the canyon below like a bright, curving ribbon in the midst of the snowy canvas, sunlight glimmering on its surface as it rushed downhill.

"There's the building site," he said, pointing a long arm past her shoulder.

She followed it and saw the main lodge of Rifle Creek Tactical, the size of a postage stamp in the middle of the cleared section of forest. "Amazing. Lucky we got out to see this today when it's so clear." There was a weather front moving in over the next few days and the forecast called for more snow later in the week.

She glanced up at him. "How do you feel? Was the

view worth it?"

He looked at her, that deep brown gaze sweeping over her face in a way that made her mouth go dry. "Definitely." She didn't think he was talking about the natural beauty before them.

Her heart tripped. Her body was humming, her muscles warm and pleasantly tired. But she didn't know what the hell to make of the way he was looking at her now, or some of the things he'd said. This was a new side to him she'd never seen before.

"How's your leg?"

That snapped her out of her reverie. "It's fine. But it can tell I had a good workout." Even with the extra precautions she'd taken to protect her stump, she'd have to give it a close inspection when she took the prosthetic and sleeve off once she got back to Tate's. Because she definitely wasn't doing it in front of Braxton.

His eyes crinkled at the corners with the hint of a smile, the sun bringing out sable highlights in the few days of inky growth on his face. The admiration and interest in his gaze made her pulse skip. He'd said some flirtatious things, but hadn't made a move. What would he do if she kissed him right now? Pull away?

Or pull her close. The possibility made her breath catch.

"Want to rest a bit before we head back down?" he asked.

"No, we should get going." The sun was already behind the treetops. Wouldn't be long until the shadows made it hard to see the trail properly. "It'll be way easier and a lot more fun on the way down, we can just coast most of the way."

"If that's what you want, sure."

She couldn't have what she really wanted, so she'd have to settle for just spending time with him and driving herself crazy. "Yeah, let's start back."

The way down was easy, with only a couple of short uphill sections requiring the use of poles. They didn't talk much, and he didn't say anything remotely flirtatious. They made it back to the truck in under half the time it had taken them to reach the lookout point, and by then she was cooled right down.

From the truck cab, she handed him an insulated thermos of honey-sweetened tea spiced with cinnamon, ginger and cardamom. "Brought you this."

"Thanks." He tipped it back as he took a sip, a quiet moan of pleasure coming from him that she'd love to hear under far more intimate circumstances. With him naked and gripping her hair as she sank down on him or took him in her mouth. "Damn, that's good."

"Right? I always make it for after I train." She drank some of her own, which was barely warm now.

He loaded their skis and poles into the bed of the truck while she went to the passenger side to quickly remove her one ski boot and custom prosthetic, swapping it to her everyday one that she'd fitted into her winter boot. When she stood again to put her weight on the prosthetic sleeve to lock it in place, she blinked to find Braxton suddenly there in front of her.

She stopped, looking up at him, her pulse skipping at the focused look on his face. She couldn't read his expression but his stare was intense. As if he had something important on his mind that he needed to tell her.

"Is...everything okay?" she asked slowly.

He shifted his feet but didn't answer, and his hesitation worried her.

"Brax? Is something wrong?"

He glanced away, ran a hand over his jaw, then focused on her again. "What you said earlier. About me being part of the family." His voice was low, taut, the muscles in his jaw and shoulders tight.

She frantically tried to gather her scattered thoughts,

wondering what had upset him. "What about it?"

"Is that how you see me? As family?"

Something in his tone, in the silent tension coming from him, gave her pause and warned her to phrase her answer carefully. Especially when she took into account the things he'd said earlier. Was he hinting that…

Voicing her feelings aloud made her feel incredibly vulnerable, but she needed to be honest right now, because this would change everything, one way or the other.

Holding his gaze, she drew a steadying breath before answering. "If you're asking if I think of you in a brotherly way, then… No." Not even a little.

He stilled, his gaze sharpening, the leap of heat of that dark stare sending a ripple of shock—and hope—through her. "So how *do* you think of me?"

She looked away, fighting a blush as her discomfort level skyrocketed. She didn't want to make a fool of herself or be humiliated if he didn't reciprocate her feelings. "I…"

"Tal. Look at me."

She did, and felt herself drowning in those deep brown eyes, all the feelings she'd repressed for years suddenly rushing to the surface.

"Say it," he rasped out.

I've wanted you forever.

The unspoken words got tangled on the tip of her tongue. But she couldn't look away. Couldn't drag her eyes from his, her pulse pounding in her ears as she waited for him to say something. Do something to put her out of her misery.

He took two steps toward her, stopping inches from her boots to reach both arms past her. He leaned in to cage her against the truck doorway with his big body, his hands on either side of her head, the muscles in his arms, shoulder and jaw standing out.

And his eyes. The sudden, volcanic heat in them

made the breath stall in her lungs.

Shock punched through her, followed by a wave of molten desire as she stared up at him, his face mere inches from hers. She had to be reading this wrong. Had to be, because he was staring at her like he wanted to devour her and was struggling to hold back.

"Tal." His voice was low, his taut expression making her heart thud against her ribs. He'd only ever looked at her like this in her dreams.

"What?" she whispered back, anticipation and need swirling inside her. *Touch me. Oh, God, touch me...*

His face was set, but the stark yearning she read in his eyes sent another rush of arousal through her. She held her breath as he lifted a hand.

He raised a hand. His fingers grazed her temple, raising goosebumps. They curled into her hair for a brief moment, then stroked a lock of it away from her cheek, the tips skimming across her skin.

Tingles burst outward from his touch. Down her neck to her chest. Her nipples tightened, her core clenching in pure need.

Tala automatically reached for his shoulders, anticipating the moment when he put his mouth on hers. She sank her fingers into the padding of his jacket, until they met the firm muscles beneath.

They were rigid under her hands, his eyes locked with hers. Over six feet of powerful, hungry male standing right in front of her, so close she could feel the warmth of his body and breath in his scent of snow, evergreen and spiced tea.

One hand still locked on the truck, he searched her eyes for a moment, then his gaze dropped to her mouth.

Her insides flipped. Barely breathing, she watched him, unconsciously leaning forward, her eyelids drooping in anticipation of the kiss she knew would be better than she'd ever imagined.

But then he lowered his arms and stepped back. She blinked, confused, and gripped the edge of the doorframe for balance, her pulse thudding and her body on edge.

He stood there before her, unmoving. Jaw taut, eyes smoldering with suppressed need.

Braxton wanted her. But not enough to cross the invisible line he'd drawn between them.

He shook his head, his expression unreadable now. Then, as if he couldn't help himself, he lifted a hand to graze the backs of his knuckles down her cheek. "I always knew you were dangerous," he murmured.

She blinked, biting back a protest as arousal, confusion and unfulfilled need pumped through her. "Me? Dangerous?" What was he talking about?

Dropping his hand, he made a low sound in his throat, a kind of frustrated growl, then turned away to head around the front of the truck. "We'd better get back before they decide to form a search party and come looking for us."

Tala collapsed backward into the passenger seat and sucked in a deep breath, her mind reeling. What the hell was he trying to do to her?

She'd give him space for now, but she wasn't letting this go. She refused to let him toy with her and her heart. If he wanted her, he would damn well be the one to make the first move.

CHAPTER NINE

Jesus, he should never have fucking touched her. Because now the hunger he'd fought to keep at bay was a million times stronger than it had been before.

Braxton groaned and ran a hand over his face as he sank deeper into the hot tub tucked under Tate's back deck, letting the steaming water envelop him up to his neck. Dinner wasn't for almost another hour, but he'd needed time alone to unwind, especially with Tala here. So he'd come out here to get away from everyone for a bit and get a grip on himself and find his missing control before he had to face her again.

He'd almost blown it earlier and was furious with himself. He'd given too much away as it was. Now Tala was no doubt confused by his hot/cold behavior. She knew he'd been a hair's breadth from kissing her.

The drive back had been strained. Neither of them had said anything when they'd gotten into the truck. Tala because she'd probably still been in shock, and he because he didn't know what the hell to say.

Just when she'd turned at him and opened her mouth to finally say something, her phone had rung. Rylee, asking for a ride from a friend's house back to Tate's.

LETHAL PROTECTOR

Tala had stayed on the phone with her until they'd arrived at her friend's place on the outskirts of town to pick Rylee up. Then they'd stopped to grab Nina some groceries downtown, and Rylee had chattered the rest of the way back to Tate's. There had been no time for him and Tala to talk, and for that he was grateful.

Shit. He'd wanted her for so damn long, had kept everything locked down tight inside him for years. Now his control was failing him.

Her comment on the trail about him being family had made him thankful he'd kept his feelings to himself this whole time. But later at the truck when she'd hinted that she wanted him, there was no way in hell he could have stopped himself from touching her.

It had taken an act of will not to kiss her. To grope around for what little self-control he had left where she was concerned and back away.

The basement door opened. He slung his head around, his whole body tightening when Tala stepped outside wearing a robe.

She froze with her hand on the doorknob, staring at him. "Oh. Sorry, I didn't know you were already in there." She started to turn away. "I'll just—"

"Wait."

She stopped and looked back at him, her expression guarded. Uncertain.

He hated being responsible for putting that look on her face. Hated feeling torn about her all the time.

Talking wasn't easy for him, especially when it came to feelings and shit. But he couldn't afford to fuck this up, and leaving things as they were would only make their situation worse. He had to find a way to fix this. "You don't need to go."

Her expression seemed a little stiff as she turned to face him. "You sure?"

"Yes." He didn't want her to avoid him. And he

needed to find his balls and level with her.

She tucked her hair behind her ear and came toward him, stopping short of the steps leading to the hot tub to wrap her arms around her waist.

It was freezing out here. She had to be cold already. "You're not coming in?"

She shook her head. "It's fine."

It wasn't fine. None of this was fine, and it was his fault. "Come in." He slid over to give her more room, putting a bit of distance between them to make her more comfortable.

She hesitated and glanced away. "I'm not sure I…"

And then it hit him. She was embarrassed to have him see her without her prosthesis when she got into the water. That bothered him. He'd been there the day she'd been wounded. He'd seen exactly what the war had cost her, and still thought she was the sexiest, most gorgeous woman in the world.

"I'll turn my back if you want," he offered.

She met his eyes again, then nodded. "Okay."

He turned away to give her some privacy, his brain supplying him with a high-def image of what she looked like as she took off the robe to reveal her bathing suit. One piece or bikini? Smooth, bare skin. Small, round breasts. Nipples taut from the cold.

Hell.

The gentle splash of water followed. He waited, still imagining what she looked like in her suit as she eased into the water. "Okay, I'm in."

Braxton turned around, and in spite of himself his gaze immediately shot down to her chest. She was in a one-piece suit, and the rounded tops of her breasts floated just above the surface of the water. Blood rushed to his groin, making his borrowed trunks too tight.

"You sore?"

He jerked his gaze up to her face, cursing himself.

She stripped him down to his basest level without even trying. "Not yet. Hoping a soak will avert that. How's your leg?"

"A little bit chafed, but not bad."

He could smell the scent of her perfume now, rising over the surface of the water with the steam. His hands itched to reach for her, to draw her into his lap and kiss those tempting lips.

And yet, even with this new tension between them, it felt right being here with her. It felt as if they belonged together. But touching her again would be a colossal mistake. If he put his hands on her again, what remained of his resolve and good intentions would evaporate.

"Why biathlon?" he asked, searching for a safe subject. He still had no idea how to broach the important one standing between them like a wall.

She shrugged. "I've always liked skiing and shooting. I was already feeling restless and looking for a challenge before Rylee left home, and biathlon seemed like a natural fit for me. But since she's been gone, it's been a godsend. I never realized just how empty I would feel, and training helps fill the void, gives me something else to focus on other than missing her and being lonely."

He hated the thought of her feeling empty and alone. It made him want to hold her even more. To kiss her and stroke her and immerse her in pleasure, and promise her she would never be alone, because she'd always have him.

Except he couldn't promise her that. And he'd be a selfish asshole to ask her to take a risk on him when he already knew how it would end. Him gone, and her kicking him to the curb one day.

I want someone who will put me first. Her words echoed in his mind.

Her eyes seemed to see straight into his soul. "Do you ever get lonely?"

He'd felt lonely most of his life. It was something

he'd learned to live with early on. Maybe that's why he was the way he was. "Sometimes," he allowed, aware that they were skating around the edge of some very thin ice right now.

"And you're not...seeing anyone now?"

He wouldn't lie to her about that, not even to make this easier. "No."

She held his gaze, as though waiting for him to elaborate, having given him the perfect opening. But he didn't know how to explain everything without hurting her.

Disappointment flashed in her eyes before she lowered her lashes. "Well. I should get out. Would you mind..." She flicked a hand at him, signaling for him to turn his back again as she reached for the top of the tub.

Don't let her go.

Without thinking, he grabbed her shoulder. She stopped and looked back at him. Her expression warned him he needed to talk. Fast.

He inhaled, a torrent of hunger ripping through him even as he fought the impulse to pull her to him. His fingers tightened on her smooth, wet skin, the urge to crush her to him and take that sexy mouth overpowering. "Tal."

Her face tensed. "What? Just say it, Brax, and put me out of my misery."

Her torment sliced him up inside. He'd never meant to hurt her. Never wanted to hurt her. "I shouldn't touch you," he rasped out, forcing himself to take his hand off her even as every cell in his body was screaming at him to drag her to him and kiss her breathless.

She frowned at him. "Why not? And don't say because I'm Tate's sister, because that's a weak excuse. We're both adults."

All the reasons for keeping his distance that had seemed so strong and important before were now evaporating as fast as the steam rising from the surface of the water around them. The insatiable hunger for her swelled inside him, a rising tide he was powerless to resist.

He shook his head, his will and iron control failing him for the first time. "I've stayed away from you like I promised myself I would. Kept my distance as long as I could, but I can't anymore. I *can't*," he rasped out, plunging one hand into the back of her hair as he pulled her close and he brought his mouth down on hers.

Tala gasped and grabbed his shoulders, the instant of surprise vanishing as she melted against him. She softened and melted into him, setting him on fire as her breasts made contact with his bare chest.

Raw need exploded through him. He pulled her closer, clamping an arm around her hips to bring her as tight to him as possible. She made a soft sound and set her hands on the sides of his face as she straddled his lap.

He went rock hard against her, her soft weight settling over the aching ridge of his cock. Oh, Christ, he needed inside her. Needed her to be *his*.

The urge to take and dominate lashed at him. He fought it back, searching for the tenderness she brought out in him. On a low groan, he shifted his grip on the back of her head and licked across her lower lip, seeking entry.

She parted her lips for him instantly, pressing closer. God help him, he obliged, delving inside to touch her tongue with his. Teasing. Hot, his heart pounding so hard he could hear it.

Tala cupped his head in her hands and stroked her tongue along his. He groaned and plunged deeper. Stroking. Claiming. Aching for more.

It was wrong. So wrong of him, but he couldn't stop. Couldn't pull back. Not with her.

Instead he slowed down, drawing it out for them both. Savoring every moment of this sensual exploration, losing himself in her.

Tala moaned softly. The plaintive sound was full of need, and it sent another wave of hunger through him, hot and heavy. She felt incredible, and the way she responded to him was so damn sexy.

But he needed to stop this before he took it too far. Because he wanted that more than he wanted his next breath. To devour her with kisses, pull her suit straps down her shoulders so he could cup her breasts and suck on her nipples. Get her as worked up as him before sliding his hand between her legs to find her clit and make her come while he drank in every sexy sound she made.

But not here in her brother's hot tub, when her brother or daughter could come out here at any moment looking for them.

With herculean effort, Braxton forced himself to break the kiss and lift his head. They stared at each other, breathing fast. Tala's cheeks were flushed, her gorgeous eyes dilated. She held his gaze, still poised on his lap, and touched her tongue to her lower lip as if still tasting him…or thinking about tasting another part of him.

He groaned and leaned in for another kiss, this one so tender and heartfelt it made his whole chest tighten. Christ, he was done for. Would do anything for her, except leave the military, and now that he'd crossed the line he might have fucked everything up between them forever.

There was no way he could walk away from this now. Not even if he knew it would lead to disaster in the end.

He cupped her cheek in his hand, gliding his thumb across her baby-smooth skin, and shook his head slightly. "This is why you're dangerous. You destroy my control, Tal. Just like I knew you would."

A slow smile spread across her face. "If you're waiting for an apology, don't hold your breath."

He groaned and touched his forehead to hers, closing his eyes. "God, Tala, I want you so damn bad."

She angled her head to kiss his cheek, the edge of his

mouth, then his lips. "Why didn't you ever say anything?" she whispered.

Exhaling, he gently grasped the back of her neck and lifted his head to look into her eyes. "Because you deserve better than me."

She drew her head back, shock washing over her face. "What? Why the hell would you even think something like that?"

He didn't want to have this conversation with her mound pressed to his cock, but there was no help for it. "Because it's true."

"No, it's not."

But it was. "I'm going to re-up after this contract. And I'm…not good at this," he managed.

She raised her eyebrows. "This? If you mean you're not good at making out, you're dead wrong."

That made him smile a little, but it faded fast as the cold weight of dread settled in his chest. "No, at relationships." It was humiliating to admit it to her.

She settled back on her heels, still perched atop him but no longer sitting directly on his erection, which was thankfully deflating now. "Why do you say that?"

His jaw tightened. She deserved to know the truth. "Because every time I try one, it never works." He glanced away. "I'm not built for it. Inside. Something's…missing, I guess."

She put a hand on the side of his face and turned it so he was looking at her again. "Nothing's missing inside you. And my relationship track record isn't exactly stellar either. I haven't been with anyone since before I was wounded."

Braxton met her eyes again, dumbfounded. Over four years. She hadn't been with anyone in over four fucking *years*? It was unthinkable. "Why not?"

She averted her gaze and eased off him, looking embarrassed as she slid to the seat a few feet away from him.

"I'm nervous, I guess. Self-conscious about my leg. But mostly..." That beautiful brown stare lifted to meet his.

He watched her, waiting. Sensing that whatever came next could change everything between them.

"Mostly it's because I don't want to be with anyone but you."

He exhaled in a rush and reached for her again, pulling her into his arms to crush her to his chest, burying his face in her soft, scented hair. "Jesus, Tal." He closed his eyes, reeling from her admission and being able to hold her like this after dying to for so long. She wanted him even though he was wrong for her. Even though he wasn't near good enough for her. "You're killing me."

She sat up and looked him in the eye, hands on his shoulders. "Where do we go from here?"

Nowhere. They should go nowhere except out of this hot tub and upstairs to eat. And then they should stay the hell away from each other before they went past the point of no return.

He'd sooner have all his limbs ripped off than never hold her or kiss her again.

The unfamiliar stirrings of fear tingled in his gut. Something he'd never experienced even on the battlefield while under fire.

There was no way he could stay away from her now. Not after she'd laid herself bare to him moments ago. But he didn't want to hurt her. Couldn't bear the thought of disappointing her and having her reject him. Not Tala. It would kill him.

He swallowed, anxiety burning in his belly. He wanted to be what she needed. Wanted to make this work somehow, but... "What if I can't give you what you want?" He was staying in the military. Wouldn't be with her for long stretches. She'd leave him for it eventually. And he would never recover.

Her smile was soft, the look in her eyes even softer.

"And what if you can?" She shook her head at him, her expression tender with a hint of exasperation. "Life is short, Brax, and I've already waited four years for you. I'd rather risk it and find out firsthand than spend the rest of my life without you and wondering what might have been. But I'm done with waiting, and done with settling for less than I deserve. So if you want me, you need to step up and be willing to put me first."

A wave of cold shot through him at her words, every reason for his previous breakups playing in his head. You're never there for me. Your unit always comes first with you. You're emotionally unavailable. You can't give me what I need. You don't know how to love someone.

Tala shrugged when he didn't answer, the motion stiff, shoulders tense. "Sorry to be so blunt. But that's what I need."

He nodded, anxiety forming a lead weight in his chest, even as he understood. His mind warned him to back away. Now. That if he really loved her, he would protect her from the pain he would inevitably cause her, no matter how hard he tried to avoid it.

She dipped her head down to kiss him. A light, quick brush of her lips. Before he could process it, she eased back to wave a hand at him. "Now turn around so I can get out and go inside to change for dinner."

He didn't want to, but he did, for her, the hunger inside him battling with his deepest fear.

Losing Tala.

He'd almost lost her that day in Afghanistan. Now he faced losing her for an entirely different reason, and it might already be too late.

Past experience had taught him that's exactly what was going to happen, no matter how hard he fought to stop it.

CHAPTER TEN

She didn't know what the hell to do.

Lost in thought, Tala pulled the down-filled jacket over her Lycra racing suit, then tugged her toque over her hair, her thick braid trailing down the center of her back. The conversation in the hot tub the other night hadn't gone well. At all.

The way he'd kissed her had all but melted her bones, but when she'd leveled with him about her expectations and what she wanted, he'd frozen up. At first, she'd regretted opening her mouth, but since then she'd decided it was a good thing she'd told him everything up front. If he couldn't handle what she wanted, then best she find that out now, before things went any further.

At least he'd accepted the symbolic olive branch she'd offered him by agreeing to go out on the trails with her today. She was looking forward to skiing in simulated competition conditions, but also nervous. They would be alone again, and she wasn't sure what to expect from him now.

It had been two days since he'd kissed her, stunning her with that volcanic heat he'd hidden from her for so long. Two days since he'd held her and told her with that tortured look in his eyes that she deserved better than him. That something was missing inside him.

Bullshit. And it broke her heart that he seemed to believe it.

He'd withdrawn from her after getting out of the hot tub, keeping a careful distance even through dinner afterward, and she hadn't wanted to alert the others to what was going on by forcing her presence on him.

But he'd watched her. Throughout the meal and everyone relaxing together in front of the fire after with a drink and goodies, she'd felt his eyes on her. And every time she met his gaze, the longing there set her heart pounding and her body on fire.

She'd been in knots ever since, dying for more of what he'd shown her, imagining them naked together. Him using that sensual mouth and strong hands all over her, and finally ease this all-consuming need he'd created inside her.

Yesterday he'd been busy with Mason and Tate working on things for their business, and she'd spent the day with Rylee and Nina, driving down to Missoula to hit a spa for massages and facials. They'd gone to a movie after, and then stopped for dinner before driving back to Rifle Creek.

By the time they'd arrived home it had been late, and Braxton was back at Avery and Mason's place. He'd been on her mind all day, as she slowly drove herself crazy wondering what was going on in his head and what he planned to do about them.

She'd thought about texting him, not wanting to give him the chance to keep pulling away. But in the end, she'd left it alone. She wasn't going to chase after him. She'd made it clear how she felt about him. The next move had to be his.

Just as she was climbing into bed last night, he'd texted her, setting off butterflies in her stomach. *Have a good time?*

Great. How was your day?

Good. Everything seems to be coming together.

But no word about whether or not he was leaning toward leaving the military to work with them full time. *Got plans tomorrow?*

No. But I miss you.

Just that simple admission had dissolved her irritation and turned her heart over. She knew it hadn't been easy for him to tell her, even via text. She needed to see him in person. *I miss you too. Want to go skiing in the backcountry for a while tomorrow? Tate told me about some good cross-country trails. I want to do some shooting too.*

I'm in. What time?

Eleven.

That was fifteen minutes from now, and she was anxious to get going.

She wanted him to put his inner baggage aside and seize this chance before it was too late. He was being pulled away overseas again far too soon as it was. Every day they had together was precious. Was he really going to waste the remaining time they had left here together?

"You picking up Brax on the way?"

She glanced toward the garage door where Rylee stood. "Yeah. Would you mind pouring my tea into the thermoses on the counter?"

"Sure." She turned away.

"You're the best daughter."

Rylee shot her a grin. "I know."

Tala returned to organizing their gear. Her biathlon equipment, but also Braxton's skiing stuff and emergency gear. Going into the backcountry required emergency supplies and provisions, just in case.

Along with the nerves in her belly, anticipation coiled, warm and fluttery. Her gut told her that today would either make them or break them. She hoped he'd seriously thought about what she'd said, and decided to give them a chance.

"Here's your tea. Nina and I made up some sandwiches with the leftover turkey, and she put some bars and cookies in there as well. Don't want you guys having to subsist just on those nasty protein bars you always take with you."

"You guys are awesome." She took the sealed plastic bags from her and packed them into the backpack Braxton would be carrying on the trails.

Opening the garage door, she carried her equipment and the backpack to Tate's truck and set everything in the bed. A cold gust of wind tugged at her. She glanced up at the sky, noted the dark gray clouds moving in. The predicted storm was supposed to hit tonight, bringing a foot or more of snow here, and even more higher up in the mountains.

When she turned back to get Braxton's equipment, Tate was already there, carrying it out for her. He set it in the truck bed and paused to sweep his gaze over her. "Tell me you've got more layers than that with you."

She grinned at his concern. "Of course I do, it's all rolled up tight in the backpack."

He gave a terse nod. "Good. And your spotter GPS?"

"Yes, Dad," she teased.

The corners of his lips curved. "Just looking out for you." He glanced up to study the sky. "Storm's moving in. I'll keep an eye on the weather report and let you guys know if anything changes. And be aware of your surroundings out there, just in case. That gang member I told you about still hasn't been located, and he was last seen by one of the construction workers heading into the mountains not far from our building site."

She'd told Tate about the footprints they'd seen. He'd sent officers up to search the area that night, but they hadn't found anything. "We will, and don't worry, we'll be back long before the storm starts. Planning to be here by seven at the latest, but hopefully sooner, because after a day on the hill I'm always starving, and Nina's an awesome cook."

"Yeah, she is." He glanced into the truck bed, and she could almost hear him taking inventory in his head. "You got everything you need?"

"Yep. Except this." She held out her arms expectantly.

He grinned and pulled her into a hug. Tate hugs were the best—with the exception of the ones from Rylee and Braxton. All different, and each savored for various reasons. "Have fun, and be gentle with Brax. He's on holiday."

She laughed and hugged him back, wishing she could talk to him about the way things stood between her and Braxton. Maybe she would tomorrow, depending on what happened today. "I will."

"Love you." He kissed the top of her head and released her.

"Love you too." He was such a softie inside, especially with his family. She loved that the most about him.

Turning, she found Nina and Rylee standing together in the doorway leading from the garage into the mudroom. "Bye," she called out when they waved to her. "Love you guys. See you in a while."

Her heart drummed faster as she neared Avery and Mason's place. She didn't want things to be strained or awkward between them.

Anxiety twisted her insides. She wanted Braxton. Had wanted him and no one else for four long years now, but it seemed like he was determined to keep walls up between them. It was making her crazy.

As soon as she pulled into the driveway, the front door opened and Braxton came out. Just the sight of him made her breath catch. He walked toward the truck with a full ruck over one broad shoulder.

Mason stepped out onto the front porch, folding his arms over his chest as he nodded at her in greeting. "Have him back by dark, okay?" he called out to her.

She smirked. "You gave him a curfew?"

"It's his own fault. Don't be late, son," he said to Braxton, who rolled his eyes.

"Yeah, don't wait up, warden." He opened the passenger door and climbed in, his gaze colliding with hers as he reached in to set the ruck on the backseat. "Hi."

"Hi," she said, her stomach muscles tensing. She couldn't get a read on him. Had no idea what was going on in his head. "You didn't need to bring anything."

"Just some extra food and survival gear. Thought I'd leave it with the snowmobiles so we've got everything in one place if we need it."

"Good idea." She backed out of the driveway, aiming for a light mood. "Oh, Mason's still there, waving at us. Wave back."

They waved at him as she drove away, only to stop when the front door of the house on the right suddenly flew open and two figures popped out. The gray-haired lady in front waved her down as she rushed to the front gate.

Tala pulled over and stopped next to it, and Braxton rolled down his window. "Pat," he said as the woman rushed for the truck. "Everything okay?"

"Oh, yes," she panted, breathless in her haste to reach them. "I just wanted to make sure we caught you to give you this on your way out. You can't ski on empty stomachs, can you?"

Braxton accepted the bag. "That's so nice of you, thanks."

She beamed at him. "Not at all. Thank *you*, for clearing our steps and walkway earlier."

"It's no problem. Mason and I will be over in the morning to clear them again for you after the storm clears up."

"That would be lovely." Her gaze cut to Tala, more than a little curiosity there. "You two have fun now." She stepped back and rushed up the walkway to stand with her sister on the top of the front steps, waving.

"You cleared their walkway, huh?" Tala said with a smile, waving at the sisters with him before pulling away.

"They were out there trying to do it themselves," he said in a tone that said he found that completely unacceptable. "What was I gonna do, stand back and let them?"

She shook her head, a fond smile in place. "Just another reason why I love you, Brax."

As soon as she said it, she wished she could take it back. She'd meant it in a friendly way, not a romantic one, but the way his face froze made her curse herself. "I meant, just another thing I admire about you," she said, wanting to smack herself.

Rather than answer, he opened the bag and peered inside it. "Want a muffin?"

"Sure." Anything to cover the awkwardness and keep her mouth busy so she couldn't put her foot in it again. "What kind are they?"

"Looks like cranberry and oatmeal. Smells like maybe some orange in them too."

"Yum. Hand it over."

He did, and it was still warm from the oven. Fragrant and delicious. And eating them took up the first few minutes of the drive and allowed her nerves to settle again. She wiped her hands on the paper napkin he gave her, then put it in the cup holder next to her. "So, what area do you want to hit?"

He pulled a map out of his jacket pocket. "Tate told me which trails he thought would be best. I've plotted a route out for us."

"Perfect."

She played it cool on the way to the building site, even though unease ground in the pit of her stomach. She'd made it clear that she wanted him. If he wanted her in return, how could he not act on it? How could he pretend they were nothing more than friends after the way he'd kissed her?

They talked about their upcoming adventure for the rest of the drive to the Rifle Creek Tactical site, both of them avoiding anything personal. By the time they arrived, Tala was ready to burst. She needed to expend some of the pressure inside her before she exploded.

She parked beside a newly built shed that housed the company's recreational vehicles. Together they unloaded their gear and packed everything onto two snowmobiles inside.

She turned on the spotter GPS so Tate could track them, tucked it away in the backpack, then tugged on her gloves and turned toward him. "Ready?"

He was already standing beside his snowmobile, tall and strong and gorgeous. "Ready. I'll take point." He straddled his vehicle, fired it up, and drove it out of the shed.

Tala followed, anticipation and excitement curling inside her. This was going to be a great day. She could feel it.

A light wind blew in their faces as they headed up the trail that led away from the building site and up the mountain. The heavy, overcast sky made it easy to see where they were going with no sun to blind them.

The fresh scents of the winter forest surrounded them as she rode after Braxton, sharp evergreen and crisp fallen snow. There was no one else around. It was just the two of them, and she couldn't wait to spend the next few hours alone with him. Building on the bond they shared. Showing him he had nothing to be afraid of when it came to a relationship with her.

He took them up to a ridge high above the building site and finally pulled underneath a rock overhang, parking his vehicle near the wall of the enclosure. He swung a long leg across the seat as he stood, watching her as she pulled up beside him and cut the engine. "All good?"

"Yes. Looking forward to slapping the boards on." She stood and unzipped her jacket.

As she stripped it off, he stilled. When she glanced over, she found him staring at her, his dark gaze sweeping over the length of her body with a heated look that made her toes curl in her ski boot. A delicious shiver sped through her that had nothing to do with the cold.

Touch me, she willed him. Just touch me.

But he didn't move. "You're not gonna wear a jacket out there?" he asked, his eyes doing another pass over her body-hugging Lycra suit. He wasn't even trying to be subtle about it now.

She'd definitely made the right choice in wearing it today. "Nope. I'll put it in your ruck, but I want to simulate competition conditions as much as possible." With the added bonus that he couldn't seem to take his eyes off her in this. She was calling it a win.

Tala liked to win. While she refused to chase Braxton, now that she knew he wanted her, she wasn't above using every weapon in her arsenal to break his control.

CHAPTER ELEVEN

They hadn't skied far up the untouched trail when Braxton slowed. Tala did the same, following his gaze to a fork just ahead. "Left or right?" he asked.

Tiny snowflakes had begun to fall from the thick gray clouds overhead, swirling in the light wind. "Right."

"Right it is," Braxton said and moved aside, waiting for her to join him. "There's an area about two klicks from here that Tate said would make a good shooting range. Wanna stop there and put some rounds downrange?"

She had no doubt he'd memorized a map of the area before coming up here. And she'd come up here to simulate a race, so a good sprint before she shot was perfect. "Love to." She tossed him a saucy look. "See if you can keep up."

He flashed a grin. "How about you give me a decent head start instead, so I can go on ahead and set up some targets for when you get there?"

Good idea. "Or that."

She stayed put while he skied off, giving him seven minutes lead-time before beginning her sprint up the trail. She started with freestyle method for the first hundred meters, then switching to classical, just as she would do in a race. Exhilaration filled her as her muscles warmed and her blood got pumping.

The snow was deeper here, a lot more difficult to ski through compared to the well-groomed biathlon trails she was used to. Her skis sank into it, making every stride more difficult. But she loved the thrill of it, the challenge of pushing herself as the cold air whipped over her face.

Most of all, she loved knowing Braxton was waiting up ahead for her.

She was panting, her heart racing by the time she spotted the clearing he'd mentioned up ahead. He was standing in the middle of it, the snowflakes falling faster now. She slowed as she approached him, practicing her easing-in technique. Shifting her focus to her breathing, resting her muscles to get her heart rate down before she reached the makeshift shooting range.

"I put the target on a tree trunk to your two-o'clock," he called out. "Not quite fifty meters, but close enough."

As a sniper, he was an expert at judging distance, so she wouldn't be surprised if he had the exact distance calculated in his head. Not wasting air to reply, she took the thin rolled-up yoga mat from the small of her back that she'd brought to serve as a shooting mat, and spread it out next to him.

Pulling in another slow breath, her heart rate dropping, she took off her backpack sling, hooked the webbing sling to the firing cuff on her upper arm and flipped the cap up on the end of the muzzle before loading a five-round clip into the chamber. The sprint had been shorter than in a real race, but the deeper snow made it feel longer. And shooting outside was always far more challenging than at an indoor range with perfect conditions and no wind to worry about.

"Light wind blowing east to west. Adjust left slightly," he told her.

Nodding, she located the paper target he'd fixed to a

tree trunk in the distance, then got onto her belly. There were all kinds of tips, tricks and questions she wanted to pick his brain about later. But first, time to see if their last lesson had stuck in her head.

She assumed her firing position and brought the rifle tight to her shoulder, making the adjustments he'd helped her with the other day.

A snowflake landed on her eyelashes. She blinked it away, staring through the sight at the target. The stock was ice cold against her cheek as she aimed at the first circle, timed her shot between heartbeats, then squeezed the trigger.

"Miss. High and to the left, five centimeters," Braxton said a few meters beside her, watching the target through a pair of binos.

Not surprising, since she'd hadn't zeroed the rifle yet. She quickly adjusted her sight, took aim again, implementing everything he'd taught her before, and fired.

"Hit, right of center. Good job."

His praise warmed her all the way to her bones. She immediately focused on the second target. Tucked her chin in a bit more and exhaled. Picked a spot between heartbeats. Fired.

"Hit, left of center."

Then the third.

"Hit, center."

God, I love this. She fired at the last two targets in succession with only a second in between.

"Both hits, dead center." He lowered the binos and met her gaze as she looked over at him, a huge grin on her face. "Look at you," he said in admiration, giving her a proud smile that made her still fast-beating heart flip-flop.

"It's my new secret weapon coach." She pushed up onto her knees to rise, already slinging her rifle onto her back.

Braxton reached down to grasp her arm and help her

to her feet. He didn't let go.

Tala stilled at the contact, her gaze shooting to his. Her insides fluttered at the yearning in his eyes. Then she laughed softly.

"What?" he asked her.

"I'm sweaty and out of breath, and have no makeup on."

"Mmm," he agreed. "And you're still the sexiest thing I've ever seen."

Her eyes widened at the compliment, but then he was bending his head and...

She sucked in a breath and grabbed hold of his sturdy shoulders as his lips came down on hers. Slow at first. Careful.

She didn't want slow *or* careful with him.

Tala reached her arms up to wind them around his neck and leaned into him, his deep groan sending a shiver through her as his lips parted, his tongue delving between hers. She flattened her body to his, barely aware of the cold snowflakes drifting down to kiss her upturned face.

Braxton made the whole world fall away. There was only him and this moment, his strong arms around her, his mouth on hers as his big body sheltered her from the cold wind.

He held her rock steady on her skis while his tongue caressed hers. Gliding. Teasing before he nipped at her lower lip, sucked at it tenderly and raised his head.

Tala blinked up at him, half-drugged with arousal, the pulse between her thighs bordering on painful and her nipples tight beads against the front of her sports bra.

"I've never wanted anyone the way I want you," he murmured, his eyes blazing with unmistakable heat.

He was telling her this now? Here, when there was nothing she could do about it? "Same."

He cupped the side of her neck with one hand, his thumb grazing across her lips. "You deserve better than me, but I can't keep my distance. Christ, Tal, I just don't wanna hurt you," he finished, anguish bleeding into his expression.

She shivered as a strong gust of wind tore over her. Her heart was still pounding, from elation now instead of exertion, and her body was cooling fast now that she'd stopped skiing. "So then, don't hurt me. And you *are* good enough for me. You're exactly right for me."

Braxton groaned and wrapped his arms around her, pulling her in for a tight hug. "Promise me I won't lose you," he whispered, crushing her to him. "No matter what happens. I couldn't take that."

The note of vulnerability in his words twisted her heart even as it swelled with hope. Did this mean he was giving them a shot? A real one? But how could he if he was going to re-up at the end of his current contract? She wasn't willing to put herself through a relationship like that.

She also didn't want to ruin the moment by pushing any harder right now.

"You won't lose me, Brax," she promised, hugging him tight. They'd started out as friends, and that meant something to her. No matter what happened between them, she couldn't see herself cutting him out of her life entirely. "Unless you cheated on me," she added. "Then you'd lose me real fast."

He relaxed his grip and lifted his head to stare down at her, equal parts heat and disbelief in his eyes, snowflakes gathering on his dark whiskers. "I've never cheated on anyone, and I would *never* do that to you."

She believed him. "Good," she murmured, giving him a little smile.

His lips curved, then he cupped the back of her head with one hand and kissed her again, making her lose track of time and space until he sighed and eased back. "We came up here to give you more practice. Up for another sprint and shoot? This time standing."

She'd rather keep kissing him, but sensed he needed breathing room while he grappled with whatever internal conflict made him think he wasn't good enough for her. "Sure."

He pinned another target for her on the same tree, then they set out on an easy ski up the trail and stopped three klicks from the clearing. On his mark she took off, pretending she was in a race.

Braxton was right behind her, keeping pace without any difficulty. In the clearing, he stopped and looked through the binos while she set up in standing position and adjusted everything according to his previous instruction.

As usual, she wasn't nearly as good as when she shot prone. She lowered the rifle with a sigh. "Meh."

"Not bad," he said, tucking the binos away. "Try again now that your heart rate's lower."

She took a fresh five-round clip from the stock, loaded it, and took aim. This time she hit four out of five. "I'll take it," she said, giving him a smile.

"Wanna keep going?"

"No, I've had enough for now. Let's head back, I want to learn some finer points of compensating for windage and air temp while we ski."

He grinned. "Sure."

He stayed beside her as they made their way back down the trail, the big ruck strapped to his back while she carried her biathlon rifle in its backpack harness. He was in the middle of answering a question about a technical point when he suddenly stopped talking and looked to the left.

Tala followed his gaze into the trees. Through them, she saw a single set of footprints emerge from the edge of the trees up ahead onto their trail. Braxton immediately stopped and moved in front of her, his posture tense, gaze alert.

LETHAL PROTECTOR

The tracks made her uneasy. She immediately thought of the fugitive Tate had mentioned earlier. They were truly in the middle of nowhere here, and a storm was about to move in.

She glanced at Braxton to get a read on his reaction, making note of their position so she could tell Tate about the tracks later on in case he wanted to look into it. "Should we…turn around and find another trail?"

He didn't answer for a moment, taking out his binos to check the trail in front of them. "The tracks lead back into the trees a ways up ahead. We'll go straight back to the truck."

He started forward, moving in front of her now in a protective move that wasn't lost on her. While she appreciated the sentiment, she wasn't exactly helpless, and she was the one with the rifle when he only had a pistol on him.

She followed him anyway, watching the prints. Sure enough, they veered off into the trees and disappeared, and when she scanned the trail up ahead of them, she didn't see any further traces that anyone had been there. "We need to call—"

"I'm calling Tate now," he said, already pulling his phone from his jacket. He explained what they'd seen, and their approximate location, plus the direction the tracks were headed in.

He answered a few questions, then paused. "Roger. We're heading straight for the truck right now anyway. See you in a while." He ended the call and kept skiing. Thankfully there were no more tracks ahead of them.

"What did he say?" she asked.

"He's calling the station to alert the guys on shift right now, but they won't be able to send out anyone to check the tracks tonight. Forecast has changed. Storm's moving in faster than anticipated. He says we need to get home."

After seeing those tracks, she was eager to get off the mountain. The last thing she wanted was to put either of them at risk by staying out here with a potential fugitive and a blizzard bearing down on them. "Let's get moving then."

"Yeah." He tucked the phone away as he skied, then glanced over and gave her a slow, sexy half-smile that sent a fresh wave of arousal through her. "You up for coming back to Mason and Avery's place with me after dinner?"

Her insides heated, images of them tangled together naked in his sheets filling her brain. "You might be able to persuade me."

He quirked a dark eyebrow, a hot gleam in his eyes. "Race you to the bottom." He shot away.

She'd already been motivated to get out of there. Now she couldn't wait to get into the truck with him. Tala sprinted after him, her whole body pulsing with anticipation of what lay ahead tonight once they were alone.

****

Jason stilled when the first shots ripped through the air, his heart rate skyrocketing. He whipped around to face the shack door, his muscles tight as steel cables.

More shots. Spaced out. Distant, but not distant enough.

He was definitely no longer alone on the mountain. Hunters?

Could be the cops.

His pulse kicked hard. A couple hours earlier he'd managed to find a spot with a weak signal for his hand-cranked radio to check the weather and the local news. Right after the forecast about the blizzard, the local radio station had talked about him.

LETHAL PROTECTOR

The cops had put out an alert about him, asking anyone who might have seen him or have information on his whereabouts to report it. Now every local yokel within thirty miles knew who he was, and that he was out here. He was trapped here for now. With the storm moving in he couldn't risk leaving yet.

But he needed to find out who was out there, and what they were shooting at.

Jaw tightening, he grabbed his heavy jacket from the peg on the wall, shrugged it on and yanked on his knit cap and gloves. The custom rifle was still in the corner near the wood-burning stove, along with his binoculars. He grabbed them both, loaded a round, and stuffed more ammo in his jacket pocket before stalking to the door.

Opening it a few inches, he paused to peer outside and make sure the coast was clear. The storm was already here. Hours earlier than expected. Overhead the sky was dark and leaden, thin flakes mixed with fat, fluffy ones as they fell in a steady curtain.

He stepped out and shut the door behind him, his breath catching at the sudden bite of cold, the wind snatching his breath away in a silver mist. His snowshoes sank only a few inches into the snow as he hugged the edge of the trees before crossing the clearing. They would still leave tracks for anyone trying to follow him, but with the snow falling faster by the minute, it wouldn't be long until they were completely covered again.

For now, he had an urgent scouting mission to accomplish.

His gloved hands tightened around the rifle as he made his way through the trees toward the trail he would take to begin his hunt. Heading in the direction the rifle shots had come from, he shoved back the fear making the hair on the back of his neck tingle.

If whoever was out here had come to find him, they would die.

CHAPTER TWELVE

Braxton was preoccupied by the deteriorating weather conditions and the possibility of a fugitive being nearby as he followed Tala back down the trail, but he hadn't seen any more tracks, and the sight of her in that body-hugging Lycra suit was distracting. The light blue fabric clung to every inch of her, and made him think about slowly peeling it off her in the basement suite at Mason and Avery's place.

Tearing his gaze from her firm, shapely ass and thighs, he glanced up at the sky through the goggles he'd put on, the snowflakes gathering on his face. Fat and fluffy now, and so thick their visibility had dropped to about fifty meters. The wind was picking up too, gusting hard and swirling the snow around.

He adjusted his goggles and stayed right behind Tala in the grooves cut by her skis. The storm had moved in a lot faster than anticipated, and they still had at least a thirty-minute ski to get back to where they'd left the snowmobiles. From there, it was easily another twenty minutes or so back to the building site. Maybe more, if the storm kept getting worse.

LETHAL PROTECTOR

Tala stayed several strides ahead of him, her technique smooth and steady, showing no signs of tiring yet. While her outfit was sexy as hell on her, it also made him worried about her core temp in these conditions.

She would be plenty warm while they were skiing, but once they got to the snowmobiles he was going to wrap her in the extra layer he'd brought in his ruck for the ride back to the truck. In these conditions, even the base layer she had underneath her suit for added warmth wasn't enough.

They rounded a bend in the trail, and ahead of them their previous tracks from the trek up were already disappearing beneath the heavy snowfall. Sheets of it dropped from drooping, snow-bound branches they passed on either side of the trail. A sharp gust of wind cut across the face of the mountain, sucking the breath from his lungs.

Then a faint, distinctive rumbling sound reached him.

Shit. "Tala, stop," he ordered, racing to catch her.

She did, turning to look back at him questioningly as he got close. "What's wr—" She froze as the sound intensified, her head whipping back around to face forward.

Braxton cut in front of her and stopped, angling his body and holding out an arm in front of her in case he suddenly needed to throw her out of the line of fire. The rumbling was louder now, getting closer, but he couldn't tell where it was coming from.

About forty meters ahead, a wall of white appeared in their line of vision, kicking up snow and other debris as the small avalanche exploded over the trail and over the edge of the cliff to plunge down the mountainside on their right.

He pushed her off the trail, backed her up against the closest thick tree trunk he could find and froze, waiting. Listening. The rumbling faded away in the distance, and the cloud of snow up the trail from the debris field began to ebb.

He waited another minute, his chest pressed to her back, then set his hand on her shoulder and squeezed. "Stay here. I'm gonna take a look."

She didn't argue or question him, but he could feel her eyes on him as he skied away, watching anxiously as he followed the trail down until he could get a good look at the damage. As soon as the extent of the avalanche became clear, he stopped.

A wall of snow, rock and tree branches stood eight feet high across the trail. More debris was still piling on from up the mountain in a sluggish stream.

There was no telling how wide the debris field was, but it didn't much matter, because the height alone made it impossible to traverse. It would be too unstable to try and climb over it, and he wasn't going to risk Tala's safety by trying. They'd have to find another route down.

He skied back to where she waited. "It's completely blocked. We'll have to go up the mountain and find another route back." He angled his back to her. "Can you grab the map for me? It's rolled up in a canister on the right side of the small pouch at the bottom."

Moving quickly, she pulled the cap free and handed him the map. He unrolled it, quickly found their location and calculated another route. He looked up at her. "Safest bet is a trail another six miles up, but I'm not sure how steep the grade is going down the mountain from there. Might be a section or two where we'll have to hike instead of ski."

He glanced down at her specialized ski prosthetic. No way she'd be able to hike on it. The end of it was small and round, like the end of a crutch. It would sink deep into the snow, and she'd have no balance or stabilization. "If that happens I'll carry you."

She nodded, face grave. "Okay. Whatever we need to do."

LETHAL PROTECTOR

He was glad she wasn't arguing or getting scared, but not surprised. Tala was the strongest woman he'd ever known. "All right. Let's head out. I'm on point." He tucked the map back into the canister, waited for her to put it in his ruck, then glanced at her. "Ready?"

"Yes," she said with a decisive nod.

Braxton headed out, paying careful attention to their surroundings. Watching for any puffs of snow rolling down the mountain above them, and listening for that telltale rumbling noise again.

The trail became intense pretty quickly as they reached an uphill section. He pushed his way up it, pausing every so often to check that Tala was still with him. She was close behind him, doggedly conquering the steep grade in spite of the wind and near white-out conditions.

He slowed to keep pace with her, already breathing hard, sweat gathering along his back, chest and face. All the while, the snow swirled around them, falling thick and fast in a white curtain, deadening all sound except for the wind. It howled down the mountainside and cut along the trail to blast them right in their faces, kicking up snow and dropping visibility to mere feet. The exposed skin on his face stung.

Within two more klicks, he knew it was too dangerous to continue. He couldn't see shit at this point and had no idea what lay ahead. If it had just been him, he would have risked it and carried on, but he wasn't willing to endanger Tala.

They needed to get out of the storm and hunker down until conditions improved enough for them to move safely. Otherwise they were just moving blind.

He paused, trying to catch his breath while he waited for her to reach him at the top of an incline. "We have to find shelter for a while," he told her.

She nodded but didn't respond, busy sucking in gasps of air.

He wished he could have given her more time to rest, but they had to keep moving and find a safer place to stop. "Come on," he said, and edged toward the inside of the trail as they rounded a bend.

A few minutes later, he spotted a slim gap between the trees to the right. Not a trail, exactly, but enough room for them to maneuver between the trunks. "This way. Tell me right away if you need help, okay?"

"Okay."

He led the way, picking his path between the trees. It was slow going, his skis plunging deep and occasionally getting caught in a branch or root hidden below the surface. At least here in the relative shelter of the evergreen the wind wasn't so fierce and the snow wasn't falling as thick.

Tala kept up with him, following him without complaint as he searched for a place to make a shelter for them. As he picked his way around a large boulder, the trees ahead opened up into a small clearing.

And then he saw it. A small wooden building set on the far side of the clearing. It looked abandoned, but he wasn't taking any chances.

He headed toward it. The wind picked up as he neared the upcoming tree line, whistling as it sliced between the trunks. At the edge of the clearing, he paused behind a tree to observe the site for a few minutes, making sure they were alone. There was no smoke coming from the tiny chimney in the roof, but a slight groove in the snow marked the place of a possible path leading toward the side of the shed.

Mindful of the tracks they'd seen earlier, he transferred both poles to his left hand and reached down to draw his pistol from the holster at his hip. Tala stayed behind him, silent.

"Stay here," he whispered.

He surveyed the clearing one last time, moving his

gaze from right to left because scanning in the opposite direction of reading forced the brain to slow down and notice more detail.

Finding nothing of concern, he skied out of the trees toward the small building. Instantly the wind blasted him, the snow coming down harder than before. He kept going, the tinted goggles allowing him to see the few feet of ground around him more easily.

There was definitely a path leading to the door, but he couldn't tell how recent it was with the new snow on top. He paused a few dozen meters from the door, listening. It definitely looked deserted.

"Hello?" he called out, pistol at the ready. His voice didn't carry, deadened by the snow. "Hello?" he repeated, a little louder.

No answer. No sound and no movement from near the shed.

He edged toward the door, still on alert. For good measure, he paused and knocked before pushing the door open.

Immediately, he tensed.

It was warm inside, the potbellied stove in the corner obviously having been recently used. And the tiny dwelling was full of supplies stacked against the walls. Along with weapons, and a backpack overflowing with stacks of cash.

He grabbed what ammo he could see, tugged the door shut and immediately backed away, his hand tightening around his weapon. His gaze cut across the small clearing to the trees he'd come from.

Tala was still there, half-hidden behind a trunk. He skied back to her, the back of his neck tingling. They had to get the hell out of here.

"What's wrong?" she whispered when he got close enough.

"Someone's holing up inside. There're weapons and

cash. Maybe drugs." He didn't like it. "We need to be long gone before whoever it is comes back."

A worried frown pulled her eyebrows together. "Think it might be the fugitive Tate told us about?"

"Good chance it is." He dumped the ammo on the ground and covered it with snow. Moving in beside her, he kept an eye on the clearing, watching for any sign of the squatter returning as he pulled out his phone. No bars. "No service. You?"

She fished hers out of his ruck and tried it. "Nothing."

They'd have to try again once they found a safer place to stop. "Okay. Let's move."

He led the way, skirting the edge of the clearing and trying to keep their ski tracks hidden from view. But on the far side, he paused, swearing silently at the recent set of footprints leading away from the shed.

A warning prickle flashed over his skin.

Braxton did an about face and headed back into the trees, searching for another path. Blizzard or not, they couldn't get out of there fast enough for his liking.

****

Jason froze steps from the edge of the clearing on his way back to the shack, his heart rocketing into his throat when through the heavy veil of falling snow he spied movement inside the trees off to his right. Two people, their silhouettes barely visible as they disappeared into the forest and were swallowed up by the shadows.

His earlier recon had given him nothing, the storm making it impossible to track anyone. But someone had found his hideout.

They couldn't find *him*.

He jerked his hunting rifle into position, finger resting on the trigger guard as he aimed at the spot he'd last seen them. The wind moaned and howled just beyond the trees, covering any sounds from their retreat.

He waited another few seconds, then edged closer to the set of tracks he'd left earlier when he'd stepped out to do the perimeter check of the area. Dread coiled tighter in his gut with every step. And when he saw the rapidly vanishing ski tracks leading to and from the shack's door, he swallowed as fear gripped him.

He stayed within the shadows on the far side of the shack as he ran toward it, his pulse thudding in his ears. Checking once to make sure he couldn't see anyone, he broke from the trees and ran for the door.

He threw it open, every muscle tight. When he saw the inside, he sagged, a shaky, relieved breath exploding from his lungs. His stash was still there, the weapons still leaning against the wall and the backpack full of cash looked untouched.

But whoever had come here had definitely seen what he'd hidden inside. The tracks led right up to the door. They would report everything, putting even more heat on him.

Stepping back outside for a moment, he turned to face the far side of the clearing, his gaze following the recent ski tracks in the snow. His instincts were screaming at him to get the hell out. That he wasn't safe here anymore.

All the while, the storm raged around him, Mother Nature in a fury. This shack and his supplies were all that stood between him and dying of hypothermia. But staying here was too risky right now, no matter how dangerous it was to leave in these conditions.

Resigned, he quickly dashed inside and shoved as much gear as he could comfortably carry into one of the backpacks, then threw a tarp over everything else. He would come back once he'd taken care of this new threat. For now, he needed to hunt the trespassers down.

He shut the shack door, gripped his precious rifle and left, leaning forward against the wind as he followed the ski tracks. They were already half-gone, rapidly filling with snow.

But inside the trees the wind no longer sliced at him, and the snow fell softly. The two sets of tracks were starkly visible.

The skiers were out of sight, but the tracks they left marked their path. He moved quickly but cautiously, watching for them ahead through the trees.

Finally, he saw them. Just a glimpse of movement through the screen of trunks a few dozen meters to the left.

Jason ducked back behind a wide trunk and risked a peek, his rifle at the ready. Two figures came into view. A man in the lead, then a woman. She had a rifle slung across her back.

His stomach tightened, his fingers flexing around his rifle. If she was armed, then he was too. They weren't from his former gang, but they could easily be undercover cops posing as skiers to search for him…and they'd just found his hideout.

If they made it down the mountain, they would send more cops up here looking for him. Maybe Feds too. As soon as the storm lifted, this place would be crawling with them.

Setting his jaw, Jason started after his targets again. Determination burned inside him, chasing away the chill of fear. To survive, he had to kill them and get back to his hideout before darkness fell.

CHAPTER THIRTEEN

Tala struggled to keep up with Braxton. This new trail wasn't a trail at all, merely space between the trees that they picked their way along. Several times the tips of her skis got caught on things under the surface of the snow.

It wasn't so bad with her left foot because she could feel immediately when there was a problem, but with her prosthetic foot she didn't feel any pressure to warn her the ski was stuck until her prosthetic "boot" came out of the binding. And she was also starting to have nerve pain at the amputation site.

Her right ski caught on something else and her ski popped off. She cursed under her breath and bent to retrieve it, stuck on whatever had caught it beneath the snow.

"You okay?" Braxton called back quietly, his voice barely carrying over the sound of the wind moving through the branches overhead.

She nodded, yanked the ski out while balancing her weight on her left leg, then pressed the tip of her prosthetic into the socket binding and carried on. Knowing the dangerous fugitive might be close by spurred her to move quickly, but she was starting to get tired. Fighting her way through the woods was tiring her out fast.

Braxton waited for her to catch up. When she stopped behind him, he searched her face in concern. "You hurt?"

"No, but I'm getting tired, and it makes me clumsy on my right leg. We need to get out of the trees and onto some kind of an actual trail again."

He nodded and paused to scan their surroundings one last time. "This way. I'll get us out of here as quick as I can."

Good. She followed him as close as she could, trusting his instincts and sense of direction. While she was pretty good with land nav, she had less experience than Braxton. He was a seasoned pro, and she had every confidence he could get them out of here and find somewhere safer to wait out the worst of the storm.

The going was rough, and by the time she glimpsed a brightening through the trees, she was panting and sweaty, her legs like lead. He kept a steady, slow pace as he picked his way toward the light source.

As they neared the edge of the tree line the wind picked up again, gusting through the trunks and branches. The veil of snow beyond the relative shelter of the forest was thick and white, obscuring everything beyond it. It could be the edge of a cliff waiting for them up ahead instead of a trail.

As Braxton neared the edge of the trees, he stopped to look back at her. His gaze suddenly snapped over her left shoulder and he went dead still. Tala instinctively froze and followed his gaze, dread curling in the pit of her stomach.

At first, she didn't see anything through the shadows. Then she caught a glimpse of movement. A shadow detaching itself from behind one tree before darting to another and disappearing again.

A human silhouette.

Sucking in a breath, she whipped back around and rushed for Braxton. He was coming back for her, his face grave.

When she was twenty feet from him, a rifle shot rang out, splintering the quiet. She jumped, her heart jolting as a shower of bark exploded from a tree trunk between them.

"Down!" he yelled.

Tala dove onto her belly just as another shot rang out, acting on reflex even as a spurt of panic punched through her, her mind taking her right back to the day she'd been wounded. The staccato rifle fire erupting around her. Raking the sides of the vehicle she was riding in. The enemy surrounding them. And then having to get out, stepping away from the vehicle...

Then a blinding flash of light, and the sensation of being thrown into the air.

Flat on her stomach, she cringed when another shot echoed through the trees, jerking her out of the memory to the present. Then Braxton was there, coming down on top of her.

Almost as soon as his weight registered across her back, it was gone. He was already up and dragging her to her right.

She tried to push upright to scramble after him but her damn right ski caught on something and her prosthetic popped out of the binding again. She tripped and fell forward, would have fallen flat on her face if he hadn't caught her and hauled her upright before she hit the ground.

Instinctively, she reached back for her ski, sucked in a gasp when the shooter fired again. This time close enough to kick up snow mere inches from where she'd just been standing, making her heart lurch.

She'd barely grabbed her fallen ski when Braxton

yanked her sideways and shoved her back to a thick tree trunk. She grabbed at the front of his jacket for balance and froze, watching him. He was staring in the direction of the shots, jaw tight.

"Put your ski on," he commanded in a low voice.

Shaking off the queasy sensation swirling in the pit of her stomach, she dropped the ski and quickly shoved her prosthetic back into the binding. But it was loose. Damaged from all the trauma it had sustained while trying to ski in the woods.

Braxton's gaze remained fixed somewhere behind them. He gripped her shoulder and hauled her up next to him, his pistol in his free hand. "When I fire at him, sprint for the trail ahead, and then turn hard left and ski downhill. Don't stop, no matter what."

She opened her mouth to argue, ready to reach for her rifle and make a stand, but he killed anything she was about to say with a warning look. "No matter what, Tal." His fingers bit into her shoulder.

Fuck. He was right, they couldn't stay here and wait to try and pick off the shooter. Smarter to get out of here and lose him in the storm.

She nodded and gathered herself, forcing back the fear, the ghostly memories of the day she was wounded still fresh in her mind as she waited for him to give her covering fire.

He squeezed her shoulder once, then angled his body between her and the shooter. Before she could say anything he darted out from behind the tree trunk and fired two shots.

Hating to leave him but counting on him to be right behind her, Tala dug her poles into the ground and shot forward, mindful of her loose right ski. Rifle fire echoed behind her. Her heart jerked but she didn't stop, just kept heading for the trail ahead.

But she couldn't resist the urge to peek over her

shoulder as she neared the tree line, worried about Braxton. Hope and relief surged when she saw him tearing after her.

She faced forward again and raced along the path she'd picked through the thinning trees. As soon as she neared it the howling wind whipped straight at her face, drowning out the thud of her pulse in her ears and momentarily stealing her breath.

Without pause, she darted out onto what she sincerely hoped was a trail and turned hard left, keeping her right ski pressed down to avoid it coming off again.

Thankfully there wasn't a cliff edge for her to sail over. If it wasn't a proper trail, it was a hell of a lot better than being stuck in the trees with a murderer shooting at them.

"Go, Tal," Braxton shouted behind her, his voice taut, urgent.

She glanced back just to make sure he was okay, then put her head down and leaned forward as she pushed up the slight incline, half-expecting to feel the burn of a bullet at any moment. The snow was falling so thick she could barely see in front of her, the wind so cold it stung her cheeks. Her legs, arms and back burned with the effort she put into making it to the top of the incline.

Finally cresting it, she sailed down the other side, relieved when the ground was right there to meet her skis. She risked a peek over her shoulder. Braxton appeared at the top of the rise, then barreled toward her down the incline at full speed. There were no more rifle shots.

She kept going and glanced around, worried. "Is he...down?" she managed between gasps, her legs and arms burning, heart slamming like a jackhammer against her ribs.

"No. I lost sight of him. Don't stop," he said tersely.

She wasn't planning on it. But now that the initial flood of adrenaline was beginning to ebb, her legs were growing weak and shaky. She didn't say anything, didn't slow, skiing along the trail as fast as she could and praying they were putting distance between them and the shooter.

The trail wound left then right, then down and to the left again. After a while when there were still no more shots, Braxton came up alongside her. "He was on foot. We should be able to lose him, but we can't slow down yet," he said over the wind.

Tala nodded, put her head down and kept pace with him as best she could. Digging deep for her stamina and ignoring the burn in her limbs and lungs, her body pushed to its limits.

She didn't know how far they went, didn't know how much time had passed since they'd left the trees, but it seemed like ages. The heavy snow made it hard because it obscured her vision and made her skis drag more. But the damn wind was killing her, like a cold knife slicing at her face and cutting through her suit.

Her face and hands were half-frozen in spite of how hard she was skiing, and so was her left foot. She was shivering so badly her jaw was trembling. The sub layer she'd put on under her suit might as well have been tissue paper for all the warmth it was trapping against her body.

She took it for as long as she could, then shook her head, knowing going any father without another layer was asking for trouble. "Jacket," she panted, hating to stop and risk the shooter possibly gaining on them—if he was even still following—but continuing like this was equally dangerous.

Braxton immediately stopped, looked behind them, then gave her his back. "In the top of my ruck."

She shrugged out of her rifle harness and fished her down jacket out with numb hands. He helped her put it on, then tugged off his gloves with his teeth and did up her zipper, watching her face. "We need to keep moving and find a way to get back down to the snowmobiles," he told her as he put his gloves back on. He had to be half-frozen too.

She nodded, trying to stop shivering, and shrugged back into her rifle harness. They had to make it back down and take the snowmobiles back to the truck before it got dark. "I'm g-good."

They started out again, the storm raging around them, showing no sign of easing. Braxton turned right at a slight fork in the trail and led her down a steep incline. At one point he pulled out his phone as he skied, but he must not have had any service because he shoved it back in his pocket and kept going.

Tala had no idea where they were, but Braxton seemed to have a direction in mind so she followed without question, unable to see what lay to their right beyond the edge of the trail. The canyon? Hopefully with the lodge at the bottom?

They skied up and down. Left and right. Over and over, until he finally paused for a breather at the top of a small ridge. He bent over a little between his planted poles and sucked in a few breaths.

She stopped beside him and did the same, too tired to bother looking behind them. They must have lost the shooter by now, or they would have known otherwise.

"Pretty sure we've lost him," he panted, then pulled in another big breath and straightened a bit. "No way he could see us through this shit anyway."

She nodded, in full agreement. She'd skied in some pretty gnarly conditions in her life, but never a full-on blizzard out in the backcountry. Without Braxton, she would be totally lost right now. Or dead.

"The snowmobiles are about three miles from here," he told her. "We just need to find a route down there." He eyed her. "Can you keep going?"

"Yeah." She didn't have the oxygen for anything more than that.

"I'll get us down as fast as I can."

Another nod, and then they were off again. They found a side trail another three klicks or so up the trail. But it wasn't pretty.

Tala stood at the edge of it, peering down the steep grade through the curtain of snow, everything in her telling her this was a really bad idea. The wind was sharper here rushing up at them, tugging at her jacket and toque. Her lips were numb, her fingers and toes practically bloodless from the cold, and her legs and arms were like lead.

Braxton glanced back and forth, all around them before settling his gaze on her. "I don't see any other way down."

Yeah, she was getting that.

"I'll go first and stop ten meters down, then call and wait for you. Go sideways, and *slow*. It's narrow and I can't see where we're going yet. I know you're tired. I know your balance is an issue. But you can't afford to slip or stumble here. Understand?"

"Got it." He wasn't being harsh, he was being real, warning her of the danger. If she did, she'd knock them both off the trail, and maybe over a cliff somewhere below. But she didn't plan on screwing up and causing either of them to fall to their death after escaping a deranged shooter in the middle of this goddamn blizzard.

She thought of Rylee. Of her daughter waiting for her right now. And Tate.

Tala straightened and mentally geared up for this next challenge. She could do this. She *would* do this. She'd survived giving birth to an eight-and-a-half-pound baby without any drugs, then having her foot and lower leg blown off in a warzone. She wasn't fucking dying out here on this mountain.

Before she even realized what he was doing, Braxton leaned in and kissed her, one hand sliding up to cup the back of her head.

She was still processing the shock of it when he lifted his head and gave her the semblance of a smile. "I'm so goddamn proud of you, sweetheart."

Sweetheart. Her insides fluttered and her heart turned over.

She opened her mouth to say something but he'd already turned away and started down the trail. She swallowed the urge to blurt out *be careful* and crept to the edge, watching anxiously.

After a few tense seconds, she lost sight of him. She waited, heart thudding.

Please let him be okay. Please let us get down safely.

"Okay, start down," he called. "Real slow. It's narrow. Stay tight to the left."

Pushing out a breath, she thought of Rylee again and began her wary descent. She angled her body to come down the trail with her skis sideways across it, her left foot on the bottom to provide her with a stronger, more stable base. With slow, careful placement, she edged her way down the incline.

Braxton finally came into view, and her heart rate slowed a little. He nodded his approval. "Good. Now stop there and wait."

She did, waiting for him to move down the trail and call out to her again. Every second, she was prepared for him to say they'd reached a dead end and would have to climb back to the top to try and find another route down.

Thankfully, that didn't happen. He descended a little at a time, stopped, and waited for her to catch up while the wind roared over them, driving snow into their faces.

It seemed to take hours to reach the bottom. By the time they made it to flat ground, her left leg was on fire from the strain of bearing her weight on the tortuous descent, and her stump was burning.

"Not far now," he told her, and turned to his left.

"This way."

She didn't know how the hell he knew where they were, but doggedly pushed her exhausted body to follow him. The burning in her left leg faded, replaced by a heavy numbness that told her she was going to be damn sore over the next few days.

"Should be just up on the left, another few hundred meters," he said over his shoulder.

She slowed when he did, could have cried from relief when the familiar outline of the rock outcropping came into view up ahead on the left. But her relief was short-lived.

Braxton swore softly. Her spine snapped taut and she dropped her poles, automatically shrugging out of her harness to grip her rifle. But as she slowed beside him, she scented the problem on the wind.

Smoke and scorched metal.

A few seconds and ten more meters later, her heart sank as the destruction became visible through the snowflakes. Just as fast, another tendril of fear snaked through her.

The shooter had been here.

Beneath the rock overhang the snow was blackened, smoke rising from the scorched remains of the one remaining snowmobile, and the pile of smoldering ashes that had been their extra emergency supplies.

Tala edged under the overhang to shield herself from the worst of the wind and snow, shoving out a hard breath. The shooter must have known a shortcut down the mountain and found their earlier tracks, leading him here somehow. It was the only explanation. And now he had a vehicle to get around on.

Her skin crawled at the thought of him still close, watching for them. She clutched her rifle, scanning uselessly through the storm in case he was out there within range, waiting to take another shot at them. If he did, this time she'd be ready.

Braxton had his phone out. He skied a short distance away, then turned in various directions, watching his phone. "No signal at all," he muttered, and came back to her.

Tala took hers out just in case, but, of course, she had no signal either so she shoved it away in her pocket. The shooter was likely long gone. He wouldn't be able to withstand this storm any better than they could.

"What do we do now?" The ride up here on the snowmobiles had taken them the better part of twenty to thirty minutes. On skis, it would be more than double that, even going downhill most of the way, and the little daylight that penetrated the storm was already fading. Within another hour, it would be full dark out here. They'd be at serious risk of hypothermia, or worse.

Catching her off guard, Braxton wrapped his arms around her and pulled her into a tight hug, his face pressed to the side of her head. She lowered her rifle and leaned into him, grateful for his warmth and strength, her cheek on his chest.

"We're gonna have to find shelter for the night," he murmured, confirming what she'd already known inside. "But not here."

No, not here. The shooter might try to come back to look for them.

Braxton eased his grip enough to lift his head and caught her chin in his gloved fingers, bringing her eyes to his. "You trust me?"

There wasn't even the slightest hesitation. "Completely." With her life.

His eyes warmed behind the goggles as the corner of his mouth kicked up. "Let's get out of here."

CHAPTER FOURTEEN

Visibility was still the shits, and it was getting dark fast. With the temperature dropping, they needed to find shelter and get out of the elements. Fast.

Braxton leaned forward against the relentless wind, its force making the icy snowflakes sting his cheeks. The hollow he'd found them in the side of the mountain wasn't deep enough to be called a cave, but at least it was large enough that they would both be able to lie down inside the rock enclosure. If they could seal the opening with branches and whatever greenery they could find, it should keep out the worst of the storm.

In theory.

At any rate, it would have to do. They were out of time, and he was worried about Tala.

The shooter was no longer their biggest threat. The storm was. Tala was smaller than him, with less muscle mass, and she had fewer layers on. The sooner he got her out of the elements and warmed up, the sooner he could breathe easier.

She stood a few meters from him, hunched over with her back to the wind, her arms wrapped around herself for warmth. He shrugged out of his ruck, quickly took out the emergency Mylar blanket and wrapped it around her.

"I'm gonna start piling up some branches," he told her over the wind. It had to be gusting around a hundred klicks an hour.

She nodded in understanding and waited while he took out the folding axe, skied over to some fallen branches and began cutting up some large evergreen boughs that had fallen onto the trail. He brought an armful back and began standing them up on end. Then he shoved them into the snow and wedged them against the mouth of the opening to form a partial windscreen across the rock opening of their makeshift shelter.

"I'll d-do that," she told him, shaking visibly as she took the next branch from him. "You go get more."

He hated that she was so cold and tired, wished he could do more to warm her up and take care of her, but she needed to keep moving and if they worked together they'd get this done much faster. Cutting the large boughs up worked up a sweat in no time.

Armful by armful he brought her the branches while the snow flew in their faces. She'd stacked the boughs close together, weaving the greenery together in a kind of blanket to help keep out the wind.

He gathered several more loads, then helped finish the first layer and started on the second. By the time they had the second one halfway done, he took her by the upper arm and pulled her toward the little opening they'd left in the branches.

"Go inside," he told her. "I'll be done here soon."

"No, I c-can—"

"Tala, *go*," he commanded, just wanting her out of the wind and cold. They both had survival training but his was more advanced, and survival in austere conditions was part of his expertise. He wanted her somewhere sheltered so she could start to warm up a little.

Thankfully she relented, took off her skis and

crawled through the opening. He pushed her skis and poles in after her, along with his ruck, then set to work finishing the second layer. When he was done, there were still gaps in the branches.

He skied farther down the trail to find more boughs, cut them up and carried them back to plug all the holes with fir and pine greenery. Soon enough the snow would pile up on the outside of the wall they'd erected, forming an insulating blanket against the elements. They'd have to maintain a hole for ventilation to stave off carbon monoxide poisoning.

After plugging the last gap as best he could, he crawled through the hole and found Tala inside with her headlamp on, the emergency blanket wrapped around her. He set his skis and poles on top of hers right next to the curtain of branches they'd erected, then set about closing the hole, leaving the top portion open for an airway.

It was still freezing inside, but at least the wind and snow were blocked by the makeshift wall. He crawled over to Tala, who was shivering as she sat on the bedroll he'd attached to his ruck. Without a word, she opened the silvery blanket and held it out to make room for him.

After digging in his ruck for all the extra clothing he'd brought, he gave her thick socks, a sweatshirt and a pair of sweatpants, along with some chemical packet hand warmers. He took off her jacket and quickly helped her get the extra layers on, then put her jacket back on, zipped it up and tucked the hand warmers into her gloves.

"That should help," he murmured, tugging her toque down a little more beneath the Mylar blanket. The other one he'd brought had been burned with the snowmobile.

"Wh-what about y-you?" she asked, her teeth chattering.

"I've got some more." He stripped off his jacket, put on the extra layer, then pulled the jacket back on.

As soon as it was zipped up and his gloves were on

with the hand warmers inside, he sat next to Tala. Hauling her into his lap, he bundled the emergency blanket around them both, his arms tight around her.

She groaned in relief and tucked in tight to him, her face pressed into his neck, gloves clenched against his chest. She was shivering hard, her body jerking with them.

Braxton laid them down on their sides and pulled his ruck into place to use as a pillow, tucking her thigh between his and holding her as close as possible. They were in for a long, cold, uncomfortable night, but at least now they were out of the elements and could share body heat.

"C-can't believe how f-fast the storm blew up," she said.

He pressed his cheek to hers, the shared body heat warming the front of him while the unyielding cold seeped along his back. "I know." The original forecast had called for the blizzard to end just before dawn. Maybe since it had started early, it would end early too. "Better?"

"Much." She wriggled in closer, flattening her body to him.

Braxton released a long breath. He'd wanted more time with her. Had never imagined a shooter coming after them. And even though this situation sucked, he was thankful he'd been with her today. Grateful that she was still alive, and that he could take care of her now.

He hadn't been able to help her after she'd been wounded. Seeing her lying in that hospital bed, he'd felt totally helpless. He'd even wondered if coming to see her was a mistake, if seeing him might upset her more.

He could still picture the look on her face when he'd stepped around the curtain. Surprise. Relief. Gratitude.

And then she'd reached for him, and there was nothing on earth that could have kept him away from her.

Duty had dragged him away from her far too soon when all he wanted was to stay, to be there for her. He still felt guilty about that, even though he hadn't had a choice. He'd done all he could for her that day and ever since, but it hadn't seemed enough. Still didn't. And all he'd been able to leave behind of himself was that damn bear she loved so much.

"What are you thinking about?" she whispered. Her shivering was subsiding.

"You." About how he was more certain of his feelings for her today than ever. Tala was it for him and always would be.

"What about me?"

"About seeing you in the hospital just before I had to leave. How much I wish I could've been there for you while you recovered." It had been a long, hard ordeal lasting the better part of two years. He'd been deployed for almost all of it, only managing to sneak in one visit to see her in Kelowna in between.

She slipped her arms around him beneath the blanket and rubbed a hand over his back, as though he was the one in need of comfort. "You were there for me."

He grunted and shook his head. "Not in person, and not nearly often enough. Not as much as I wanted to be. I thought about you every single day." He hugged her close, burying his face in the side of her neck. Thinking of her had gotten him through some of the hardest times of his deployments. "I wished I could trade places with you so you wouldn't have to suffer anymore."

She squeezed him, her shivers lessening even more. "It was awful, not gonna lie, but it made me into who I am today. I'm stronger now for it all."

"You sure as hell are." He sighed, savoring the feel of her wrapped around him, soaking up their shared warmth as the wind howled beyond their enclosure. "You hungry?"

"Yeah. What've we got?"

Not as much as they would have if the emergency

supplies he'd left with the snowmobiles hadn't been burned to ash. Right about now, he would have killed for those extra layers and blankets. He hoped the asshole responsible was currently freezing to death out in the storm somewhere. "Let's take a look."

He tucked the edges of the thin blanket around her to minimize the cold air seeping in as he sat them up and reached into his ruck. The sandwiches Nina and Rylee had made them were frozen solid, but the trail mix and protein bars were still edible. "Think the tea's still liquid enough to drink it?" he asked, pulling out both thermoses.

"Oh, God, I hope so." She tucked the edges of the blanket under her chin and stuck her hands through to take a thermos. She shook it, groaned in relief. "There's definitely liquid in there somewhere." Uncapping it, she tipped it to her lips and closed her eyes, a moan rising from her throat. "I swear that's the best thing I've ever tasted."

He took a sip of his own, and agreed. It was like chai without the milk. Spicy, sweet and delicious. After the ordeal they'd just been through, the sugar in the honey was a godsend.

Eating the trail mix with numb fingers, however, was a challenge. He ended up taking off his gloves and feeding her little bits of nuts, dried fruit and dark chocolate by hand, not wanting her to remove her own gloves.

"Your fingers are like icicles," she said in a worried voice, capturing his hand between her gloved ones. She brought them to her mouth to kiss his fingers, then rubbed them gently.

They were too cold to feel anything, but his heart squeezed at her effort. "Keep eating," he told her, pulling his hand free to get her another mouthful. "You need the calories." He fed her until she refused to eat any more, then ate the rest and nearly broke his teeth trying to chew the frozen protein bar.

After that, he took a ski pole and poked it through the snow covering the ventilation hole in the door they'd constructed. "What time is it?" she murmured sleepily when he eased back to lie down behind her again.

"Little after seven, I think." Their phones had no service out here. Hopefully Tate would still be able to get their location on the GPS spotter, but no one would be able to come looking until the storm ended. "Sore?"

"A little." She sighed. "Seems like it should be the middle of the night."

He drew her tighter into his body, tucked them into a tight ball and wrapped his arms around her. Blizzard or not, holding her like this was heaven. He just wished they were somewhere safe and warm so he could peel all their layers off and show her how much he loved her.

Yeah, he loved her, and he'd known it for a long time now. Even knowing all the reasons he should keep his distance, and that she deserved more than what he could give her, he still loved her. That would never change, no matter what happened between them.

Even if she couldn't be his.

"Where were you going that day, anyway?" Tala asked him after a minute.

"What day?"

"When you saw me in the hospital."

His mind snapped him back in time. "We went out to hunt down the cell responsible for the attack on the convoy."

"Oh."

"After that, we went after the cell that made and planted the IEDs." He paused, his muscles tightening. "Including the mine you stepped on."

She turned her head to try and look at him, the low beam of her headlamp casting a ring of light on the rock ceiling above them. "And did you get them?" she asked quietly.

A surge of savage satisfaction shot through him. "Oh yeah."

That mission was still vivid in his mind. He remembered the exact smell of the arid air as he'd waited in his sniper hide on a low ridge overlooking the village, reporting observations from him and his spotter to the rest of the team. And when they'd positively ID'd the head bomb maker entering that village, Braxton had laid in position for another twenty-one hours waiting for his target to come back out.

It was still the single most satisfying shot he'd ever taken in his career. Too bad the fucker he'd shot had never known what hit him. He'd been dead before he hit the ground from the bullet Braxton put through his C-spine.

It hadn't changed anything for Tala. She'd still lost her foot and lower leg. Had still gone through endless months of agony through other surgeries and painful, grueling rehab before she could finally walk with a prosthetic. But at least the man responsible for her suffering had paid with his life. At least Braxton had been able to give her that.

"I made sure you got justice for what happened," he told her in a low voice, hoping the glimpse into his darker nature wouldn't alarm her. "It was all I could give you."

She turned over fully to face him, angling her headlamp upward so it hit the far wall instead of his face. "What do you mean? Who did you kill?"

She was so beautiful and strong. A proud survivor. "The lead bomb maker. Former Afghan National Army, trained by the U.S." It was all classified but he didn't give a fuck. She deserved to know. He hoped it brought her at least a little peace after all she'd been through.

Tala trailed her gloved fingers down the side of his face, her gaze searching his. "You couldn't tell me before."

"No."

"You shouldn't have even told me now, should you?"

"No."

A soft smile curved her lips. They were no longer purple from the cold, but a dark pink, and all he could think about was kissing them. Sliding his tongue between them to taste her again. "I'm glad he's dead. So thank you. For what you did, and for telling me."

He'd do anything for her. Had already killed for her once, and would do it again if the fugitive up the mountain came after them again. No one was ever touching her again while he was here.

She shifted closer, her gaze still locked with his as her thigh pressed against his groin, and his entire body tightened. Blood rushed between his legs, making his cock go rock hard inside his ski pants and sweats. And suddenly everything but her fell away, leaving nothing but the desire raging inside him.

Shifting his hands up to palm the back of her head, he fused their mouths together, unleashing some of his hunger for her. Enough to make his heart pound and his muscles bunch. Letting her see what she did to him. What she meant to him. Showing her how much he wanted her.

Tala made a quiet, sexy purring sound and twined her tongue with his, all but melting into his body. Soft where he was hard. Warm where he was cold.

Her kiss and touch melted the frozen place inside him, making him ache for so much more. She tasted of sweet spices and every guilty fantasy he'd had of her for the past four years.

One hand slid down to cup her ass and squeeze it as he pressed her hips to the throbbing length of his erection. That Lycra suit had been driving him crazy all afternoon, and now he could finally feel her firm curves the way he'd been dying to.

But it wasn't enough. He wanted closer. Deeper.

Barely clinging to his control, he rocked his hips into her, aching to rip the layers of clothing away so he could plunge inside her. Claim her. Bathe in her warmth and feel her wrapped around him completely while he gave her enough pleasure to make her forget where they were and that they were trapped out here in a blizzard with a madman somewhere on this mountain.

He groaned into her mouth as he kissed her, resenting the gloves that kept him from being able to explore her the way he wanted. And if he didn't slow this down now, he might lose his head and not be able to stop until he was buried inside her.

Instead he slowed the kiss, gentled it, until she strained in his arms, her body rubbing against his the most incredibly erotic torture. Then he kissed his way across her face and down her jaw to the sensitive place below her jaw.

"Dammit, I wish we were in a big warm bed right now," he breathed, his cock so hard it hurt.

She rubbed her covered core along his thigh, a needy sigh escaping. "I really want to risk getting you naked right now, but I'm afraid we'd freeze to death," she muttered.

He laughed, drawing a startled look from her. Hell, it surprised him too, but it was so damn funny, and it felt good. He hadn't laughed in too long.

She pressed her hips and belly tighter to his erection, grinning at him as she nudged it. "You won't leave me hanging when we get home, right?"

"That's a promise I can't wait to keep, sweetheart."

Her gaze softened. She kissed him again. Gently. Slowly. Then snuggled back against his chest and cuddled in close with a gentle sigh. "This whole situation blows, but I'm really glad you're with me right now, Brax. I wouldn't want to be here with anyone but you."

He kissed the top of her toque-covered head, that all-too familiar pressure filling his chest. "Me too. Now try to get some sleep. I'll take the first watch."

"Okay." Her face was pressed to the base of his neck, her exhalations warming his skin.

Minutes passed with nothing but their quiet breathing filling the enclosure and the sound of the wind outside. Tala's body was relaxed against him. He thought she'd fallen asleep until she spoke.

"Rylee and my brother are gonna freak when we don't show up soon," she murmured drowsily. "Tate'll be out here at first light if the storm lets up by then."

Braxton was counting on it.

****

Neither of them were answering their phones. Not that they could probably get a signal in this storm.

Tate slipped his phone back into his jeans pocket and turned away from the front window where he'd been keeping watch, hoping to see the headlights of his truck coming down the road. Eight inches of snow had already fallen here and the wind was shearing snow-laden branches off the trees.

Up where Brax and Tala were, it would be a lot worse.

"Anything?"

He glanced over his shoulder as Nina came into the family room. "No." And that made him damn worried.

She wrapped her arms around his waist from behind and flattened herself to the back of him, her cheek pressed between his shoulder blades. "I'm sure they're okay. They'll probably pull into the driveway any minute now."

"They're not in the truck. They're not even anywhere close to it."

"What?" She eased away and he turned to meet her gaze.

"The GPS spotter says they're still thirteen miles from the building site." He'd been tracking them all afternoon to keep tabs on them. Then, a little over an hour ago, they'd either stopped or the signal had dropped.

Her eyes widened, then she looked at the darkened front windows as the snow flew thick and fast outside. "What happened?"

"Dunno. Could just be the storm blew up too fast for them to get back to the truck." Could be they'd lost visibility. Could be one of them was hurt. Or maybe something had happened to Tala's prosthetic, making it impossible for her to ski back down.

Or it could mean the fugitive killer had found them.

Nina reached for his hand and squeezed it, her face full of worry. "What can I do?"

"Did you hear from them?"

They both turned at Rylee's voice behind them. His niece stood in the kitchen doorway, her arms around her middle, watching them anxiously.

"Not yet. But I've got their location." He gave her a reassuring smile. The kid had been through too much these past few months. He wasn't going to add to her trauma by saying something was wrong and that her mother was missing in a fucking blizzard with a possible murderer on the loose in the same area. "Don't worry. If they're not back soon, Mase and I'll go out as soon as the storm lets up. But I'm sure they're fine. They took lots of supplies with them. They're both trained in winter survival, and Braxton's an expert. They'll be fine."

She watched him for a long moment, as if trying to decide whether he was bullshitting her or not. "She's not answering my calls or texts."

"They won't have reception where they are. And the cold saps battery life, so her phone might be dead."

Rylee pushed out a breath, then nodded. "You'll tell me the second you hear anything?"

"Of course."

He waited until she'd gone down the hall, listened for the sound of her door shutting. But Nina spoke first. "Tate, what do you need me to do?"

He loved that she was ready and willing to help him with whatever needed to be done. "Get food and some blankets together. I'm gonna go organize the rest of what I need and call Mason."

She leaned up on tiptoe to brush a soft kiss on his mouth. "On it."

He dialed Mason's number as he strode for the garage, his mind churning. "Hey, I can't reach either of them and they're still thirteen miles from the building site. Get whatever you need together now, because as of right now we're both on alert. As soon as this storm breaks, we're going after them."

CHAPTER FIFTEEN

Tala woke with a shiver after falling into another fitful doze and immediately regretted waking, gritting her teeth against the pain in her right leg. Thin, dark gray light seeped through the hole at the top of the door they'd built.

Morning was finally approaching, after an endless and completely miserable night.

Braxton shifted on the bedroll they were lying on and wordlessly pulled her tighter into his body. The Mylar blanket had come loose around them. He tucked it back around her shoulders and lifted his top leg to let her sandwich her thigh between his.

Another time it might have been arousing as hell to wake up next to him like this. Right now, it was all about survival and sharing body heat.

She burrowed into him and pressed her face into the base of his neck, trying to ignore the pain coming from her stump. Her nose and lips were numb from the cold. The chemical pouches were no longer keeping her hands warm, and her left foot felt like a block of ice. Her back and shoulder muscles ached from overdoing it yesterday. But the pain in her leg eclipsed every other discomfort.

She shifted, trying to escape it, or at least find a position that made it more bearable. Nothing helped.

Squeezing her eyes shut, she focused on the feel of Braxton, hoping to distract herself from the pain as she'd done during those first few weeks after being wounded.

When she shifted restlessly again, Braxton eased away slightly to look down into her face. The tiny amount of light coming in through their air hole above them allowed her to see the shape of his eyes. "What's wrong?" he whispered.

"Hurts," she muttered.

"What does?"

"My stump."

His arms came all the way around her, then he was sitting up and pulling her with him. "Is something wrong?"

Yes. "It sometimes g-gets like this." She'd overdone it yesterday. And she hadn't taken off the liner to let the skin breathe and check or clean it because it had been too damn cold. "The cold's m-making it worse."

He hugged her to his chest, tucking her across his lap so that her stump wasn't pressed against anything. "Can I do something to make it better?"

She shook her head, willing the pain to go away. A combination of sharp, lightning nerve pain shooting up what remained of her leg, and a deep, horrible ache that signaled bone pain.

"Should we check it?"

"No," she said, too sharply. Not only did she not want him seeing it, she didn't want anything to touch it. Any additional stimulation right now would make the pain unbearable.

"Are you going to be able to ski on it?"

She'd have to if she wanted off this mountain, but she was dreading putting her prosthetic back on right now. "Yes. What time is it?"

He reached up to unzip his jacket and pull out his phone where he'd kept it against his chest to stay warm. She'd tucked hers into the front of her sports bra to try and conserve whatever battery life remained. "Almost oh-six-hundred-hours. Still no service."

He put it away, zipped back up and immediately drew her close, holding her to him while he rubbed his gloved hands rapidly up and down her back. Trying to warm and comfort her. "Wind's died down some. I just cleared the air hole again before you woke up. It's still snowing out there, but not as bad as it was last night."

She drew a deep breath, mentally gearing up for the trek ahead. "We going to get moving?"

"I want to wait for it to die down just a little more. Then if you're up to it, yes."

"I'm up to it." She was sore and would pay for it all the way down the mountain, but she had no choice but to put her prosthetic back on and ski out of here. "Think the shooter's still out there?" That and the cold had kept her from sleeping in anything more than little snatches all night, even with Braxton right here.

"Doubtful. If he's not a total idiot he would have gone back to that shed for the night. And if he doesn't want to get arrested, he'll be out of there long before this storm is over."

She pressed her face to the front of his jacket and forced herself to take slow, deep breaths. Her pain tolerance was generally high, but nerve and bone pain were the worst. She had prescription meds for the infrequent times it got this bad. Unfortunately, she didn't have them with her.

"I wish I could make it stop," he murmured, holding her tight to his powerful body. "I wish I could make *all* of this go away."

Her, too. "J-just think of the stories we can t-tell after this. We can be all, 'Remember that time when we got s-stuck on the mountain in the middle of a blizzard and a wanted murderer tried to k-kill us, so we holed up in a cave and nearly froze to death?'."

His low chuckle gusted against her ear. "Maybe we should write a book about it together."

"They'll make it into a m-movie."

"They would if they're smart." He nuzzled the side of her neck, his whiskers scraping pleasantly, sending a different kind of shiver through her.

They lapsed into quiet after that. She closed her eyes, trying to disassociate from her physical discomfort, but exhausted as she was, the pain wouldn't allow her to doze off again.

She kept breathing through it and toughed it out, thinking about Rylee and her brother. "Tate and Rylee are going to be freaking out right now."

"He was probably already doing that by about nineteen-hundred-hours last night when we didn't show up and he couldn't reach us."

Maybe she'd be able to get a cell signal a little farther down the mountain, so she could at least text him to say they were alive. "He and Mase will come looking for us as soon as the storm eases enough for them to get up here."

"Yeah. We'll probably run into them on the way down."

"I hope Rylee's not too upset." The thought of her daughter in distress tore at her. But she was so glad Rylee had declined the invitation to come up here with them yesterday. Tala would never want her going through something like this.

"We'll get you back to her as soon as possible." He rubbed her back again, more slowly now. A soothing motion meant to comfort and lull. "Can you go back to sleep if I lie us down again?"

"No. But you go ahead and get some more sleep. I'll

keep watch."

"I'm okay. Just worried about you."

She liked that he cared so much. "I'm tougher than I look."

"Don't I know it."

She didn't know what the cryptic comment meant, but there was a note of respect in his tone so she didn't ask him what he meant by it. Instead, she closed her eyes and focused on him to try and push the sharpest edge of the pain away.

She concentrated on his warmth. The strength of his arms around her. Sheltering and protecting her with his body.

More than anything, she tried not to think of him walking away when this was over. Back to war. Maybe never to return.

Her eyes popped open when he shifted under her sometime later. It seemed a bit brighter inside the enclosure now.

"Sorry, just had to clear the air hole again," he said, setting the ski pole down in front of them.

She couldn't believe she'd dozed off. "It's okay." Her eyelids felt heavy and swollen, and the pain in her leg increased with her alertness.

"It's starting to get light out now. Snow's slowed a bit more." He ran a hand up and down her spine. "Can you ski on your right leg right now?"

"Yes." It would hurt, but tough shit for her. She wanted out of here and to get back to her daughter.

"Eat something first." He reached into his ruck to get another bag of trail mix. "Can you manage—"

"Yes." She took the bag from him, clumsily opened it with her gloves, then popped a handful in her mouth. After scooping up another big handful, she gave it back to him.

He left the blanket around her while he rolled up the

bedroll and packed up what little they'd used overnight. She checked the two socks she'd pulled over the liner on her stump to make sure there were no wrinkles in them, then reached for her prosthetic, bracing for the coming pain.

She pressed her lips together as she pulled it on, then set her hands on the bedroll to push upright. Braxton was right there to help scoop her up and set her on her feet. She gripped his arm while she sank her weight down on her right leg, locking the pin into the prosthetic socket.

Pain shot from the stump and up her leg, making her inhale sharply. *Shit.*

Braxton steadied her with an arm across the middle of her back. "Tal."

She clenched her jaw, didn't look at him. "No, I'm okay." She could do this. She'd been through a lot worse. All she had to do was tough it out until they got to the truck. Then she could take everything off, and once back at Tate's place, she could take some meds.

"If it's too much we can wait here until the storm breaks. Maybe then we can reach Tate and they'll bring snowmobiles up to get us."

She shook her head, adamant. "No, I want to get going now." Waiting here in the cold would only make it worse. At least once they were moving, she would get a bit warmer, and maybe the pain would decrease after a while too. It depended.

His dark brown eyes held hers, his eyebrows pulled together in a concerned frown. "If it gets too bad, I'll carry you."

She gave a terse nod, not wanting to talk anymore, and reached for her right ski. The binding wobbled when she set the foot of her prosthetic into it. Her leg howled in protest with the movement, pain forking through it, and when she reached down for her poles, all the muscles in her arms and across her back knotted and ached.

Hell. This was gonna suck so bad on the way down.

She reached for her goggles next, tugging them in place. Gearing up to face the elements once more. *You can do this, Tal. You're going home to Rylee.*

When she straightened, Braxton was standing at the entrance, watching her through his own goggles. "Ready?"

As she'd ever be. "Yeah."

He pulled aside some of the branches, opening a doorway of sorts. The bitter wind raced through the opening, momentarily stealing her breath, but he was right, it had died down some, and the snow had slowed enough to allow her to partially see their surroundings in the predawn light. But the landscape they emerged into from the enclosure was completely unrecognizable from the night before.

Snowdrifts taller than her obscured her view along the side of the mountain. "We heading left?" That was the direction they'd come here from last night.

He nodded and struggled his way through the deep snow toward where the trail had been. "Stay in my tracks. And if you need to stop, tell me right away."

"Okay."

It was the toughest skiing she'd ever done. Every single stride sent a combination of pain through her stump, and the fresh, deep snow made it extra difficult to maneuver her skis.

She blocked it all out. Blocked out everything but her determination to keep going, telling herself that each painful stride forward meant being one step closer to finishing and getting back to Rylee.

Braxton kept a steady, methodical pace, looking back frequently to check on her. But as they wound their way around a curve in the trail, Tala's nape began to tingle.

She looked around instinctively, her pulse thudding

in her ears. There was no sound but the wind and her labored breaths. Nothing moved around them except the drifting snowflakes and the evergreen boughs waving in the wind.

But she knew without a doubt that they weren't alone out here.

****

"What is it? Did you hear something?" Nina mumbled sleepily beside him, pushing up on one elbow in their bed.

It was too dark to see her face, but the sky was already beginning to lighten outside their master bedroom window. Eight inches of new snow clung to the bottom of the sill. "No. But it's almost dawn and the storm's finally easing. I have to go."

Tate stood and grabbed the cold weather gear he'd put on the dresser last night. He'd barely slept, kept waking up soon after he dozed off and checking his phone, hoping he'd find a message from either Tala or Brax. But he'd heard nothing all night, and according to the GPS spotter, they were still out there, in the same place it had last pinged them ten hours ago.

His gut told him there was more to this than the storm. That something else had caused them to take shelter up there. He and Mason needed to get out there and find them A-fucking-SAP.

He dressed and hurried into the kitchen, already on the phone. Three different calls put everyone involved in the search effort into motion, and everything was ready to begin. He'd coordinated everything with the department last night, with cops and local search and rescue volunteers.

Several on-duty officers would be helping, along with a half-dozen more who were technically on holiday but were coming out today as volunteers. Tate and Mason were going up now, and everyone else was meeting at the building site at eight. They would start at the area where Tala and Brax's GPS spotter last pinged their location, and work outward from there.

Tate wolfed down half a turkey sandwich on his way through the kitchen, his gaze straying out to the back deck. They had well over eighteen inches of snow out there and it was still coming down, though not as bad as before. The backyard was littered with broken boughs and branches brought down by the near hurricane-force winds.

The storm had been intense. When Tal and Brax hadn't been able to make it down the mountain, they would have taken shelter somewhere through the night.

Unless something happened to them.

He was at the counter pouring thermoses full of hot coffee to take with him when Nina came in, her fluffy yellow robe with pink roses on it belted around her waist. "Don't worry about that," she said. "Rylee and I will bring up food and drinks for everyone. We've got it covered." She wound her arms around him from behind, her right hand rubbing his chest in a soothing circle.

He set a hand on hers, squeezed. "You don't need to do that."

"We want to. Avery's already going to be handling all the search party coordination at the building site. Rylee and I are going to help her. I just wish I could do more."

He turned around and took her face in his hands. She had the biggest heart of anyone he knew, and knowing she cared so much made him love her even more. "Love you, sunshine."

She smiled up at him, her brown eyes worried. "Love you back. And you need to promise me you'll be careful."

He stroked his thumb across her petal-soft cheek, impatient to get going. By the time he and Mason reached the building site, it would be sunrise. "I promise." He kissed her gently. "Let Rylee sleep as long as you can." He didn't want his niece worrying a second longer than she had to. And maybe, if he was lucky, by the time she awoke, he would have Tala back here to greet her.

"I will." Nina lifted up on her toes to brush a kiss across his mouth, her hands squeezing his shoulders. "You go find them, Tate, and bring them home."

That's exactly what he was going to do.

CHAPTER SIXTEEN

Jason hunched over to try and protect himself from the icy wind as he drove the snowmobile down an incline, heading for a trail he knew of farther down the mountain. He just hoped it was still unblocked, because if it wasn't, he would have to backtrack to his starting point and try another direction.

Urgency pumped through him. The storm had cost him precious time already, preventing him from getting out of here last night as planned.

He should have been in Idaho by now, on a nice warm bus heading to meet his sister in California. Instead he was stuck out here, half-frozen and forced to find an alternative route out of these damn mountains.

His fingers were like ice inside his insulated gloves. Last night had been the coldest, longest night of his life. The weather had forced him to go back to the shack. Even inside it he'd half-frozen to death.

He'd run out of fuel for the wood-burning stove at around one in the morning. Soon after that, the wind had torn part of the roof off. He'd spent the rest of the night huddled next to the barely-warm stove beneath a nest of tarps and blankets, wondering if he'd make it to morning.

Now dawn was approaching. Moving around in the daylight increased the risk of being seen. He didn't know what had happened to the two people he'd gone after yesterday, but since he'd taken one snowmobile and burned the rest of their shit, they'd probably frozen to death.

The snowmobile tipped forward as he started down the slope. Snow sprayed him as the vehicle tore through the powder covering the denser snow beneath. Just as he was about to reach the bottom, the skis hit something. The handlebars snapped sideways, making the vehicle torque in midair.

He flew off the seat, the breath whooshing from his lungs when he plowed face first into the thick powder. Immediately he shoved up and struggled to his feet, shaken. Snow seeped down into the collar of his jacket and up his sleeves, the intense cold burning his already chilly skin.

The snowmobile was lying on its side a dozen feet away. He trudged over to it and yanked out the rifle that was now sticking end up out of the snow. Slinging it across his back, he grabbed the handlebars of the snowmobile and struggled to wrestle it back onto its treads.

Finally he succeeded, panting and sweating, the melting snow inside his clothes creating icy rivulets along his skin. But the snowmobile wouldn't start. He tried everything he knew to get it going, and the bastard wouldn't turn over.

"Fuck!" he snarled, and began gathering up the contents of the backpack that had strewn everywhere during the crash. The snowmobile had been his only chance of getting out of here without the cops hot on his trail, and now he was back to being on foot. In the middle of a goddamn blizzard.

Straightening, he stared through the swirling snow at the shadowy peaks rising ahead of him. He'd never make it to the pass on foot. Not with the weather turned to shit and his only shelter ruined.

His heart sank, his frustration building, rising in a red tide of anger. He needed to find shelter and hide until he could find another way out of here, but the only other building he knew of within reach right now was a partially-constructed one down in the valley near the creek. He'd have to go back down the mountain and risk taking the shortcut again to get there.

Anger pulsed through him, helping to counteract the cold and the bitter sting of disappointment. He was down, but not out. He still had a rifle and supplies, and he knew how to survive.

He shrugged into his backpack and slung the rifle over his shoulder before starting his retreat back the way he'd come. With every single step, he plunged thigh-deep into the snow. Covering fifty feet felt like he'd trudged the length of a football field. But he kept going, stopping when he couldn't catch his breath, then carrying on.

It took him over an hour to reach the start of the shortcut. Because of the incline the snow hadn't settled as thickly on it. He half-jogged, half-skidded his way down the trail he knew by heart. But when he finally emerged onto the wider trail at the bottom, his racing heart stuttered to a halt.

Ski tracks. Two sets. Leading down the same trail he had to take.

He reached back for his rifle, his gaze jerking left and right as he searched for the skiers. Had to be the same people as yesterday. No way anyone else would have been up here so early, in this same spot in these conditions. How the hell had they made it through the night out here?

His pulse thudded in his ears. They'd seen him. Might be able to ID him, and would definitely be able to give his location away now that he was stranded. And now they were between him and the only place of refuge he knew of for miles around.

He tightened his grip on his weapon, mind made up. They had to die.

There was no other way for him to escape. He had to kill them both and get down to that building to hide until it was safe enough to move again.

Moving with purpose, he started down the trail. Following the tracks, his rifle at the ready.

When he crested a slight ridge partway down the trail, he paused to scan below him. Through the falling snow his gaze immediately shot to the two figures skiing down the trail almost directly beneath him.

He swallowed, his heart rate kicking up. He stepped closer to the edge of the ridge, carefully feeling along with his right boot to make sure he didn't step on unstable ground. There was no sound but the dying wind.

They hadn't seen him. Didn't know he was up here. His conscience needled him. It almost seemed unfair for him to pick them off this way, but he had no choice.

Jason tugged off his right glove with his teeth, brought the rifle to his shoulder and took aim at the man. He was out front. Bigger, an easier target. And once Jason killed him, the woman would likely freeze in terror or stop to try and help him, making her an easy kill.

He angled his body to make the shot, his index finger shifting from the trigger guard to curve around the trigger.

The ground shifted beneath his right boot.

He lowered the rifle and jerked back, the momentum making him tumble into the snow. He jerked his head up in terror to see the edge crumbling inches from his feet. Disappearing a bit at a time and plunging down the cliff face.

Jason frantically scrambled away as the ground in front of him disintegrated and tumbled down right where his targets were.

"HALFWAY THERE," BRAXTON said to Tala

over his shoulder, trying to encourage her. Her lips had a purple cast from the cold and she was pale. And even though she was still hurting, she refused to let him carry her.

She nodded in answer and kept coming, her strides awkward and jerky. Partly from the ruined binding he'd wrapped some duct tape around a while back to try and hold it together, but mostly because of her leg.

"Tal, let me carry you," he said again. The storm was definitely easing now, giving them a bit of visibility to work with. He could ski with her on piggyback, or even across his shoulders. "At least for a while."

She shook her head. "Don't stop," she panted. "Keep going."

While he loved and admired her determination and inner strength, he hated to see her hurting, and worried she was doing long-term damage by insisting on continuing to ski with her leg the way it was now.

He stopped and turned to face her, ignoring the way her lips thinned and her jaw flexed. "Stop," he commanded her, unable to stand it any longer.

"I can…keep going," she insisted stubbornly.

He reached out and wrapped a hand around her nape to bring her to a halt, her eyes raising to his inside her goggles. "Do you think I'll see you as weak if I carry you? Is that the problem?"

She averted her gaze. "No. I can do this."

"And I don't want you in any more pain than you already are." He released her to shift the straps of his ruck. Then he reached for her, intending to pull her onto his back, and he heard it.

A shifting sound, then a low, ominous rumble overhead.

Tala's head snapped up, and when he followed her gaze, his heart seized.

A wall of white was barreling down the cliff straight

at them. Less than two-hundred-yards and closing, fast.

"Move!" he shouted, grabbing her arm to fling her in front of him.

She scrambled to get her skis in place, then began frantically using her poles to get momentum. Braxton was faster, helping her with a shove on the back just beneath her rifle harness.

But he wasn't fast enough.

Before he'd gone a dozen strides, the wall of debris reached him. It picked him up, pushing upward like a rising wave. He had just enough time to throw his arm at Tala, catching her across the back to fling her out of the way.

His last sight of her was falling forward, her skis coming loose as she plunged headfirst away from the debris flow. Then the wall closed over him. Engulfing him from all sides in a crushing embrace.

He couldn't see. Couldn't move. Couldn't breathe as it trapped him, carrying him down the slope like a pebble caught in a raging river.

It was like being caught in a frozen washing machine. Instinctively he fought to bring his arms up and cover his face and head.

Rocks and branches slammed into him from all sides, punching the air from his lungs. Over and over he tumbled, losing all sense of direction, unable to escape.

Endless seconds later, he slammed into what felt like a wall beneath him and plunged to an abrupt stop.

He wasn't sure if it knocked him out, but when he opened his eyes again, pain flashed through his back and ribs. He was trapped in freezing, pitch blackness, struggling to suck in air through the tiny pocket he'd created in front of his face with his hands.

Through the panic flooding him, his brain kicked back into gear.

Tala! She was alone, helpless if her prosthetic was

broken, and might have been caught in the avalanche with him.

Fight or flight kicked in, the need to get to her eating him alive. *Get out. You have to get the fuck out. Tala needs you.*

He struggled to move his limbs, fighting the crushing wall of snow entombing him. Every move cost him. Using up the air he'd managed to save. Already he was light-headed, his precious oxygen supply rapidly dwindling to nothing.

And the whole time he fought to get free, his mind screamed at him. Warning him that he was running out of time.

If he couldn't get out in the next minute, he wasn't getting out at all.

CHAPTER SEVENTEEN

Terror rocketed through Tala as she hit the snow, getting a face full of icy powder. She shoved up and rolled to her side to see what had happened, her gut clenching when she saw the huge pile of debris and nothing else. "Braxton!"

She couldn't see him. Only the river of snow, rock and tree matter still spilling down the hillside, piled up at least seven feet high across the trail. "No, no, no," she breathed, desperate to find him, refusing to believe he could be dead.

Her right ski had come off when he'd shoved her out of the way, and been swept up in the avalanche. She flung off the left one, now useless.

Unable to walk without a foot at the end of her prosthetic, she flipped onto her knees and crawled as fast as she could to the huge pile of snow studded with rock and branches, frantically scanning for any sign of him.

She couldn't see anything. "Braxton!" *Please let him be okay...* She had to find him. Had to get him out before he suffocated.

Her heart pounded so hard against her ribs it felt bruised as she searched for some sign, anything that might help her locate him beneath the rubble. She crawled partway up the debris mound and started digging with her hands, shoving big sweeps of snow and bits of branches aside with her arms when it didn't seem to move fast enough. She could feel the seconds slipping past, time she didn't have to waste.

As she swept another armful off to the side, her gaze caught on something sticking out of the mound.

A ski tip.

She lunged over to it and frantically began digging the snow away from it. "Braxton, can you hear me?" she called out.

No answer, only the wind swirling around her and her pulse hammering in her ears.

She kept digging. The ski came loose. She yanked it out, tossed it behind her and hurriedly scooped the snow away from that same spot, praying she would be able to find him. It had to have been well over a minute since she'd started digging.

Her hand touched something hard. A ski pole.

Dammit, she had to be close to him. She pulled it free and resumed digging, every heartbeat feeling like an eternity. The pain in her leg was forgotten. There was no cold, no exhaustion, nothing but the icy terror gripping her that she wouldn't be able to get to Braxton in time.

Then she saw it. Faint movement in the snow just to the left of where she was digging.

She sucked in a breath and plunged her arm deep into the snow there. Her hand met something firm. She grabbed it. Pulled.

Her heart jumped when her fingers closed around the puffy material of a jacket. "*Brax.*"

Tala dug as hard and fast as she could, desperation driving her. He didn't have any air in there. Wouldn't be able to breathe. *Come on, come on*, she ordered herself, pushing harder, faster.

She uncovered part of his arm. Shoved her hand through the snow to grope around. She needed to uncover his face. Give him room to breathe.

Sweat gathering along her spine as she fought to free him. His upper arm. Shoulder. Neck.

He wasn't moving.

"Brax, come *on*," she urged him as she uncovered the side of his face, her voice shredding. He couldn't be dead. She couldn't take that.

She thought his hand moved slightly. Hope leaped inside her. "Brax, wake up. You have to wake up," she ordered, fighting back tears. She kept working, moving fast but carefully now so as not to hurt him. *Please, please…*

His other glove was cupped in front of his face. As if he'd tried to create an air pocket as the snow closed over him.

Her chest hitched, scalding tears burning the backs of her eyes. She pulled his hand away from his face. Blood was trickling down it from a gash over his right eyebrow, and he had several scrapes on his cheeks. She kept digging, managed to remove the snow away from his head, still covered by his knit cap.

Her breathing hitched when his eyelids fluttered. She seized his face in her hands, cupping it, careful not to move him in case he had a neck or spinal injury. "Wake up. I need you to open your eyes and look at me," she begged.

His eyelids flickered. Then his eyes cracked open, his gaze blurry as he slowly focused on her.

"You're okay," she told him, though he probably wasn't—how could he be after being buried in all this? "Just stay with me. Stay with me, we need to get you out of here." Shit, what was she going to do?

There was no cell reception here, they had no medical supplies other than basic things in his ruck—wherever that was now—and she could no longer ski down for help. How was she going to get him down the mountain safely? Maybe she could lash the skis together with something and lay him down on them, then push him across the snow on her hands and knees.

His gaze cleared a little more as he blinked up at her, a low groan coming from his throat. "Tal."

"Yes." She leaned down and put her nose and forehead against his, then covered his face with kisses, not caring about the blood, just happy he was still alive. "Where does it hurt?"

"My...back."

Her stomach dropped. "Your spine?"

"Don't know." He moved a little, bringing his arms up.

Yes! "That's it, nice and slow," she encouraged, shoving back her emotions. She needed to hold it together. Had to get him out and then find help somehow.

She scooped more snow away from him and he started moving more. Finally, she was able to reach in and wrap her arms around his ribs. "I'm scared to move you."

He shook his head. "I can move." His jaw clenched. She could feel the muscles in his arms and back bunching beneath his jacket as he struggled to get free while she kept pulling snow and branches away from him.

After a few minutes, Braxton leaned to the side and managed to crawl out under his own power. She knelt beside him, holding her breath as she scanned him for injuries. His jacket was torn up in spots, and his ruck and pistol were nowhere to be seen.

She pulled off her gloves and ran her frozen hands along his arms, spine and legs, checking them for more blood. They came away clean. But he could be bleeding under his clothes, or inside somewhere. "Do you hurt bad anywhere besides your back?"

"I'm okay," he managed.

He definitely wasn't okay. Might have internal damage they didn't know about. But she couldn't treat that and had nothing to wrap him in to keep him warm. "Just lie still. I—"

She jerked, sucking in a sharp breath when a gunshot cracked through the icy air. The bullet hit meters to their left, kicking up a burst of snow where Braxton had just crawled out of.

Tala dove on top of him, instinctively curling her arms around his head to shield him. He groaned and pushed her off him. "Go," he commanded, shoving her behind him. "Get behind cover."

"I'm not leaving you." She grabbed him by the wrist and pulled, intending to drag him to safety.

Another shot rang out, pinging off a rock outcropping mere feet away.

Braxton put his hands on her shoulders and pushed, his face taut. "Go!"

Ignoring him, she glanced up. Saw the shooter standing above them on the ridge and her blood iced over. "He's up there!"

Braxton tried to grab her but she wrenched away and shrugged her harness from her shoulders, reaching for her rifle. The shooter was farther away than the fifty yards she was accurate at, but it didn't matter.

She was going to stop him right here and now.

****

A few minutes after leaving the building site, Mason stopped his snowmobile beside Tate and waited for his friend to consult their map one more time. Repeated attempts to reach Braxton's or Tala's cell phones had failed, and now the GPS spotter wasn't working either.

He and Tate each had rucks full of food, blankets, clothing and medical supplies. They were also both

LETHAL PROTECTOR

armed, with a rifle and sidearm. Now it was just a matter of finding their friends.

He tugged off his gloves and blew on his hands to warm them. Shit, it was cold. Dawn was here, giving them lots of daylight for the search, and the weather was finally improving some.

The storm was slowly dying, but it had stalled over the area instead of moving on as the original forecast had predicted. The bitter wind still gusted around them but nothing like last night, and the snow had become a steady, gentle fall.

Back at the building site, all the other volunteers were assembling with their equipment. Avery was coordinating the initial search effort. As soon as everyone headed out, she would head up with Tate's neighbor, Curt, on other snowmobiles to a different trail in case Braxton and Tala were on that one instead.

Tate rolled the map back up and tucked it inside his jacket. "Last ping from the GPS spotter put them seven miles from here. We'll start there and work our way down."

Mason nodded, was about to answer, when the unmistakable sound of a rifle shot echoed in the distance. His head jerked up, then he looked sharply at Tate, and from the look in his friend's eyes, Mason knew they were thinking the same thing.

No fucking way it was a hunter or sport shooter out here in these conditions. And that meant the fugitive gang member might have found Tala and Braxton.

Before he could say anything, another shot cracked through the air.

Shit. "Northeast?" Mason said, trying to locate where the shots were coming from.

Tate's jaw clenched, his gaze now trained in that direction up the trail. "Yep."

Then came the distinctive, high-pitched pop of another weapon. He snapped his gaze back to Tate. "Hear that?" He'd recognize that sound anywhere.

A .22. And hearing it now in answer to the other rifle made his guts clench.

"Tala," Tate blurted, and took off.

Mason fired up his snowmobile and tore after him, their treads kicking up rooster tails of fresh powder behind them as they raced along the access trail that would get them up to the ridge where the shots seemed to be coming from. Until those shots, they'd been searching blind out here, hoping for a miracle.

Now the miracle would be if Tala and Braxton were still alive when he and Tate reached them.

CHAPTER EIGHTEEN

Dammit, he'd missed! The angle was all wrong, and the wind wasn't helping. Neither was his wounded shoulder, and the snow kept trying to glue his eyelashes together.

Jason clenched his jaw to keep it from shivering and painfully shrugged off the backpack full of cash and ammo he'd been carrying, setting it aside in the snow. He needed to reposition himself to get a better shot.

Inching closer toward the edge of the cliff, he kept well away from the lip. He'd been damn lucky he hadn't fallen to his death when the avalanche started.

Somehow, the man and woman were both still alive down there. He couldn't afford to let them live. He wanted this over and done with so he could get off this fucking mountain and find another way out.

Leaning as much of his weight as he dared onto his front foot, he brought his rifle to his shoulder and took aim once more. Shock punched through him when he found the woman aiming right at him.

Just as he went to pull the trigger, she fired.

The bullet came within inches of hitting him in the hip, pinging off a rock right next to him. Instinct made him dive out of the way, landing on his belly in the snow.

Almost instantly, he heard the crumbling sound again. He jerked his head up, stared in horror at the lip of the cliff as it began to shift and buckle.

"Shit," he breathed, scrambling away on his hands and knees until he could get to his feet. His gaze snagged on the backpack, precariously close to where the snowpack was crumbling away.

His heart lurched. *No!*

He lunged for it, skidding to his knees in the snow. The straps remained inches from his straining fingers. A different sort of fear shot through him. He needed what was in that backpack to get out of here. Couldn't make it without it.

Cursing mentally, he flopped to his belly and inched forward, his heart threatening to explode as the ground kept giving way. The abyss coming closer and closer.

His wounded shoulder ached as he reached out, stretching as far as he could. Finally, his fingers brushed the straps. He curled them around it, scrambled to his feet and darted for more stable ground.

The rumbling got louder, the ground undulating beneath his feet. He took three more running steps, then dove for solid ground on his belly, skidding across the snow with the backpack clutched tight in his fist.

Shaking all over, he rolled to his side just in time to see another slide tumble down the cliff face behind him.

BRAXTON FELT LIKE he'd been hit by a truck.

He was dizzy, still trying to get his bearings when Tala wrenched away from him and flopped into a prone shooting stance with her rifle to her shoulder. Biting back a curse, he shot a hand out, intending to grab her and haul her behind whatever cover he could find, but it was too late.

The pop of her shot punched through the air. He

jerked his gaze upward just in time to see the shooter dive away from the bullet and disappear from view.

"Missed him," Tala muttered, anger clear in her voice. She kept her cheek pressed to the stock, watching, ready to take another shot.

A cracking sound wrenched his attention back up to the cliff edge just as the lip began to give way again.

Christ.

He lunged forward to grab Tala by the back of her jacket, yanking her out of the way milliseconds before the plume of debris hit beside them.

They hit the snow just as the deadly river of snow and rock rushed down the hill, mere feet behind them. He wrapped his arms around her and tucked her into his body as they rolled away from it, trying to shield her from anything poking out of the ground.

Her rifle jammed into his chest, and her weight drove it in harder. He sucked in a breath and clamped his jaw tight, still rolling them.

Pain shot through every single bruise and contusion on his back, chest and hips, but he didn't let go. Didn't stop. All that mattered was protecting Tala.

After another few seconds they finally came to a stop on their sides, with Tala's face shoved into his shoulder. The sliding sound of the snow behind them stopped.

Tala shoved up onto an elbow to peer down at him. "You okay?" she asked worriedly, cradling the side of his face in the palm of her glove.

"Yeah," he muttered, even though everything throbbed and ached. He lifted his head to take a look behind them and blinked until his blurry vision sharpened. The mini avalanche had stopped but the shooter was probably still up there somewhere.

They needed cover. Now.

His back and shoulders felt like they'd been beaten with a hammer. He winced, woozy as hell. He didn't think he had a concussion but his head was pounding. "Gotta move," he told her.

"To where?"

He spotted a group of boulders nearby. Not big enough to afford them total protection, but better than nothing. Looking up at the ridge, there was no sign of the shooter.

He put a hand on Tala's shoulder and pushed her away from him gently. "Get behind those rocks."

She lifted up onto her hip and looked behind her. Seeing them, she flipped over, put her rifle harness back on and started crawling for the rocks. Unable to walk without her right ski.

Braxton rolled painfully to his hands and knees and followed. He'd lost his pistol in the initial avalanche. All they had now was Tala's .22 and what little ammo she had left, against a shooter with a high-powered rifle. He was dizzy enough that he wasn't sure he could even hit anything right now.

Tala scooted behind the rocks and made as much room for him as she could. "I don't see him," she whispered, shrugging out of her harness and bringing her rifle into position again.

He leaned to the side slightly to see around the rocks and followed her gaze, a sense of vertigo hitting him. Immediately he closed his eyes, sucking in a deep breath as a wave of nausea swirled in his stomach.

When he opened his eyes a few moments later, the world spun for a few seconds. He shook it off, squinting at the ridge above them.

For a few minutes there was nothing. Just the snow falling softly. Then he caught a flash of movement on the top of the ridge.

His muscles tensed and he opened his mouth to warn Tala, reaching a hand out to flatten it against her back. Ready to throw himself on top of her.

"I see him," she murmured, the calm determination in her voice impressing him.

Bastard still wasn't giving up. Braxton lost sight of him for a few seconds. Then a slight shadow appeared in the snow near the edge of the ridge. "He's moving to the right," he whispered. "Eighty yards. Wind's gusting between forty-five and fifty klicks from the northeast. Adjust right to counter."

Tala tracked the target without answering. Braxton bit back other corrections, not wanting to distract her, itching to take the shot himself in spite of the vertigo. And when the asshole suddenly rose onto his knee to take a shot at them, Tala honed her aim and pulled the trigger.

Hit. Braxton heard the round strike. Saw the shooter disappear from view.

Tala raised her head slightly, rifle still to her shoulder. "Did I hit him?" she whispered.

"Damn right, you did. Low center mass, right." He stayed low on his belly, watching, acting as her spotter as the tense seconds ticked past. Nothing happened. No more movement. No shadows. "He's down."

"Dead?"

"If he's not, he will be soon." At any rate, Braxton didn't plan to wait here a minute longer to find out. "Let's go."

She locked eyes with him, her forehead creased in a deep frown. "Go where? Neither of us can ski."

"We'll move out on foot."

"But I can't, I—"

"I'll carry you."

"No." She shook her head, adamant.

"Yes. We're leaving, *now*." He shoved to his feet and reached for her, seizing her wrist and pulling her upright. A wave of dizziness hit him. He swayed a second, then the world righted itself. "Hurry."

She hesitated another moment, then slipped her harness back on and grabbed hold of his shoulders when he pulled her toward his back. "Brax, are you sure…"

"Get on," he said gruffly, still woozy and nauseated and not wanting to waste energy on arguing.

Tala gingerly wound her arms around the front of his neck. He leaned forward at the waist slightly and held his arms back a little, bracing himself for the coming pain.

Tala jumped up. He caught her under the thighs and sucked in a breath as her weight landed against his bruised back, lighting up every sore spot. "Are you okay?" she demanded, holding on tight with her arms and squeezing his waist with her thighs.

He didn't answer, merely turned and began walking down the slope with her clinging to his back, concentrating on keeping them both upright. And with every step he hoped the building site was a lot closer than he thought it was.

He would get her out of here safely if it was the last thing he did.

****

He was hurting bad. Tala knew it by the way Braxton held himself, by the shallow breaths he took as he carried her, slogging through the thigh-deep snow.

He could only go fifty meters or so each time before he had to stop and rest. She would slide off him and give him a minute to catch his breath, taking her rifle off her back and watching their six, just in case.

There was still no sign of the shooter. If she'd hit him center mass, then he was probably dead by now. Tala couldn't believe she might have killed a man today, but she wasn't sorry. She'd done what she'd had to in order to protect her and Braxton.

"Okay," Braxton said, his lips pressed into a thin line

as he slowly straightened and gave her his back again.

She slung her rifle harness on and hopped up on his back, her thighs quivering with the effort of keeping her legs locked around his waist. Her stump was still driving her insane with that blend of deep bone pain and electric shocks that sizzled up the back of her thigh.

She hated that she couldn't walk on her own, that she was slowing their descent down and exhausting Braxton when he was clearly already in pain.

But he didn't complain. Didn't swear or mutter, only the occasional low groan escaping him as he trudged downhill. All the while, she held on tight, trying to make it as easy on him as possible.

At least the wind and snow had eased up finally, no longer slicing at them like an icy blade. She was still cold, but being plastered to Braxton's broad back helped, and every step took them closer to the bottom of the mountain.

Now that the storm was dying out she could at least see around them, but not far enough to orient herself. With the map and GPS spotter gone and no cell service, she had no clue where they were at this point. The avalanche had messed up her sense of direction, and nothing about their current surroundings was familiar because of all the new snow.

All she knew was they needed to move downhill to reach the valley, and then hopefully they'd be able to call for help or at least be able to figure out where the building site was. Rylee and Tate must be going insane with worry right now.

She jerked when her cell phone began buzzing against her chest. "My phone," she said to Braxton, unwrapping one arm from his chest to tug at her jacket zipper. "It's working."

Braxton stopped. She slid off him, holding onto his shoulder with one hand to steady herself as she reached into the front of her jacket and beneath the sweatshirt and

Lycra suit to retrieve her phone from inside her sports bra. It was still buzzing when she pulled it out.

Over a dozen messages showed up, most from Tate. Some from Rylee.

Relief punched through her, so powerful she sagged a little. "The last message is from Tate, sent thirty-five minutes ago. He and Mason were leaving the building site on snowmobiles, heading up to look for us at the last position the GPS spotter marked us at."

She tried calling but he didn't pick up. So she typed back a quick response saying they were okay but in need of a ride back to the building site. She couldn't give them an exact location, but they were somewhere between the last known position and the building site.

She looked at Braxton, hope a painful pressure rising inside her ribcage. She wanted off this damn mountain as soon as possible, to get Braxton checked out. "They have to be close."

He nodded once, opened his mouth to say something.

A loud crack sliced through the air, and shards of bark exploded from the tree less than a foot from Tala's left shoulder.

CHAPTER NINETEEN

"*Down!*" Braxton grabbed Tala around the ribs and dove to the ground.

A throttled cry escaped him as they hit, his back taking the brunt of the impact on the compact snow they'd been standing on. Tala scrambled up beside him on her hands and knees but he knocked her flat and covered her as more bullets ripped past them.

Her rifle harness had come off when they'd first landed, now lying in the snow between them. Her face was pale, her movements uncoordinated as she reached for her weapon.

Braxton pinned her flat against the ground, stilling her movement. "Stay put," he growled, covering her head with his arms. He'd heard and seen Tala's bullet hit the shooter. How the hell was he still coming after them?

Another round pinged off a rock just behind them. He lifted his weight off her slightly, allowing her to move. As soon as she got to her hands and knees he put a hand on her ass and shoved her toward the trees. "Go, go," he commanded.

She scuttled behind one of the trunks and laid flat on her stomach, still holding her weapon as Braxton moved in behind another tree to her left. Keeping himself between her and the shooter he couldn't see. Where was he? The bastard hadn't fired in the past fifteen seconds. He could be on the move through the screen of trees separating them.

Braxton peered around the trunk, looking in the direction the shots had come from. His vision wasn't quite right, and he was still dizzy.

A second later, he caught a flash of movement as a shadow detached from a tree in the distance. He ducked. An instant later, a bullet slammed into the trunk he was hiding behind, inches above his head.

Way too close. The asshole had a bead on them.

Braxton clenched his jaw, wishing he had his sniper rifle to hunt this bastard down.

"Did you see him?" Tala asked anxiously, pinned down beside him.

"For a second. Hundred-ten meters, moving to our right." Hidden in shadow now. It made Braxton uneasy not to have a visual on him.

"He's too far away for me," Tala said, her face tight as she pushed her rifle at him. "You have to take him out."

He took it, slipping into sniper mode the instant his hands closed around the weapon, fighting past the dizziness that kept coming in waves. "How many rounds do you have left?" He tugged off his gloves, the need for accuracy superseding the need to protect them from frostbite.

"Two."

Damn. This range was the upper limit for a lethal shot with a .22. His hands were slightly unsteady as he settled into a prone shooting position, shivers ripping through him. He brought the butt of the rifle to his shoulder and pressed his cheek to the side of the stock.

Beside him, Tala was still and silent, watchful. He had to block his awareness of her out. Had to block out everything except the threat in front of them.

His focus shrank to his narrow field of fire as he stared through the sight, searching for his target. The small weapon felt foreign in his grip. Dainty. But it was all they had, so he'd have to make it work. Because he only had two shots left, and if he missed both, they were dead.

He settled into the zone and locked in, pushing away all his physical discomfort. Watching. Waiting for his target to make a mistake. He was a master sniper. Patience was his domain.

A couple minutes later, he thought he saw movement, a shadow slipping in between the trees out there in the distance. He kept his finger on the trigger guard and blinked to clear the haze in his vision, the cold seeping into his skin. If he and Tala were going to make it out of here, he had to get a clean hit.

Through the sight, he spotted the barrel of a weapon as it appeared from behind a tree trunk. "Stay down," he snapped at Tala.

She flattened herself into the snow just as the shooter fired. She sucked in a breath when the round struck the trunk he was hiding behind, but otherwise didn't make a sound.

Braxton kept his gaze locked on his target, the cold and pain pushed to the back of his consciousness. He was battered and bruised, but still in the fight. And he would protect Tala with his last breath if necessary.

The cold bit into him. Shortening his breath and making his lungs ache. Just as his muscles tensed, screaming at him to move to lessen the pain, his target finally grew impatient and made his first mistake.

Asshole tried to move closer through the screen of trees to get a better angle on them, giving Braxton his first sighting in the past ten minutes. He tracked his prey with complete focus, patiently waiting for the next mistake.

This time he didn't have to wait long.

The shooter must have been frustrated by his inability to line up a good shot, because he emerged partially from behind cover, crouching on one knee to bring his weapon up.

Braxton adjusted his aim for dead center mass. The wind was gusting. Easily able to push a .22 round off course at this distance.

The shooter fired, bark splintering mere inches from Braxton's head. Braxton didn't move. Remained totally motionless, his training and discipline giving him the advantage.

That's right. Come on. Little more.

The shooter edged out more from behind cover and took aim straight at him. Braxton could practically feel the enemy's crosshairs lining up on his head.

You're mine.

He focused on his breathing, feeling the rhythm of his heartbeat. His finger curving around the trigger.

The shooter fired again, the shot sizzling past Braxton's ear, then emerged from the trees to fire another round.

Braxton squeezed the trigger just as the bullet slammed into the tree above his right ear. The shooter jerked sideways.

Hit. High and right.

He quickly adjusted the sight to compensate. If the bastard had survived Tala's shot, then he might be wearing a vest. Braxton would have to make a head shot to take him down.

The shooter was struggling to his feet, his left arm dangling at his side. He whirled, struggled to bring the rifle to his shoulder, and Braxton finally had the opening he needed.

Exhaling fully, he squeezed the trigger between heartbeats.

The shooter's head snapped back, blood spattering the pristine white of the snow. He dropped and lay on his back, unmoving.

"He's down," Tala breathed.

Braxton shoved up and reached for her arm, ready to haul her upright and get moving. But when she wrapped her gloved fingers around his forearm, their gazes locked, instantly snapping him out of operator mode. His heart shredded at the shimmer of tears in her eyes.

"You got him," she whispered.

He crushed her to his chest, allowing himself a relieved exhale even as he hated that she'd had to go through all of this. "You okay?"

She nodded, her body trembling from the cold and maybe shock. He couldn't wait to get her off this fucking mountain and warmed up back at Tate's place. Safe, where nothing and no one could ever hurt her. "Just…the shots c-coming at us. It brought it all b-back. The day I was h-hit," she said in a rush as shivers racked her.

Yeah. Yeah, of course it would bring it all back. Shit, he wished he could have spared her this additional trauma. All he could do was hold her tight, thankful she was alive and safe in his arms.

He loved her so fucking much it hurt. And he was going to tell her as soon as this was over. Couldn't wait another day, no matter what barriers still lay between them. She meant too much to him.

"He's gone," he murmured. "And no one's ever going to shoot at you again."

She drew a deep breath and lifted her head to peer up at him. The wobbly, brave smile she gave him damn near split his chest wide open. "I d-don't know about you, but I'm fr-freezing. Let's get the hell out of here, h-huh?"

****

Tala's trembling eased a few minutes after Braxton resumed carrying her down the trail once more, changing from a blend of cold and fear to merely from the cold. Her head spun with everything that had happened over the last day. At how close they'd both come to dying—several times.

Before leaving a few minutes ago, she'd taken out her cell phone to call Tate, but the battery was now dead. Her brother and Mason were out here right now looking for them. They couldn't be far away.

The faint sound of engines in the distance carried on the wind. Tala lifted her head, her pulse skipping. "Hear that?"

Braxton stopped and slid her off his back with a low groan, wincing as he bent over to suck in air. She held onto his shoulder to keep her balance as she stood on her left foot, hope swelling inside her ribcage. "Has to be Tate and Mason." *Had* to be. She refused to accept any other outcome. They were finally getting out of here.

The sound of the engines grew louder, then, finally, two little dots appeared on a trail below them in the distance. Tala and Braxton both called out and waved their arms to get the drivers' attention. "Did they see us?"

"Guess we'll find out."

Tala all but held her breath as the minutes dragged by with agonizing slowness as they waited to see whether the drivers came closer.

Her heart sank when they disappeared from view around a curve in the trail below, but a minute later it swelled as they came around the bend up ahead. She hugged Braxton in relief and happiness, mindful that he was sore, and choked back tears.

Tate and Mason roared up to them and stopped close by.

"Shit, are you guys okay?" Tate demanded, raking his gaze over them as he jumped off his snowmobile.

LETHAL PROTECTOR

Tala swallowed a sob and opened her arms, balanced on her left leg. Tate caught her to him, crushed her to his chest and held her upright as she sagged in his hold.

"Tal. Are you hurt?" His voice was taut, urgent.

She shook her head, unable to get her voice to work, afraid she would lose it and burst into tears at any second. She held onto him, aware of Mason checking on Braxton beside her.

Exhaustion hit her hard all of a sudden, as if her body and subconscious knew she was safe now and could let go. She could hear Braxton's deep voice explaining what had happened. How they had been caught in the storm. The shooter. Overnighting in their makeshift shelter. Then everything that had happened over the past two hours.

Tala shuddered, burying her face in her brother's chest. She'd almost lost Braxton out here. A few times she'd wondered if they would both die out here.

"An avalanche?" Mason blurted. "Jesus, no wonder you look like hell."

"What about the shooter?" Tate demanded, his muscles tense.

"Dead," Braxton answered. "About two klicks behind us."

"You take him out?" Mason asked.

"Yeah."

"Good. Fucker. Come on."

Tala lifted her head to see Braxton trudging for Mason's snowmobile. He climbed on and caught her gaze, gave her a little smile that belied the exhaustion on his blood-stained face. A rush of emotion slammed into her, her heart swelling until it was on the verge of exploding.

She loved him. Completely and without reservation. She was done with holding back. If having him meant making more sacrifices, then so be it. She needed him.

Tate put a hand on the side of her face, bringing her

attention back to him. His hazel eyes were full of concern. "You sure you're not hurt?"

She blew out an unsteady breath, willing the searing pressure in her chest to ease. It wasn't too late. She would talk to Braxton once they were alone tonight. "Yeah." Her stump was killing her and she was cold and bruised in a few spots, but that was nothing compared to what could have happened. "Just glad it's over."

"Let's get you warmed up." He bent and lifted her into his arms, then carried her to his snowmobile and placed her down on the back of the seat. He bundled her up in a couple blankets and handed her a thermos. "Coffee with sugar. I didn't have time to make your tea before I headed out."

"Thanks," she murmured. "How's Rylee?"

"She'll be fantastic once she finds out you're okay." He squeezed her shoulder and pulled out a radio. "I'm just going to alert the others and get a team up here to deal with the body."

She nodded, and as soon as he began talking into the radio, her attention strayed back to Braxton. He was seated on the back of the other snowmobile while Mason put a bandage on the cut over his eye. His dark brown gaze snagged hers and locked there, and the answering swell of emotion inside her made it hard to breathe.

He'd saved her life so many times. The harrowing experience out here together had merely intensified everything that had already been there between them.

She'd never loved anyone the way she did him. What the hell was she going to do if he still didn't want a relationship after everything they'd been through?

There were so many unfinished things between them. She was desperate to change that. To put all this behind them so they could be alone. To make something real and lasting together.

She also wanted him naked and on top of her as soon

as possible. His weight and warmth holding her down while he filled her, temporarily erasing what they'd just gone through and replacing it with something she'd craved for years. She wanted that so badly she could scarcely breathe.

Tate finished talking, put the radio away and tugged on his gloves as he turned to the others. "Let's head back down. Avery's sending a team up here to deal with everything else." He glanced down at her, his hard features softening with love and relief. "Real glad you're okay, Tal."

She smiled at him. "Me too. And you can thank Braxton for that."

"I plan to. Now, let's get you guys down the hill so you can get checked out and then back to Rifle Creek." He climbed on in front of her and started the engine. "Hold on."

She looped her arms around his middle and leaned her cheek against his back, allowing her eyes to close. "Love you, Tater."

"Love you too." Tate turned them around and sped back down the hill, Mason with Braxton right behind them.

The cold air whipped over her face but the rest of her was warming up beneath the blankets. Exhaustion weighed down her limbs and eyelids. Twice she caught herself drifting off, managed to shake herself awake by pure will.

It seemed like no time at all before they reached the end of the trail. The building site came into view, now a hive of activity, full of people.

Tate drove straight to the waiting ambulance someone had called, and Tala spotted Rylee standing near it with Nina. She gave a glad cry and pushed up onto her left foot as soon as Tate stopped the vehicle.

Rylee raced over and flung her arms around Tala, her face streaked with tears. "You're really okay?" she choked out, hugging her hard.

Tala squeezed her daughter tight and closed her eyes, her own eyes stinging. "Yeah. Promise."

Nina came up and engulfed them both in a fierce embrace. "Thank God you're both okay."

Yes. After everything that had happened, it truly seemed like a miracle that she and Braxton had made it out alive.

Tate waited for them to stop hugging, then immediately bent and lifted her in his arms. "Rest of the hugs will have to wait. We're transporting them both to Missoula to get checked out, and then I'll need to take their statements before I bring them home after that." He began carrying her to the back of the waiting ambulance.

"I don't need an ambulance," she protested, dreading the thought of being poked and prodded in the back of a cold vehicle all the way to Missoula. And knowing she was about to be in another hospital sent a cold shiver through her. She'd had enough of hospitals for several lifetimes. "Just take me to the hospital in your truck."

"Nope, you're going in the ambulance," he told her gruffly. "*Both* of you, and don't bother arguing. I'll follow you down."

She snapped her mouth shut and waved at Rylee, who was watching her anxiously with Nina, giving her daughter a reassuring smile. "I'm fine, sweetheart. I'll be back before you know it," she called out. Then to her brother, "Make sure she's okay."

"Nina, Avery and Mason will keep her company until we get back."

Braxton was walking toward the ambulance as Tate carried her there, and she was thankful they at least wouldn't be separated. Her brother placed her on the edge of the rear deck, and Braxton lowered himself next to her, wincing.

She tugged off her gloves and reached for his hand,

twining their fingers together. Hers were numb, their hands both half-frozen, but she needed the connection anyway.

"Tal," he said, and she lifted her gaze to his. He set his other hand on the side of her face, his expression so intent her heart began to pound. "I love you."

Shock ripped through her, even as joy eclipsed it. "You do?" she whispered, her voice rough.

"Yeah. I'm in love with you, and have been for a long time. I needed you to know."

Her throat thickened. She'd never expected him to say it first. Had never imagined he would admit it out loud. "I love you too. So much. Have for a long time," she managed.

A slow smile tugged at one corner of his mouth. "Yeah?"

"Yeah." Her laugh was cut off abruptly when his lips closed over hers. She melted into him, holding his head in her hands as she kissed him back, pouring all her love into it and not caring who saw them.

Just when things were starting to get good, the moment when everything around them began to fall away, the paramedics converged on them to begin their initial assessment. They broke apart, still gazing into each other's eyes, and she couldn't wait for this all to be done so they could finally be alone to finish what they'd started.

Frustrated, Tala answered various questions for the paramedic, her gaze wandering over the crowd of people in the background as the woman checked her over. She spotted Rylee, Tate and Nina talking together over to the right near Tate's truck. Then Mason appeared with Avery, who waved at her and gave her a big smile as Tate's neighbor, Curt, stepped up next to Avery, holding a rifle.

It humbled Tala, to know so many people cared. They had all come together to find her and Braxton and bring them down the mountain safely. And for that she was unspeakably grateful. But the reality was, she owed her life to Braxton and no one else. She never would have made it without him.

The paramedics finished their initial assessment. Watching her, Braxton brought her hand to his lips and kissed it, closing his eyes as his lips lingered on her cold skin.

She squeezed his fingers in return, wishing they had some privacy so she could say all the things crowding her heart and throat. They loved each other and now their feelings were finally out in the open.

"We made it," she whispered to him, torn between wanting to sleep for two days, and just be alone in bed together. Also for two days, and shut out the rest of the world for a while.

He lowered her hand, one side of his mouth tugging upward, the yearning and devotion in his gaze almost undoing her. He loved her. Hopefully, enough to fight for a future together. "We sure as hell did."

"Let us through," an assertive female voice called out from the back of the crowd.

Tala looked up to see Pat and her quiet sister pushing through the knot of people, their arms laden with blankets and a big basket.

"Lord, you two are a sight for sore eyes," Pat said when she reached the back of the ambulance, her tone almost scolding as she looked from Tala to Braxton. "We were worried sick. Stayed up all night, baking and finishing up some repairs on these old patchwork quilts because we didn't know what else to do to help. Here."

She shook out the one she was holding and draped it around Tala's shoulders. "Now you," she said to Braxton, taking the second quilt from her sister and wrapping it around him. "There."

"And this is for both of you," Bev said softly, holding

out the basket to them. "We thought you would be hungry."

Braxton took it with an appreciative groan. "I don't know what you put in here, but I don't even care, because I already can't wait to taste it," he told them.

The sisters beamed at him, then Pat sobered and shook her head, clucking her tongue. "Poor things, stranded out in that blizzard with a cold-blooded murderer on your trail." She shuddered, then stopped and raised an eyebrow. "Well, go on, I know you both have to be starving."

Tala opened the basket to find homemade rolls that were still a little warm, along with a carefully wrapped crock of butter and jam, some decorated gingerbread cookies—

She stopped and lifted out the cookie on top. A female gingerbread person…missing a foot.

She looked at Pat, surprised. Had it been deliberate?

"It came off as I was icing her," Bev blurted, her cheeks turning a darker shade of pink as she wrung her hands in distress. "I was going to stick it back on with more icing, but then I thought I shouldn't because it made her just like you. So I left it alone."

Oh, hell.

Tala stared at the shy woman, momentarily rendered speechless by her thoughtfulness. But when she looked down at the cookie, the gingerbread amputee with her little chocolate candy buttons and the wide icing smile and the huge pink icing heart in the center of her chest, something cracked inside her.

Everything hit her all at once in a rush. Exhaustion. Relief. Gratitude. And the lingering anxiety about what would happen with her and Braxton.

She hadn't felt brave out there, but she'd done her best. And now that she and Braxton had both finally admitted their true feelings, they only had a few more days left together before the military took him from her and he headed back to a war zone on the other side of the world.

Tears blurred her vision, scalding hot. She clapped a hand over her face to hide them, and Bev let out a horrified gasp. She tried to shake her head, opened her mouth to explain that it wasn't the cookie, that the gesture touched her deeply, but she couldn't speak.

Braxton's low chuckle came from beside her, then his long, strong arm curled around her shoulders and tugged her into his side. Tala buried her face in his sturdy shoulder as the floodgates opened, the cookie still grasped in her right hand.

"Don't worry, ladies," Braxton told them, nuzzling the top of Tala's head. "I think it's safe to say she loves it."

CHAPTER TWENTY

"I can confirm that the shooter was Jason Fenwick, the missing fugitive we've been searching for. His body has been recovered and we've got a team up there searching the hunting shed and surrounding area now," Tate said to him.

Braxton nodded. Tate was involved with the investigation, but another officer had taken Braxton's statement earlier, and someone else had taken Tala's.

"And you were right, he was wearing a vest. It took a round low center mass, just like you said."

So Tala had definitely hit him.

Braxton nodded, filing the information away, proud as hell of his lady. But right now, more than anything else he was itching to sign the paperwork for his release so he could get the hell out of here and be with Tala. His scans were clean, his core temp was back to normal, and they'd given him pain meds and anti-inflammatories for his bruises and contusions.

"How's Tala?" He needed to see her. It had been over four hours since they'd been separated, and it felt more like four days. He was dying to hold her again, and to get her alone either back at Tate's or Mason's place. He had a lot of things to say, and they had a lot to talk about.

Right after he got her naked and underneath him. He didn't care if his back and ribs were black and blue or if his head was still pounding, he needed skin on skin with her, to give her every ounce of pleasure he could, and then bury himself as deep as he could get in her delectable body.

His pulse pounded at the thought, need and impatience riding him.

"Better now that they gave her something for the bone and nerve pain. No long-term damage done, she just needs a few days without her prosthetic to let her skin heal and take pressure off the stump."

Good. He'd make sure she stayed off her feet. If he had his way, she wouldn't leave his bed at all until he had to fly back to Ottawa, but he couldn't be a selfish asshole. Rylee and Tate would want to spend time with her too before she flew back to Kelowna at the end of the week. "Are they discharging her yet?"

"They're in the process of it now. As soon as you're both cleared, I'll have you out of here and in the truck. You hungry? I can grab you something while we wait."

"No, I'm good." He'd wolfed down a couple sandwiches and a hot bowl of soup earlier, soon after they'd admitted him. Now he just needed Tala, and eventually, some sleep with her tucked against him.

Tate eyed him. "How you feeling?"

"All right." His back and the right side of his ribs throbbed the worst. The skin there was already turning interesting shades of blue and purple.

Thankfully his concussion had only been mild, and now that he was warmed up and hydrated again, the headache was only a dull throb and his vision was back to normal. He'd be sore for a few days yet, but should be back to pretty much normal by the time he flew to Ottawa on his way overseas to finish his tour.

He was already dreading the moment he had to leave Tala to finish his tour and the remainder of his contract. But she'd told him she loved him, so hopefully she would be willing to wait for him. Although, he wouldn't hold it against her if she wasn't.

His job was high risk, and his future was still uncertain. He was so damn torn. While he loved what he did and knew he'd miss it if he gave it up, he could never give Tala up. Not unless she wanted him to, and fuck, that would rip his heart out.

"What do you know about Fenwick's background?" Braxton asked, putting all that aside for now. "He knew what he was doing out there. A lot more than your average street thug."

Tate nodded. "Intel says he learned survival and firearms training in his teens from an expert, likely a SOF veteran. He's also got a younger sister he was close to. He's been supporting her for years, and that's how he got involved with his gang. We just found her out in California. Apparently, he'd sent her there a few days ago by bus. The plan was to meet her there once he felt safe enough to leave the hunting shed, and start over there together. But the storm messed up his timeline."

Yeah, along with his and Tala's. "Any idea why he targeted us?"

"We think he assumed you were either cops, or going to report him. You'd seen him and his hideaway, and he knew he couldn't get out of the area before you reported him."

"So he thought he'd just take us out and what? Escape on foot over the mountains?"

"Until he stole your snowmobile."

Hell. So he and Tala had just been in the wrong place at the wrong time. He shook his head, incredulous.

Tate laid a hand on Braxton's shoulder. "I'm just gonna go check on Tala. You need anything?"

"No." But as his buddy turned away, Braxton grabbed his arm. "Wait."

Tate stopped and looked at him. When Braxton didn't say anything, Tate raised his eyebrows. "What?"

"Look, I need to tell you something." He ran a hand over his scruffy jaw and shifted his weight. This wasn't how he'd wanted this conversation to happen, but he needed to come clean with Tate here and now, before things went any further. Braxton respected the hell out of him, and he valued their friendship. "It's about me and Tala."

Tate turned to face him fully, his expression turning wary. "What about you?"

"I'm in love with her. And I finally told her so."

His buddy's eyes widened in shock. "Oh." He stared at Braxton for a long moment. "Is this… I mean, how long have you…?"

"Since last summer."

Tate looked stunned. "That's a long time."

"Yeah."

He shook his head. "I didn't know."

"I didn't want you to. I didn't want anyone to. Anyway, I just needed you to know, because I'm still not sure how things are going to go between us yet. I've still got the rest of this contract to finish, and after that, I'd planned to re-up…" He drew a breath. "But no matter what happens, just know that I love her and that I'd do anything for her."

Tate nodded, still looking a little astonished. "Okay, man. I appreciate you telling me. And does Tal… I think she's had a thing for you for a long time, but is she on the same page as you?"

"Yes." He still didn't feel like he deserved it, but he was going to do everything in his power to hold onto her.

Tate's shoulders eased and a smile tugged at the corners of his mouth. "That's good." He chuckled, a grin breaking across his face. "Hell, that's awesome."

"I'd never hurt her. Not on purpose." It was the accidental possibility that worried him. He'd fucked up every single relationship he'd ever been in, but he'd never felt this way about anyone. He couldn't afford to fuck this up.

Tate's smile faded, his expression growing serious. He put a hand on Braxton's shoulder again. Squeezed gently, his gaze steady. "I know. Now let me go see if they've released her so we can get you both back to Rifle Creek."

Hell yes.

As soon as Tate had gone, Braxton blew out a deep breath and ran a hand over his face, feeling drained. Tate had taken that way better than he'd expected, and it felt like a giant weight had been taken off his shoulders.

Tala definitely deserved more than he could give her, but that was twice Braxton had almost lost her, and no matter if there was still a risk of losing her later on, he wasn't holding back with her anymore.

He lowered himself into a chair to wait, bouncing one foot up and down to burn off a mixture of nerves and anticipation. Tonight was going to change everything between them.

There was no way he could keep from crossing the final line with her now. Not after everything they'd been through together. She'd been so fucking brave out there, so strong in the face of everything thrown at them. She awed and humbled him and he couldn't wait to worship every last inch of her when they got back to Rifle Creek.

He shot to his feet when she appeared around the corner with Tate a few minutes later, his arm around her shoulders. She had her regular prosthetic on but she was limping noticeably, still sore and probably raw from the prolonged friction it had undergone during their ordeal. She must have refused the wheelchair the hospital staff had offered.

The instant she saw him, her steps faltered, and a big smile broke over her face. So full of love that his heart flipped in his chest.

Braxton smiled back, his feet already carrying him to her. Tate withdrew his arm from her shoulders and stepped aside, the nonverbal equivalent of giving them his blessing.

"How you feeling?" he asked her, stopping in front of her to cradle the side of her neck in his hand, his thumb sweeping across her cheek. Her color was way better, her cheeks a soft pink and her eyes were bright.

Longing and heat filled her gaze, instantly making his pulse pound. "I'm good. How are you?"

"Just a few bumps and bruises." He reached for her, drawing her tight against his chest and locked his arms around her, burying his face in her silky hair. He could still smell the faint scent of her shampoo. "Ready to get out of here?"

"*Yes.*"

He kept her tight against his side as they walked out to Tate's truck, and the initial awkwardness of showing his affection in front of Tala's brother faded quickly. Tate opened the front passenger door for her but she shook her head. "I'll ride in the back with Brax."

His chest hitched at knowing she wanted to be close to him. He boosted her into the backseat, then climbed in beside her and immediately drew her into his arms. She cuddled into him with a contented sigh that eased something deep inside him, her cheek nestled right over his heart.

Tate handed him a blanket and he tucked it around her, awed by the strength and determination in such a fragile body, and humbled at finally being able to hold her openly like this.

Tate got them right to the road back to Rifle Creek. Braxton leaned his back against the door, angling them so that Tala could recline a bit, and stroked his fingers through her rich brown hair.

He knew the moment she dropped off to sleep, her lips parting slightly, her breathing deep and even. He glanced up to meet Tate's gaze in the rearview mirror, and caught the faint smile on his buddy's face before he focused back on the road.

Braxton kissed the top of Tala's head and leaned his against the doorframe with a sigh, allowing his eyes to close. Tala was safe, warm, and curled up in his arms. That was all he needed right now.

He came awake sometime later when the truck slowed. Opening his eyes, he saw they were already in Rifle Creek. His back and ribs ached like a bitch and his muscles were stiff from staying in one position for so long, but Tala was still sound asleep, a dead weight against his chest, and he didn't want to disturb her.

He shifted slightly to brace them when Tate made a turn and she woke anyway, blinking groggily. "Where are we?" she murmured.

"Almost home." He couldn't wait to be alone with her.

She sat up and looked at her brother, rubbing the back of her neck. "I'm gonna stay with Brax tonight. Maybe for the next few days."

The announcement surprised and pleased Braxton, and Tate met her gaze in the rearview mirror for a moment before focusing back on the road. "Okay. Want me to stop at our place first, and grab you a bag of stuff?"

"No. I'll borrow whatever I need from Avery, and maybe Rylee can bring me a bag tomorrow." She settled back against the seat, reaching for his hand, and Braxton twined their fingers together. His blood was already heating, anticipating the moment when he finally got her alone in his suite.

They arrived at Avery and Mason's place a few

minutes later, and everything happened in a blur. After filling Avery and Mason in on everything they'd missed, Avery whisked Tala into the upstairs part of the house to get whatever she needed. Meanwhile, Braxton went downstairs and took a long, hot shower, letting the heat of the water ease some of the tension and soreness out of his battered muscles.

Pulling on some flannel pajama pants and a T-shirt, he walked into the bedroom, only to stop dead when he saw Tala already curled up in his bed, facing him under the covers, her prosthetic leg propped against the wall next to the headboard.

She was fast asleep, her hair spilling across the pillow. And someone must have run over to Tate's to get her things, because Sergeant Stumpy was sitting on his pillow.

Braxton's heart turned over at the sight of her asleep in his bed like she belonged there. He put the bear on the bedside table and slid carefully in beside Tala. Easing an arm around her back, his body hardened at the feel of her, blood rushing to his cock. She smelled like soap, shampoo and toothpaste, clean and delicious.

He ached to wake her with kisses, bring her into that dreamy state of arousal that let her float while he slowly explored every inch of her satiny skin. Find every spot that made her sigh and gasp, then slowly enjoy those tempting nipples he'd been dreaming about before kissing his way down between her thighs and savoring her until she came on his tongue.

Her eyelashes fluttered and she blinked at him, focusing briefly on his face before giving him a sleepy smile. "Hi," she murmured, eyes half-closed.

"Hi." He drew her closer, tucking her head against his chest, the rightness of it settling deep inside him.

Damn, she felt incredible, like she'd been made for him. And even better, she loved him. His cock pulsed, aching to be buried inside her, but that could wait. They had a few more days left together before he had to leave. She was completely exhausted and they both needed sleep.

"Love you," she mumbled.

He squeezed his eyes shut, unable to believe how lucky he was. "Love you too," he whispered, and held her close, praying she was willing to make things work and stick with him while he was away.

Because living without her wouldn't be living at all.

CHAPTER TWENTY-ONE

Tala drifted slowly toward consciousness, surrounded by warmth. Gradually, she became aware of a low-grade pain in her right leg, and then more, expanding out to various other places across her body.

The mountain. The blizzard and the shooter.

A chill shot through her. She opened her eyes to find her cheek resting on the hard plane of a muscular chest.

Braxton. He was here beside her. They were safe. Alone.

She relaxed, banishing the frightening memories because they didn't belong here. Now it was just her and Braxton. She intended to enjoy him to the fullest while she still had him.

Heat spread through her, pooling low in her belly. She eased a hand up the soft T-shirt covering his broad back, mindful of his bruises, wishing he was naked too.

He tensed slightly as he awoke, then a deep, satisfied rumble sounded in his chest as he drew her closer. "Hey."

"Hey," she murmured, snuggling closer. Her whole body tingled with anticipation, a hot throb blooming between her thighs. He felt even better than she'd imagined, warm and solid and…hard all over, the unmistakable ridge of his erection cradled against her belly. "What time is it?"

"Little after seven."

So they'd only slept a little over an hour. She should be exhausted still, but instead she was wide awake, arousal pumping through her like warm honey. Everything that had happened up 'til now had led them to this moment. To here and now, the two of them alone in this bed, and she couldn't wait a moment longer to have him.

She slid a hand up to stroke his hair. Braxton made a deep sound low in his throat and cupped the back of her head, then his mouth was on hers. She moaned and parted her lips, fire streaking through her as their tongues touched. Her breasts ached, the nipples tight as she rubbed them against his covered chest.

Frustrated at not being able to feel his skin against hers, she reached for the bottom of his shirt and impatiently dragged it up his body. He helped her, breaking the kiss just long enough for him to fling it over his head, then he was kissing her again, his hands cradling her face as he rolled them until she was on her back and he was settled between her legs.

Tala gasped as his weight sank on top of her, his erection pressed to her throbbing core. She angled her hips to rub against him, a shudder rolling through her at the contact.

Yes. More. So much more.

Braxton stroked her tongue with his one last time, then nipped her lower lip and began nibbling his way across her jaw to the side of her throat. She tipped her head to the side and palmed the back of his head, gasping as his lips and tongue hit a sensitive spot that sent streamers of pleasure shooting across her skin. She felt like she was dissolving, every stroke of his lips and tongue melting her bones.

He shifted one hand down to brush his fingers along

her right collarbone, along her sternum and followed it down to the curve of her breast. She sucked in a breath when he cupped it in his big hand, glanced down in time to see the taut, absorbed look on his face as he stared at her naked flesh and swept his thumb across the rigid nipple.

Her toes curled. She bit her lip, then whimpered as he lowered his head and captured the aching peak in his mouth. Heat engulfed her, roaring through her veins and settling in her swelling clit. She was already wet and aching for him. He sucked on her slowly, as if savoring a piece of candy, his tongue caressing with each decadent pull of his mouth.

"Braxton," she whispered, her heart threatening to pound out of her chest.

He made a deep sound of enjoyment and kept sucking, shifting his hand to her other breast and playing with the nipple while he enjoyed her other one. Tala reached up to grip his shoulders, remembered at the last moment how battered he was, and gently coasted her palms down the length of his naked back, enjoying the feel of all that smooth, hot skin shifting over bunching muscle.

She curled her fingers in the waistband of his pants and shoved them down, then sucked in a breath and grabbed his hips when his mouth switched to her other nipple. Pleasure shot through her, streaking down to the slick folds between her legs.

His hands closed around her ribcage. He lifted his head, the molten heat in his gaze as he looked up at her stealing her breath. "Condom."

"On the bedside table," she whispered in a rush. "I brought it down last night."

"God, I love you," he breathed, and went right back to what he'd been doing.

She smiled and let her head drop back into the pillow as he released her throbbing nipple to kiss his way down her stomach, one of his hands leading the way to the center of her body, his fingertips skimming over her heated flesh.

She sank her teeth into her lower lip, her muscles tensing in anticipation as those talented fingers stroked and teased her hipbone, the inside of her thigh, following it down to her knee before easing back up and stopping several inches from where she was wet and needy.

His tongue dragged over the tender skin beneath her navel. Her abs contracted, her rapid breathing filling the air as she waited for the touch she'd fantasized about for four endless years.

Then his hand shifted. His fingertips grazed the edge of her soaked folds. She squeezed her eyes shut and moaned, tilting her hips, dying for more.

"So pretty, baby," he whispered as he sank to his knees on the floor at the end of the bed and pulled her hips toward the edge. His fingers kept teasing, gliding up and down, making her wetter, hotter. "I'm gonna lick you all up, until you come on my tongue."

She couldn't answer, could only lock her fingers on his hair and wait, her whole body drawn taut in anticipation of that first touch of his lips and tongue on her aching clit. His fingers stroked lower, easing just inside her as his tongue flicked the swollen knot.

Tala cried out, fisting his hair and opening wider for him. His mouth settled over her more firmly, but his tongue was oh-so soft as he caressed her clit. She shuddered.

Slow, tender circles, growing smaller and smaller until he found exactly the right spot that made her arch and whimper, her muscles trembling with every tiny flutter of his tongue. He kept going, his fingertips stroking just inside her body, curving upward to hit the spot that threatened to make her explode.

"Brax," she pleaded, her voice ragged and breathless.

She'd gone so long without him, and only had a short time left before he was leaving again. "Let me touch you. I need to touch you. Want you inside me."

He delivered one last devastating caress with his tongue, then lifted his head and leaned down to suck a taut nipple into his mouth while he shoved his pants down his thighs. She tried to sit up, desperate to get her hands on him, but he held her down with a hand on her stomach and a warning growl and kept his mouth right where it was, allowing her only to touch him where she could reach.

She stroked her palms over his broad, bunched shoulders, over the corded muscle on either side of his spine before coming back up and dipping around to map the front of him. The hard mounds of his pecs, and the flat, ridged abs beneath.

She leaned to the side, her hungry gaze latching onto the rigid length of his cock standing proudly against his lower belly.

Her hand closed around him, her core clenching at how thick and hard he was. Braxton froze, a groan ripping free. His eyes were squeezed shut, an expression of blissful agony on his face as she gripped him, then eased up and stroked down his length.

He shuddered and pushed into her fist, his forehead pressed to her stomach. "Tal," he groaned. His hand closed around hers, squeezing to stop her. Pulling in a deep breath, he raised his head, and their gazes locked.

"Make me come," she whispered, rocking her hips, feeling more sensual, powerful and beautiful than she ever had in her life. All because of him.

He released her hand with a growl to grab the condom from the nightstand, shuddering again when she stroked him with one hand and dropped the other to her clit. His gaze zeroed in on her fingers as she circled the throbbing bud, the incredible arousal on his face making it even hotter.

She moaned as pleasure swirled through her. Braxton tore open the condom and rolled it on, then tugged her even farther toward him so that her ass was almost off the bed. "Hand me a pillow," he said in a deep, sexy voice.

She flung a hand out to grab one and gave it to him. He lifted her hips and shoved it beneath her lower back, arching her spine, then leaned one hand on the bed beside her ribcage and positioned the head of his cock against her.

Tala curled a hand around his hip and looked up at him, her heart knocking against her ribs when their gazes connected. She needed him. Needed to hold him inside her. His face was tense, his jaw taut, eyes blazing as he eased forward, lodging the thick head of his cock inside her.

Her mouth opened, eyes slamming shut at the incredible sensation. Heat and fullness, a delicious stretching that filled her, easing the hungry ache initially, and then making it a whole lot worse. She grabbed his shoulder, a wave of emotion hitting her. "Brax…"

A deep, hot kiss cut her off, a deep sound of pleasure coming from his chest. "Let me."

She nodded and stroked her clit faster, arching her hips to fight for more of him. Then her eyes sprang open when he pushed her hand away.

"Let me," he repeated, his voice deep and sexy. Holding her gaze, he slid a hand under her hips and eased his lower body forward, seating himself deep inside her.

She made a soft, pleading sound and tightened her grip on his shoulder, wanting to rock and thrust. He stopped her, watching her as he shifted his weight until his pelvis was tight against hers and the base of his cock nestled against her swollen clit.

"Eyes on me, Tal," he rasped out, his jaw tight.

She met his gaze, her heart threatening to explode, her body dying for the release he'd been building her to.

But he didn't thrust. Instead he…rubbed. Rocking his pelvis against her, stroking her with his cock while his body caressed her clit.

Tala whimpered, her whole body trembling at the incredible pleasure streaking through her. All she could do was cling to him and angle her hips so that he hit exactly the right place. She was worried it wouldn't work for her but he was so damn hard inside her, every single brush of their bodies hitting both her sweet spots.

"Brax," she sobbed, shaking as the sensation built and built and built. She loved him so much.

"Love you," he rasped out. "Just let me love you." His mouth captured hers, his tongue twining with hers as her core clenched around him and the pleasure detonated. She tore her mouth free, crying out her release as she shattered.

When it finally began to ebb, she collapsed against the bed and forced her eyes open. Braxton's face was inches from hers. He was breathing hard, his jaw clenched, those gorgeous dark eyes staring into hers, his big body on edge.

Tenderness flooded her. She curled a hand around the back of his neck and drew him down for a kiss, winding her weakened legs around his waist. He moaned into her mouth, drew his hips back slightly and then thrust deep, finally allowing himself to seek his own pleasure.

Tala stayed with him, kissing and caressing while his rhythm sped up, his thrusts becoming longer, deeper. Raw, deep sounds of pleasure came from his throat each time he drove into her.

She knew the exact moment he reached the edge. He plunged deep and froze, his breath hissing between his teeth, then an agonized groan ripped from him as he shuddered and began pulsing deep inside her.

She drew him close, cradling his head on her shoulder, his face pressed into her neck while it tore through him. His body slowly relaxed, the weight of his head and torso becoming heavier as his ragged gasps warmed her skin.

Tala kissed wherever her lips could reach, letting her hands drift over the damp skin of his back and shoulders. That had been so good. Incredible considering it had been their first time. Her heart had never felt so full, or her body so sated.

"I love you so much," she whispered, already dreading the moment he would leave in a few more days. She wasn't sure her heart could take it after all they'd been through and how long they'd already waited for each other.

He buried his face in her neck and slid his arms beneath her to wrap all the way around her, locking her in a fierce hug that made her feel utterly safe and adored. "Ah, Christ, I don't want to leave you."

Her heart hitched, her hands pausing on his back. Did he mean because of his tour? Or something else? They hadn't talked about the future. She didn't know what—

Braxton raised his head to look down at her. "We have to make this work somehow." He took her face in his hands, his expression desperate. "Say you'll help me make this work, Tal, because I can't lose you. And if leaving the military after this contract is what it takes to have you, then—"

"No," she said, surprising them both. But she couldn't bear to make him give up the thing he loved as much as her.

Until yesterday, she'd been so sure about what she wanted, about the boundaries she'd decided on and that she wasn't willing to come in second in Braxton's life. But what they'd just gone through had changed everything. And she knew what being part of his unit and serving his country meant to him.

Forcing him to give that up for her was selfish and

he would grow to resent her for it. If he wanted to stay in, then he should, and she would just have to deal with it. Because there was no way she was letting him go now.

"We'll make it work," she whispered. He was worth it.

He exhaled hard and pressed his face into the side of her neck, his relief palpable. "Thank God."

She held him, a sense of peace spreading through her now that she'd made the decision and given her word. "I'll wait as long as it takes as long as I know we'll be together when you come home."

"We will be."

With Rylee off to college now, she was free to move anywhere to be with him. "I feel like I've been waiting for you my whole life," she whispered unsteadily. For this moment, and the future they would build together.

He lifted his head to stare down at her, a loving smile curving his lips. "Same. And I promise to be worth the wait."

EPILOGUE

Almost there. Keep going.

The muscles in Tala's arms and legs burned as she pushed up the final slope of the course. Panting, she reached the top, and the range came into view up ahead.

She pushed hard, trying to make up some of the time she'd lost on this last climb. It was a beautiful, clear day at the end of March, and she had a lot of support behind her. Including Braxton, from the other side of the world.

She couldn't let her supporters or herself down after all the hard work and sacrifice she'd put in over the last fourteen months. Not when she was so close to achieving her goal.

She changed her strides to long glides as she skied down the slope and began her easing-in procedure as she approached the range, consciously slowing her breathing to get her heart rate down. Her stump was starting to bother her, and her body was tired from completing most of the twenty-kilometer individual course, her muscles feeling like rubber from the prolonged exertion.

But the worst was behind her. This was her final competition of the season, and she was down to her last five shots. She'd done well so far. Maybe her best result ever. She just hoped it was enough.

Everything was riding on her final time here in Whistler. If she finished in the top twenty, she had a real shot at making the national masters team. If not...she'd have to wait another year to try and make the squad.

Shoving those thoughts aside, she focused on the task before her as she eased into the range, took off her harness and assumed her standing shooting position. Her goggles cut the glare of the sun overhead, and the wind flags on the range were only moving slightly. The conditions were almost ideal. Her greatest enemy right now was the fatigue.

She readied her rifle, put it to her shoulder and tucked her left elbow into her hip, making all the adjustments she'd practiced so much since working with Braxton. Angling her body, she slowed her breathing even more. Conscious of every heartbeat as she zeroed in on the first target.

The world shrank to the view through her sight, and the line of circular targets at the end of her lane.

She fired.

Hit.

She pulled the bolt and took aim at number two. Fired.

Hit.

She loaded the next round. Fired at the third target.

Hit.

Four.

Miss.

Dammit! That would add a minute penalty to her total time.

With effort, she shelved her disappointment and frustration, channeling it into pure focus as she took aim at her last target and squeezed the trigger.

Hit.

Two other athletes were just leaving the range ahead of her. She shrugged the rifle harness back on, then grabbed her poles and hit the course, striding hard as she left the range. She needed to sprint as hard as she could to the finish line to try to make up for the penalty she'd incurred.

Her legs burned with each stride, her tired arms powering her forward with the poles. She pushed herself harder. Faster.

The burn in her muscles grew every second but it was only for a little longer. She could do this. Rylee and the others would be waiting at the finish line, cheering her on with her coach.

She'd done her best today. Whatever happened, she could hold her head high knowing that.

She rounded the final turn and the finish line came into view. She sucked in an aching lungful of air and dug deep, her endurance pushed to its limit.

Almost there, Tal. Give it everything you've got left and finish strong.

People were standing on either side of the finish line. She poured everything she had into the final sprint.

Soon the faces came into focus. She spotted Rylee with Tate and Nina right up front on the left. Her parents. Avery and her coach beside them.

"Come on, Mom! You got this!" Rylee screamed jumping up and down, the red pom-pom on her Team Canada toque bobbing.

"Come on, Tal!" Tate's deep voice carried to her. "Finish strong!"

She put her head down, gritted her teeth and gave it one final burst of energy. The other two competitors were nearly to the line now.

They crossed it one after the other, only a second apart. What place were they? How far behind them was she?

It felt like her whole body was on fire as she focused on the finish line, so close yet so far, her heart racing so fast it felt on the verge of exploding. Three more hard strides and she leaned forward, straining, reaching for the finish...

Her skis crossed the line and she immediately bent at the waist to rest her forearms on her thighs as she coasted to a stop, completely out of breath and ready to collapse. Gasping, she fought to suck in air and closed her eyes, afraid to open them and look at the board to see where she'd placed.

Her eyes snapped open at a flurry of movement to her left. She started to smile as Rylee ran toward her, then jerked, startled as someone appeared on her right and caught her arms to help steady her. She looked up at him, her heart jolting in shock.

Braxton.

She gaped at him for an instant, still gasping for air, convinced she was hallucinating. He wasn't due back from the Middle East for at least another two weeks, and then he had a few more days at Dwyer Hill before he could get time to fly out here to B.C. once his current contract finished.

He grinned down at her, his teeth a white slash against his dark beard. "Hey, sweetheart."

"Oh my God," she blurted, flinging her arms around him.

He caught her with a deep chuckle and hugged her close, his embrace solid, achingly familiar. "You were incredible out there. I'm *so* damn proud of you."

Her throat closed up. Tears flooded her eyes. She scrunched her face and hid it in the side of his neck. "What are you doing here?" she demanded shakily.

"I pulled some strings and managed to get back early for a few days' leave before I have to be back at base." He ran a hand up and down her back, seeming not to care that she was covered in sweat. "Wanted to be here for your last race and surprise you."

She kept hugging him, vaguely aware of how ridiculous she probably looked, clinging to him in full gear with her rifle still on and her poles dangling down his back. But she couldn't let go. It had been months since she'd last seen him, since she'd last held him. "I *missed* you."

"Missed you too." He squeezed her, then eased away slightly with a grin. "Hi."

She smiled too and pulled him down for a kiss. She was a sweaty, exhausted mess, but she'd never been happier and luckily he didn't mind.

Belatedly remembering the race and the stakes involved, she pulled back and blurted, "Wait, what was my time?"

"Take a look and find out."

Holding onto his muscular shoulders for support, she looked over at the board and anxiously scanned the final list of names and times, listed from first place to last. Top twenty. Was she in the top twenty?

She gasped, her eyes jerking back to Braxton when she saw where her name was listed. "Fifteenth? I came in *fifteenth*?" It was her best finish yet.

The edge of his mouth curved, his eyes warm as melted chocolate. "Hell yeah, you did."

With a glad cry she flung her arms around his neck, hopping up and down. She'd met her goal. And with that finish she had a solid chance.

Someone cleared their throat beside them. Tala eased back down and looked over to see Rylee there with her parents, Tate, Nina and Avery. "Hey," she said with a grin, her arms still around Braxton's neck.

Rylee impatiently tugged her arms free and engulfed her in a big hug. "I'm so proud of you. You kicked ass!"

Tala laughed and hugged her. "Thanks, babe. Love you. Thanks so much for coming today." She looked at the others over Rylee's shoulder. "All of you."

"Wouldn't miss it for the world," her dad said, his arm around her mom's shoulders. "Now, Braxton, take my baby girl over to her gear so she can hydrate and catch her breath. We'll all be over to visit once you've had a chance to rest a bit."

"You heard him. Let's get you off those skis," Braxton said to her, taking her by the arm to tow her over to wherever her coach must have set her equipment. "Tired?" he asked with a smile that made her heart flip-flop.

She still couldn't believe he was here. "Destroyed. But happy." She pulled off her glove and stroked her hand over his bearded cheek as he escorted her around the corner, away from the crowd. "If I'd known you were waiting for me at the finish line I would probably have cut two minutes off my time."

He laughed. "Figured it was best you didn't know. Didn't want to risk distracting you during such a big race."

Just another reason why she loved him. He was always thinking of her, even when he was far away.

Rylee jogged over to hand her a thermos. "Your après-ski tea."

"*Thank* you. This is why you're my favorite daughter." Tala swallowed the first sip with a satisfied groan as Braxton pulled her around the bend, still fizzing with excitement over him being here, and her finish time. It had been a long, hard road getting here—for them and her biathlon career—but worth every struggle and sacrifice.

"And I brought you this as well." Rylee handed her a small hand towel.

"Thanks." Tala mopped at her face and neck, already fantasizing about the long, hot shower waiting for her back at her hotel room.

Except now she was imagining Braxton in it with

her, the water sluicing over his naked body. Him massaging soap all over her wet skin, his mouth busy on all her most sensitive areas until she was desperate and trembling, then pinning her to the wall and driving inside her. Filling her up with his thickness. Making up for all this time they'd been apart.

But before they could go back to the hotel she needed to get out of her skis, visit with her family and talk with her coach about the race. "Any idea where my stuff is?" She looked around, unsure where her coach had left it. She didn't see him anywhere. Where was he?

She glanced at Rylee. "You seen Harry?"

Her daughter had a weird expression on her face. A little mischievous. Or maybe secretive. "What? No. But I'm sure he's around somewhere."

"What about Mason?"

"He's around somewhere too." Rylee glanced at Braxton, a distinctly knowing gleam in her eyes. What was going on?

"Harry's over this way, I think," Braxton said, taking Tala by the elbow and leading her away from her daughter.

Tala let him pull her, glad to rest her shaky legs and eager to get off her skis. But when they rounded the corner of the trail, Harry wasn't there, and neither was her stuff. In fact, they were all alone on the empty, snow-covered trail, bordered on both sides by underbrush and tall evergreens.

This couldn't be right. "I don't think—"

Braxton pulled her to the side and stepped in front of her, a smile tugging at his lips as he took her hands in his. She blinked up at him, opened her mouth to ask what he was smiling at, then stopped and waited. "What?" she blurted when he didn't say anything.

"Do you know how much I love you?" he began in a low voice.

She nodded, her pulse picking up again. What was going on?

"Good." His eyes twinkled. "Because I'm not re-upping. I'm getting out."

She gaped at him, eyes widening. She must have heard wrong. "What?"

He grinned. "It's official. The paperwork's being processed now."

A wave of joy crashed through her, but she quickly dismissed it, unsure if this was really cause for celebration. He'd seemed so sure about wanting to stay in before, about not being ready to get out yet. And as much as she would love for him to leave the military to be with her, she didn't want him to do something he would regret later. She never wanted him to resent her or feel that she'd held him back.

"Brax, are you…sure?" she whispered, searching his eyes.

He dipped his head in an assertive nod she knew well. "Positive." He trailed his fingertips down the side of her face. "I love you, and I want you more than anything else. Just let me finalize everything, and I'm out. I'll move to Kelowna with you. We can live there full-time, or in Rifle Creek part of the year. Whatever we want."

We. She loved the sound of that. But she didn't care where they lived, Kelowna or Rifle Creek or somewhere else. Just as long as she was with him.

Tears pricked the backs of her eyes even as a tremulous smile spread across her face. He loved her enough that he was going to leave the military. Giving up the career he'd dedicated his life to, and the sense of belonging he'd found there, so that they could be together.

Like the tattoo on his forearm and the motto he'd lived by for so many years, that told her so much more than words ever could. *Facta Non Verba.*

"Whatever we want?" She'd been afraid to even let

herself hope for this, let alone so soon. Was this really happening? It was better than if he'd gotten down on one knee and proposed.

"Anything. Just as long as we're together." His expression was intent as he gazed down at her. "We've been through so much, and we've waited a long time to be with each other. I don't want to wait anymore, Tal. You're the most important thing in my life, and I want to spend the rest of it with you."

The tears slipped over as she found her voice. "I want that too."

She laughed through her tears and flung her arms around his neck to kiss him. He pulled her tight to his body as his lips closed over hers, warm and firm, the hint of tongue sending a rush of heat shooting between her thighs. This man lit her up so fast, her body *and* her heart. She was so damn lucky.

Excited squeals from behind her jerked her back to the present. She looked over her shoulder to find Rylee, her mom, Nina and Avery all rushing at them, grinning from ear to ear. A second later, she was engulfed in a giant group hug.

"Mase, did you get it?" Braxton called out.

"Yeah, got everything!" a voice replied from the bushes.

She turned, surprised, and stared in astonishment as he crawled out wearing a Ghillie suit, perfectly camouflaged amongst the brush he'd been hiding in, with an expensive-looking camera with a telephoto lens in his hands. "Mason?"

His teeth were startlingly white in his camo-painted face. "Surprise. Wanted to capture your reaction on video, because this is epic." He hugged her first, then dragged Braxton into one, slapping his back. "Congrats, man. You're gonna love retirement. Tate and I promise not to work you too hard in your golden years with RTC."

Avery shook her head at her fiancé and gave Tala an apologetic smile. "I tried to talk him out of it, but he was hell bent on doing this." She gestured to the Ghillie suit.

Mason shrugged and looped an arm around Avery's shoulders, an unrepentant grin on his face. "Didn't want to spoil the surprise by risking you seeing me. I got some amazing shots of you on the course earlier too." He lifted the camera. "Angle just now was awesome, by the way. Wait until you see the look on your face when he tells you."

Tala laughed, so happy she could burst. "You've made a memorable event even more unforgettable."

Rylee turned away slightly, her gaze on someone over her shoulder. Tala followed it to find her coach striding up, smiling broadly, and another man next to him. Tala's breath caught even as her heart stuttered.

The national team coach.

"Congratulations, Tala," Harry said, pulling her into a hug as the others fell back to give them some privacy. "That was one hell of a race. I'm real proud of you."

"Thanks. Were you in on this too?" she asked him, nodding at Braxton.

Harry's eyes twinkled. "Maybe."

No maybe about it. He, Braxton and her friends and family had absolutely all conspired together to pull off this surprise, and she loved everything about it.

"You remember Randy," he said, gesturing to the tall man next to him.

"Yes. Hi." She shook the hand he offered, a swarm of butterflies doing a nervous loop-de-loop in her stomach.

He gave her a warm smile, his eyes full of admiration. "Fantastic race, Tala. The whole coaching staff is incredibly impressed by your performance, and especially how far you've progressed over the last year. So impressed, we'd like to officially offer you a spot on the Canadian Masters National Team."

Tala cried out, her hands flying to her mouth as everyone around her burst into cheers. A second later, she was engulfed in the center of another ecstatic group hug.

She closed her eyes and stood there in the middle of it, memorizing the moment. Absorbing the sense of accomplishment, and the love and joy of the people who meant the most to her in the world.

When everyone finally stepped back to give her room to breathe, she still couldn't take it all in. She'd done it. Made the national masters team. The Winter World Masters Games were next year, games specifically for athletes over age thirty. And now her Paralympic dream was within reach as well.

She looked up into Braxton's face, shaking her spinning head. "I can't believe it. Can't take it all in."

He settled his big hands on her hips, the love in his eyes melting her insides. "Believe it, sweetheart, because you deserve it. You made it all happen."

Tala grinned and cupped his face between her hands as his mouth came down on hers. She was back in Braxton's arms, and for the first time ever, he was all hers.

As incredible as it seemed, her dreams were finally coming true. And now she had the man of her dreams to share them with for the rest of their lives.

—**The End**—

Dear reader,

Thank you for reading *Lethal Protector*. I hope you enjoyed the **Rifle Creek Series**. To read an excerpt of the first book in my next series, turn the page.

If you'd like to stay in touch with me and be the first to learn about new releases you can:

Join my newsletter at:
http://kayleacross.com/v2/newsletter/

Find me on Facebook:
https://www.facebook.com/KayleaCrossAuthor/

Follow me on Twitter:
https://twitter.com/kayleacross

Follow me on Instagram:
https://www.instagram.com/kaylea_cross_author/

Also, please consider leaving a review at your favorite online book retailer. It helps other readers discover new books.

Happy reading,
Kaylea

Excerpt from

UNDERCURRENT

Kill Devil Hills Series #1
By Kaylea Cross
Copyright © 2021 Kaylea Cross

CHAPTER ONE

He hadn't outrun the past yet. But he kept trying anyway.

The rhythmic slap of his shoes against the cool pavement settled into a monotonous background noise as Bowie jogged up the quiet residential street. All the houses he passed were dark, no one else stirring yet in his neighborhood. Ahead of him, the eastern sky was aglow with the approaching dawn. The early May morning air was cool against his skin, carrying the briny scent of the sound behind him.

Last night his demons had taunted him mercilessly. When the weight of the memories became too much, this was the only way he knew how to chase them away.

Maintaining his pace, he cleared his mind of everything, exhaustion bringing the numbness that finally allowed him to sink into the closest thing to peace he could reach these days. At the top of the hill he circled back along the footpath that skirted the canal as the birds began to sing, the marsh and inlets glowing with the orange and gold of dawn.

His two-story house stood at the bottom of the hill,

backing onto the sound. He bent over in front of it to catch his breath while the cool breeze washed over his sweaty skin, staring at the house. Ghosts were waiting inside for him. But at least now he could handle confronting them again.

The quiet of the empty house surrounded him as he entered the small, spotless kitchen. Through the window above the sink, the surface of the canal rippled in the breeze as it flowed past at the end of the dock where his Hurricane sport boat was moored.

It was his baby and he loved being out on the water, but he barely took it out anymore. Going out there alone just made him miss his family more, and the good times they'd had together fishing or racing across the water.

He grabbed a cold bottle of water from the fridge and stood there while the stillness settled around him. It suited him. The solitude. He was meant to be alone. And if he ever needed a reminder of that, all he had to do was glance over at the stained-glass panel hanging in the window beside the French door leading outside.

Against his will, his gaze shifted to it. To the familiar patterns of blues, greens and purples locked together forever between lead lines, the morning light making the pieces glow like jewels and reflecting on the floor and walls.

That all-too familiar hollow feeling filled his gut. So constant he barely took notice of it anymore.

Tearing his gaze away from it, he walked to the French door and stepped outside into the backyard. Immediately it was easier to breathe, the salty scent of the water soothing him as he crossed the back lawn, the dew cool under his bare feet. His steps echoed slightly on the wooden planks of the dock, mixing with birdsong as he walked to the end of it, then sank down to dangle his legs over the edge next to his boat.

A cool breath of air rose from the water, the surface

so calm it looked like a mirror. He sipped his chilled water, absorbing the fragile sense of peace, knowing it wouldn't last. It never did. And soon other thoughts and worries began to intrude. Like his sister, Harper. She was still up north in Boston. He hadn't heard from her in over a week, even though he'd called and texted. That was unusual, and he couldn't shake the sense that something was wrong.

Gradually the neighborhood began to wake around him, signaling the end of his solitude. He got up and returned to his empty house, the invisible weight settling back in his chest. He still loved this place. Even if the memories it held were bittersweet.

After a long, hot shower, he got ready and drove up the winding road to work. He parked out back of the garage, climbed out of his '69 Challenger and took a deep breath of the spring air. The warmer weather meant the town of Kill Devil Hills was enjoying the last few days of quiet before the hordes of tourists descended on the Outer Banks for the summer.

It also signaled the imminent approach of a painful anniversary he was dreading.

Pushing the past from his mind, he walked into the garage he owned, sliding his sunglasses up on top of his ball cap. The moment he stepped inside, a cool blast of air from the A/C hit him, bringing with it the comforting smells of motor oil and rubber.

Barb, his twenty-year-old receptionist looked up from her phone at the front desk and put on a sunny smile for him. "Morning."

He'd hired her at the end of the college semester to take care of the phone and scheduling, both of which he hated. She'd work through the summer until school went back at the end of August. Then he'd have to either handle it himself or find someone else again. "Morning. Did that supplier call with the delivery date yet on that part I need for the Vette?"

"Not yet."

Figured. And he couldn't do anything else with it until the part arrived. "What's the schedule like for today?"

"Umm..." She set her phone down and pulled up the appointment program on the computer. "You're fully booked until noon tomorrow, and only one slot left tomorrow afternoon."

At least business was steady. "Brian in yet?" His other full-time mechanic, and the only other employee he trusted to do body work besides him.

"Not until ten."

"All right. Let me know if that supplier calls."

"Will do." She picked up her phone before he'd even turned away and started scrolling through whatever she was looking at. But the place was clean and the phone was quiet, so he didn't say anything.

The garage area was still dark when he walked through the door. He flipped on the lights and turned on the stereo. Classic rock filled the space as he put on his coveralls and gathered his tools for his first project of the day—finishing up an upgraded rebuild on the carburetor of a '67 Camaro.

He worked on vehicles of all types, but his first love was muscle and classic cars, and over the years he'd built a solid reputation for it. People from up and down the Outer Banks and beyond brought their classic cars to him.

An hour later he stood at his workbench, wrestling with a stubborn, rusted bolt when a familiar voice spoke from behind him.

"Damn, how's a man supposed to hear himself think with all this racket going on back here?"

He straightened in surprise and turned to find his brother standing in the doorway. A grin immediately spread over his face, the lingering heaviness in his chest lifting. It had been a damn long time since they'd seen each other in person. Too long.

He set down his wrench. Chase wore his usual outfit of jeans, a T-shirt and boots, and yet still managed to look like he'd just stepped off a Hollywood movie set. "What the hell are you doing in town?" Last he'd heard, Chase had been on location in L.A. working on a big-budget action movie. He hurriedly wiped his hands on a rag from his hip pocket as his brother crossed to him.

"Wanted to surprise you. Surprise." Chase gave him a tight, back-slapping hug that Bowie had needed far more than he'd realized, then stepped back to grin at him, the glare of the overhead lights glinting on the golden-brown stubble on his jaw. He shook his head. "Wow. You should talk to management, because I think the boss has been working you too hard. You look like hell, man."

"I appreciate that, thanks," he said dryly. "You just come by to hassle me?"

"Pretty much, yeah. I'm in between shoots, so I thought I'd come annoy you for a while during my downtime."

"Lucky me." Bowie was damn glad to see him. After leaving the Marine Corps with an honorable discharge, solid skill set and combat experience, Chase was now an up and coming stuntman in increasingly high demand and didn't get a lot of downtime these days. As a result, he rarely came home anymore.

But just because his brother had showed up unexpectedly didn't mean he could quit for the day, even if he was the boss. *Especially* because he was the boss. "I'm just finishing up the carb on this one," he said, nodding at the Camaro. "Wanna gimme a hand?"

"You gonna pay me for my time?"

He snorted. "Not a chance."

Chase's lips quirked. "Some things never change. But all right, since I've got nothing better to do and I'm bored, I'll help y'out for a while." He grabbed a spare pair of coveralls from a hook on the wall and pulled them on.

"You finished that latest movie yet?" Bowie asked as he bent back over the parts laid out on the workbench and resumed his task.

"Wrapped up two days ago, over a week ahead of schedule. I have to be on location in New York for another one at the end of the week." He came to the workbench and peered down at what Bowie was doing. "So what've we got here?"

Time and distance fell away as soon as they began to work together, and within minutes it was like they hadn't been apart at all for the past seven months. They'd always worked together well, even back in the days when they used to help their dad on old cars before the heart attack had taken him, shattering their world.

He and Chase slipped back into that same easy rhythm now, his brother anticipating what tool he needed before he could even ask for it. Bowie was solitary by nature, except with family.

His brother and sister meant everything to him. Didn't matter how long they went without seeing each other. They all kept in touch, and their bond was unbreakable. No matter what else Bowie did with his life, that bond would be the legacy he was most proud of. So Harper's recent silence was weighing heavy on his mind.

"You keeping busy here?" Chase asked later as he helped install the air filter under the Camaro's hood.

"It's been steady." He made enough to pay all the bills and put some aside for the future.

Not that he got excited about that or the prospect of retiring one day, since work was all he had now. But it was better that way. It's what he deserved, and he'd made peace with that a long time ago.

"What about you, they doing up a star for you on the Walk of Fame yet?" he teased.

Chase chuckled, holding the filter steady while

Bowie anchored the lid in place. "Not yet. Hopefully soon."

Bowie was damn proud of both his siblings and all they'd accomplished after leaving home. He didn't regret choosing to stay here while they left to follow their dreams. All he'd ever wanted was to help them realize their dreams and keep their family unit strong. "You heard from Harp lately?"

Chase looked up at him. "Not for about a week now. You?"

"Same." It didn't feel right. Harper had retreated into herself since her husband had been killed overseas a little over a year ago, but it wasn't like her to be out of contact with them for this long.

They stared at each other a moment. "Think something's wrong?" Chase asked.

"Hope not. Might take a few days off and go up there if I don't hear from her soon."

"If you do, let me know. I'll see if I can carve out enough time in between filming days to meet you."

He nodded and paused in the act of setting his wrench down on the workbench at the sound of an old motor outside, driving along the side of the garage. He and Chase looked at each other, both of them trying to figure out what it was, an old game they'd played since Chase was young.

Chase pursed his lips in thought. "Mini?"

Bowie shook his head. "Nah. Wrong pitch."

A minute later Barb appeared in the doorway in her shorts and tank top. She aimed a megawatt smile at Chase, twirling a lock of her long blond hair in her fingers before turning her attention to Bowie. "There's a lady here to see you about her car."

"Be right there." He wiped his hands on a rag and followed her, Chase right behind him. No surprise. His little brother was notoriously nosy.

UNDERCURRENT

The instant Bowie walked around the corner and saw the woman in question, his feet stopped moving. Chase was so close behind him he had to veer to the side at the last second to avoid hitting him. "You forget how to walk or something?" he said to Bowie on a laugh.

Bowie didn't answer, too busy staring at the newcomer. Because it was impossible not to.

She was a bit younger than him, maybe early thirties, dressed in a black fifties-style halter dress with cherries on it, the fabric hugging incredibly lush curves before stopping just below her knees. Both rounded arms were covered in colorful tats from shoulder to elbow. Her shapely calves were bare, leading his eyes down to the sexy, lipstick-red heels on her feet.

With effort, Bowie dragged his gaze back up to her face. Her long, deep brown hair was pulled back from her face in a red cloth headband, except for a shock of white that fell over the right side of her forehead. Heavy black eyeliner defined her upper lids, emphasizing incredible pale green eyes that had him frozen where he stood. A small gold hoop glinted in the side of her nose, and her lips were slicked with glossy red lipstick.

When he didn't say anything she raised her eyebrows at him in question. "Mr. Davenport?"

Her accent instantly told him she was from somewhere out west, if he wasn't mistaken. And shit, he was staring like an idiot. "Yeah, that's me. How can I help you?" he managed once he got his brain back in gear.

"My car needs some work. She's old."

"You came to the right place. I'm his younger brother, by the way. Chase," his brother said, hurrying forward to extend his hand.

She shook it, gave him a polite smile and then dismissed him, focusing back on Bowie. It surprised him as much as it did Chase. His charismatic, Hollywood-handsome brother wasn't used to being dismissed by the ladies. "I just got into town a few days ago. When I asked around, your name kept coming up as the best with old cars. I don't have an appointment, but I thought I'd come by and see if—"

"What kind of car?" Bowie asked, more intrigued by her than the mystery car parked outside. He couldn't remember the last time that had happened.

"'59 Morris."

British car. Chase hadn't been that far off after all. "Sure, I'll take a look."

She turned away and started for the door, the full skirt of the dress swaying with each step. Bowie followed, unable to tear his eyes from her hips and the tantalizing indent of her waist emphasized by the shiny red belt around it. Damn, those curves should be illegal.

He beat her to the door by a second and held it open for her. She was pretty tall. In her heels she was almost at eye level with him, and he was six-two.

"Thank you," she murmured and stepped through, giving him a whiff of delicious, sweet-tart citrus on the way past.

He darted a glance back at his brother, who grinned at him, and fought a smile. Wasn't every day a woman like that walked into his garage.

The noon heat hit him as soon as he stepped outside, and found the lady standing beside a fire engine-red Morris Minor Traveller. "A Woody," he murmured, unable to hold back a smile. The quintessential surfer vehicle, its back half framed by iconic wood accents.

She nodded and gave him a pleased smile. "Yes, this is Priscilla." She ran a hand over the curve of the hood, her glossy nails almost a perfect match for the paint color as her fingers caressed it. Bowie wouldn't mind having her stroke him like that.

"Is something wrong with her?" he asked.

UNDERCURRENT

"Apart from being old? I'm not sure, I've only had her a couple days. She makes a strange sound when I accelerate. I wanted to get her checked out and fixed up, just to be on the safe side." She ran her hand over the edge of the roof, the motion elegant and sensual at the same time. "She's sentimental to me."

"She's a beauty." Not nearly as gorgeous as her owner, but still. "Pop the hood for me."

She opened the driver's door and leaned over to pop the latch, giving him a view of the muscles in her bare calves in those sexy heels, the nip of her waist and the flare of her skirt giving him an instant visual of what she'd look like underneath it. Full, lush curves a man could explore for hours. Curves he could wrap his hands around and hold onto while he eased into her from behind.

The thought came unbidden, startling him. He hadn't thought those kinds of things about someone he'd just met in forever.

Behind him, Chase cleared his throat. Bowie snapped to attention and walked around to the driver's side door as the woman straightened. He slid into the caramel-colored seat, once again getting a whiff of her clean, tart scent. Yum. "Let's start her up and see what the old girl tells us."

He fired up the engine. The starter took a few seconds to catch. There was a definite lag, and when he gave it gas, the high-pitched squeal indicated a potential problem with the belts.

After giving a few other things a cursory check, he turned off the ignition and looked up at the woman. She stood next to Chase, completely ignoring his brother as she cupped her elbows, her full attention on Bowie.

He felt the impact of that pale green gaze all the way to his center. "I'd say she definitely needs a little TLC."

"I know you've barely looked at her, but can you give me a ballpark estimate of cost, just so I have an idea of what I'm looking at?"

He named a price range. "I've got time to look at her early tomorrow afternoon, if that works."

"That's perfect." With that she turned and headed straight back inside. Chase lunged over to grab the door for her. Bowie managed to beat him through it, entering right behind the woman, and came to stand at the desk with her while she booked the appointment.

"What's your name?" Barb asked her with a bright smile.

"Aspen Savich."

Aspen. A name as unique and sexy as she was.

Barb typed in her name and cell number, then looked at Bowie. "Do you figure you'll have it ready by closing tomorrow night?"

"Barring any unforeseen problems or special parts I need to order in, yeah." He turned back to Aspen, caught off guard by the strange tug deep in his gut when their gazes connected. He'd forgotten what that felt like. "But if I come across a problem I'll call to check with you before doing anything. Right now I'm just thinking a basic tune-up and checking the belts, nothing too bad."

She nodded. "Sounds good. Thanks very much."

"No problem." He held out his hand. "I'm Bowie, by the way."

She gave him a mysterious smile, those pale green eyes holding a trace of amusement as she accepted his hand. "I know," she murmured.

The moment their palms touched, he felt that tug deep inside him again. Her skin was soft and warm.

Withdrawing her hand, she glanced at the three of them. "Thanks a lot. I'll see you tomorrow." Those eyes shifted to him again, and this time there was no mistaking the leap of attraction inside him. He didn't like it. "Unless I hear from you sooner."

With those enigmatic parting words, she slid a pair

of oversized dark sunglasses on and walked out. Bowie stared at the closed door for a long moment, her scent still lingering faintly in the air. The sound of the Morris starting shook him out of his stupor and he spun around to head back to the shop.

Chase was right behind him. "Forget what I asked about the business earlier. Based on what I just saw, I'd say business is *real* good." He chuckled, eyes twinkling.

Bowie grunted and gave him a sharp look, annoyed at himself. For gawking like an idiot, but more for his weird reaction to her. He hadn't reacted to anyone like that since—

Simultaneous blades of guilt and pain sliced through him. He locked the door to the past shut in his mind, and blocked any more thoughts of Aspen Savich. She was just another client. "Stop yammerin' and get your lazy ass back to work," he grumbled. "This ain't Hollywood—we gotta actually work for our money around here."

The amused, knowing look Chase shot him didn't help settle Bowie's unease. He didn't want to react to Aspen like that, or any other woman.

That part of him should have died years ago, with the woman he'd planned to spend the rest of his life with.

End Excerpt

About the Author

NY Times and USA Today Bestselling author Kaylea Cross writes edge-of-your-seat military romantic suspense. Her work has won many awards, including the Daphne du Maurier Award of Excellence, and has been nominated multiple times for the National Readers' Choice Awards. A Registered Massage Therapist by trade, Kaylea is also an avid gardener, artist, Civil War buff, Special Ops aficionado, belly dance enthusiast and former nationally-carded softball pitcher. She lives in Vancouver, BC with her husband and family.

You can visit Kaylea at www.kayleacross.com. If you would like to be notified of future releases, please join her newsletter: http://kayleacross.com/v2/newsletter/

COMPLETE BOOKLIST

ROMANTIC SUSPENSE

Kill Devil Hills Series
Undercurrent
Submerged
Adrift

Rifle Creek Series
Lethal Edge
Lethal Temptation
Lethal Protector

Vengeance Series
Stealing Vengeance
Covert Vengeance
Explosive Vengeance
Toxic Vengeance
Beautiful Vengeance

Crimson Point Series
Fractured Honor
Buried Lies
Shattered Vows
Rocky Ground
Broken Bonds

DEA FAST Series
Falling Fast
Fast Kill
Stand Fast
Strike Fast
Fast Fury
Fast Justice

Fast Vengeance

Colebrook Siblings Trilogy
Brody's Vow
Wyatt's Stand
Easton's Claim

Hostage Rescue Team Series
Marked
Targeted
Hunted
Disavowed
Avenged
Exposed
Seized
Wanted
Betrayed
Reclaimed
Shattered
Guarded

Titanium Security Series
Ignited
Singed
Burned
Extinguished
Rekindled
Blindsided: A Titanium Christmas novella

Bagram Special Ops Series
Deadly Descent
Tactical Strike
Lethal Pursuit
Danger Close
Collateral Damage

Never Surrender (a MacKenzie Family novella)

Suspense Series
Out of Her League
Cover of Darkness
No Turning Back
Relentless
Absolution
Silent Night, Deadly Night

PARANORMAL ROMANCE

Empowered Series
Darkest Caress

HISTORICAL ROMANCE

The Vacant Chair

EROTIC ROMANCE (writing as *Callie Croix*)

Deacon's Touch
Dillon's Claim
No Holds Barred
Touch Me
Let Me In
Covert Seduction

Made in the USA
Las Vegas, NV
22 February 2021